WHAT THE MEDIA SAYS ABOUT *VOICES OF THE SURVIVORS*:

"Dr Easteal's book is a distressing but authoritative account that sends survivors one simple, positive message: you're not alone and nor should you be. It's both a tribute to those survivors who tragically maintain their silence and an indictment on a society that doesn't listen. Men and women alike should be encouraged to read it—lawyers, judges and the police should be forced to do so."

Julie Beun-Chown
International Women's Feature Service

"Her dry and measured style goes immediately to the heart of the matter . . ."

Susan Powell
Australian Bookseller and Publisher

"It's a deeply disturbing expose of male attitudes towards women."

Bob Hefner
Canberra Times

"A harrowing read yet these survivors no longer suffer in silence. May the sharing of the painful secrets help others release their uncalled-for shame and regain themselves. May their combined voices be a catalyst for attitudinal change against the abuse of power."

Kerrie Wilson
ABC TV News

T0166914

Patricia Easteal is currently a Senior Criminologist at the Australian Institute of Criminology. Trained as a Legal Anthropologist in the USA, Dr Easteal was formerly a lecturer in Women's Studies and Ethnic Studies at an American university. In Australia she has conducted major research projects on women in prison, rape, domestic violence and homicide between adult sexual intimates. She has published a number of books and articles on these and related issues. An articulate advocate for women, Dr Easteal enjoys many media and public speaking appearances. She brings to these talks and her writing both academic expertise and her personal experiences as a woman, survivor, feminist, volunteer worker with survivors of sexual assault, addiction and/or domestic violence. As a mother of four, she attributes her sanity and occasional serenity to aerobics and self-help, peer support groups.

Books by the same author:

Policing: The Occupation and the Introduction of Female Officers, An Anthropological Study.

Vietnamese Refugees in Australia: Crime Rates of Minors and Youths in New South Wales.

The Future of Immigration Detention Centres in Australia, with J. Mugford, S. Pinto, I. Potas, A. Vining, & P. Wilson.

Crime Prevention and Public Transportation.

The Forgotten Few: Migrant Women in Australian Prisons.

Women and the Law, editor with S. McKillop.

Killing the Beloved: Homicide between Adult Sexual Intimates.

ACT Domestic Violence Research: Report to the ACT Community Law Reform Committee, with J. Mugford, & A. Edwards.

Without Consent: Confronting Adult Sexual Violence, editor.

Shattered Dreams.

The Criminal Justice System in a Multicultural Society, editor with S. Gerull.

VOICES OF THE SURVIVORS

Patricia Easteal

PINIFEX PRESS
Australia

Spinifex Press Pty Ltd,
504 Queensberry Street,
North Melbourne, Vic. 3051
Australia

Copyright © Australian Institute of Criminology 1994

The moral right of the author Patricia Easteal has been asserted.

Cover designed by Lin Tobias
Typeset by the Australian Institute of Criminology in Palatino 8/10 pt
Production by Morgan Blackthorne Productions
Printed in Australia by Australian Print Group

National Library of Australia
Cataloguing-in-Publication entry:
CIP
Easteal, Patricia,
Voices of the survivors.

Bibliography
ISBN 1 875559 24 8
1. Rape victims - Australia. 2. Rape - Australia. 3. Sex crimes - Australia. 4. Abused women - Australia. I. Title.

364.15320994

Contents

ACKNOWLEDGMENTS

The title of this book indicates the principal recipients of my gratitude: the survivors. These courageous individuals who wrote to the Australian Institute of Criminology have given us a special part of themselves to share. I hope that the process was cathartic for you and has helped the wounds to heal.

Thank you to the Australian Broadcasting Corporation, and particularly David Goldie, for approaching the Australian Institute of Criminology to run a questionnaire for sexual assault survivors and to the Murdoch newspaper chain for printing the surveys. And thanks to the AIC Director, Professor Duncan Chappell, for endorsing the research project and approving my time spent on *Voices of the Survivors*. Other AIC staff assistance has been invaluable: Garry Raffaele for liaising with the ABC; Jill Place for her incredible stamina shown in keying the thousands of pages; Jennifer Hallinan's computing expertise; many casual workers and work experience students; and special, special thanks to Diana Nelson, assistant extraordinaire!

I am grateful to Susan Hawthorne and Renate Klein from Spinifex who encouraged me to write *Voices of the Survivors*. Also, thank you to all those beautiful women who work in the field of sexual assault for reading early drafts and encouraging me. To friends and sisters in recovery and/or survivorship who were there at the other end of the phone—a lifeline—when the pain became too great: you are all very special people.

I have the (sometimes debatable) joy of sharing life with my four children, Jesse, Brian, Ashley and David, who are always there to provide comedic or other distractions from the sorrows and anger of my work and my past. Thanks 'guys'. Also thank you to my two best friends: first, my partner, Simon, you have held my hand and provided emotional support as I trudged the often weary path and second, HP for carrying me when it all became too much.

The promises do all come true.

ACKNOWLEDGMENTS

1

OUT OF THE SHADOWS

I <u>AM</u> a survivor with a capital 'S'. In fact as I completed
these six questionnaires I rang the sexual assault clinic to
touch base and just talk for a few moments to 're-ground'
myself from the anger and fear. I hope, GOD! I hope you
will use this and the other courageous women and men who
disclose their agony to help others.

The fear of sexual assault or rape is a part of every woman's
life. In a plethora of ways that fear constricts and restricts
females' mobility and manner of living. 'Don't walk alone at
night', 'Don't talk to strangers', 'Don't hitchhike', 'Don't dress
in a provocative way' are just a few of the rules with which
girls are socialised. And, the reality is that rape is indeed a
threat for every female in Australia: the advice above is solid
and well-meaning although, in many ways, it is based upon
stereotypes about sexual assault which are not true and which
act insidiously to impute blame on the victim. Such false
beliefs flourish in the darkness of ignorance. Like a fungus,
erroneous stereotypes do indeed proliferate within a shadowy
environment that promotes secrecy.

One of the purposes of the following pages is to tear down
the myths about rape by confronting the faulty views of what
rape is, who rapes, why men rape, and the rape's impact on
the victim or survivor. 'Wait', you may be saying, 'Why bother
to show how untrue these beliefs are? How is that going to
assist future victims or those who are already survivors?'
Answer: One of the only means available to reduce sexual
assault and to enhance the probability that its victims will
report it to authorities is through knocking down the false
images of rape that act to perpetuate it in society. At a more
individual level, one of the only means available to ameliorate

the inner shame carried by so many victims is to allow many of their voices to be heard.

Given these premises, let us briefly look at some of the principal myths.

WHAT IS RAPE?

There are a multitude of definitions of rape, both legally and within the folk mores of a culture. In this book rape is defined as *the penetration of the mouth, vagina or anus by any part of the attacker's body or by an object used by the attacker, without the consent of the victim.* It must be noted, however, that this definition should not be interpreted as implying that sexual assault without penetration is any less of a criminal act with equally devastating consequences upon its survivors.

The latter part of the definition, *without the consent*, does not have universal consensus. Some believe that such a differentiation between rape and sex places the burden on the woman to prove that she did effectively communicate her lack of consent (McSherry 1993). Currently, most states' statutes relating to sexual assault do centre on the issue of consent and rape is defined in that manner.

What does *without consent* involve and/or what does it not require?

Myth: Rape requires physical force.
Studies have shown that in the majority of rapes, the perpetrator does not use force which results in physical injuries (Weekley 1986). The threat of force and death and the intimidation inherent in gender stratification is sufficient. In reality many covert forms of coercion and force may be used in rape. It is the victim's fear of the assault and its outcome that renders her passive—not compliant—but without consent. Since many victims of rape are also survivors of incest and other sexual abuse they may 'shut down' their emotions and bodies at the onset of a rape. In addition, many other women

have been socialised not to be aggressive or assertive. Consequently female passivity is a quite common response to male violence.

Myth: Rape requires physical resistance by the victim.
As discussed later, this myth unfortunately is still accepted by segments of the criminal justice system. The survivor who does not evidence injuries which she acquired through resistance becomes the incredible victim. This image is a by-product of the previous myth which mandates physical force as an element of sexual assault. The reality is far different. Almost three-quarters of the victims in a Victorian phone-in reported that 'they felt an overwhelming sense of powerlessness' (Corbett 1993); therefore they did not physically resist.

Rape is the only criminal act which has required resistance to be present in order to substantiate that a crime occurred.

Myth: Rape requires a weapon.
Various surveys of victims have shown that the vast majority of sexual assaults do not involve the use of a weapon.

Other pervasive myths concern the nature of the act of rape itself.

Myth: Rape is a sexual act.
This myth is reinforced by certain stereotypes about male sexuality such as men's inability to control themselves if they are aroused. These are all false images. Rape is not a sexual act. Rape is an act of violence which uses sex as a weapon. Rape is motivated by aggression and by the desire to exert power and humiliate. Just as wife battering had to be taken out of the privacy of the home and made a crime in order to effect any change, rape must be taken out of the sexual realm and

placed where it rightfully belongs: in the domain of violence against women.

The latter view of rape as a sexual act is perhaps one of the most pervasive, enduring, and damaging myths. It contributes directly to another misunderstanding about the crime.

Myth: Since rape is a sexual crime, the victim in some way may precipitate the offence through arousing the male in a provocative manner.

This erroneous belief has a serious impact on how people view both the crime, the rapist and the victim. It also affects the survivor's view of herself. She often accepts self-blame since she has not succeeded in controlling the male's behaviour and has somehow provoked it (Carmody 1984). It is crucially important that this myth is dispelled since it also influences the response of the criminal justice system.

Myth: Since rape is provoked by the victim, it is usually a spontaneous act.

This belief is obviously false since it is dependent in large part on the preceding premise concerning victim precipitation. Sexual assaults are not usually done spontaneously or impulsively; studies have shown that in most instances, rape is premeditated and often involves a pre-rape time period of interaction with the victim (Cobb & Schauer 1977; Flowers 1987).

Myth: Aboriginal women (or, for example, Afro-American women in the United States of America) are more highly sexed than 'white' women and therefore are always willing to have sex; thus they precipitate it by their sexual behaviour.

This myth is compatible with the theory that victims of sexual assault tend to be those with less power in the society. Myths about non-white women's sexuality justified the colonial males' oppression, subjugation, and on-going rape.

4

To reiterate, rape is an act of violence which is most commonly directed by males toward women. The woman is not responsible for her victimisation in any way.

WHO IS THE RAPIST?

A number of authors have created typologies of rapists. The variety is clearly indicative of a lack of consensus by specialists in this field. That is one of the reasons why these will not be presented. The other reason lies in the aetiology of these schemata; imprisoned rapists. Since it is now clear that the arrested population is not necessarily representative of the entire class of rapists due to under-reporting of acquaintance, date, family member and marital rape, the reliability of such typologies must be questioned.

Myth: The rapist is usually a stranger.
False. A plethora of research both overseas and in Australia has established that the majority of sexual assaults are perpetrated by acquaintances, relatives, dates, or marital partners. The erroneous image of the rapist as a stranger stems in part from the fact that those perpetrators are more likely to be reported to the police (Bownes, O'Gorman & Sayers 1991). However, various victim surveys show a different picture: in a regional study, 29 per cent of callers had been sexually abused by their husbands (Matchett 1988); whereas in a nation-wide victim survey in the United States only 22 per cent had been raped by strangers (Crime Victims Research & Treatment Center 1992); whilst in one Australian study more than a half of the victims knew or were related to the attacker (Green 1987). Reported rapes in New South Wales were analysed and it was ascertained that only one quarter involved strangers (Bonney 1985). The Australian Crime Victim Survey results were markedly similar with only a quarter of the crimes of rape or attempted rape perpetrated by strangers (Walker 1993).

Differences have been found in elements of the rape and in its impact on the victim based upon her relationship to the perpetrator. Some of these contrasts are in part responsible for the relatively low reporting of 'date' rape. For example, 'date' or acquaintance rapes are more likely to involve verbal threats than either a weapon or physical injuries. The attackers are also more likely to threaten the victim about disclosing (Bownes, O'Gorman & Sayers 1991).

Low levels of reporting are also a consequence of the victim's inability to perceive herself as a rape victim. Several studies have shown that people are more likely to label an act as rape if the victim protested both verbally and physically early in the scenario, and if the male arranged the date but the female paid her own way (Shotland & Goodstein 1983; Muehlenhard 1989). The victim has also been socialised with these fallacious concepts; even if she does label the act as a rape she might be reluctant to go to the police since she might believe either in her own partial responsibility or that the police would blame her.

Marital rape has been found to be a component in a high number of marriages that involve physical battering (Bowker 1983). It has been estimated that 10 to 14 per cent of all married women have been or will be raped by their spouse (Finkelhor 1985). Although marital rape involves more violence and physical injuries than acquaintance rape, its even lower rate of reporting can be attributed to both the isolation of the battered woman and to the on-going societal assumption that husbands are immune from sexual assault charges.

Myth: Rapists have pathological personalities and tend to come from the lower class.

The myth that the men who rape are mentally ill is not substantiated by the data: only a small minority of perpetrators are psychopathic (Stewart 1990). Empirical research has not found any consistent type of person or personality profile that distinguishes rapists from other males. One study looked at self-reported sexual aggression in men and found that class, education, and occupation were not significant variables (Alder 1985). Aggression was most strongly correlated with having sexually aggressive friends. It has been noted that rapists are more likely to adhere to the myths about sexual assault and to hold callous beliefs about rape (Chappell 1989).

IMPACT ON THE VICTIM

Myth: All women really want to be raped.
False.

Myth: Women ask to be raped.
False.

Rape is a crime which has devastating effects upon the survivor. It has been described as 'the beginning of a nightmare' (Main 1991). The following table outlines the possible consequences of rape. It represents an integration of numerous sources in the literature. (*See* Table 1)

The effects may vary depending upon a few variables: the relationship of the rapist to the survivor; the brutality of the crime; ego strength and the support or lack of support that the victim receives from those to whom she discloses (Girelli et al. 1981; Scott & Hewitt 1983; Stewart 1990). Some of these symptoms are short-term; others have been documented as lasting for years—possibly for the survivor's entire life.

Victims who do not report the crime experience more personality disorder, isolation and self-blame (Peretti & Cozzens 1983). It must also be noted that being raped by one's spouse does not ameliorate the trauma for the victim. Studies have shown that the long term effects are in fact more severe and longer term since marital rape involves betrayal, isolation and living with the rapist (Finkelhor 1985).

7

Survivors of rape must not be compelled by the myths into self-blame. Passivity, marriage, victim's appearance or behaviour should not be interpreted as consent.

Table 1: The potential impact of rape on the victim

Emotional
Depression, fear, anxiety, lack of trust, withdrawn behaviour, shame, self-blame (greater for acquaintance rape victims), guilt, humiliation, anger, rage, feelings of betrayal, (for marital rape), perception of the world as malevolent, low self-worth, phobias.

Physical
Headaches, muscle tension, gastro-intestinal upset, genital/urinary complaints, pregnancy, disease, injuries.

Behavioural
Suicidal actions, anorexia, alcohol and drug addiction, isolating oneself (for marital rape), eating disorders, sleeping disorders, effects of phobias, nightmares.

Note: This table was compiled from the following sources: A.W. Burgess & L.O. Holmstrom 1977, *Criminal Justice Newsletter* 1992; D. Finkelhor 1985; S.A. Girelli et al. 1986; M.P. Koss 1989, B.D. Mishkin 1989; Report on Sexual Assault Phone-In 1984; M.A. Young 1991.

HIGH INCIDENCE AND HIGH UNDER-REPORTING

The nature of rape makes it an extremely problematic crime to measure. Due both to the ambiguity about what it is and to the societal and criminal justice response which, at best, could be labelled ambivalent, sexual assault is grossly under-reported by its victims. There is reason to suspect, from international crime surveys, that Australia has a particularly high incidence of sexual assault, certainly higher than the United Kingdom although probably third to the United States and New Zealand (Main 1991; Weatherburn & Devery 1991). The combined sample of the 1989 and 1992 national crime victim surveys showed that about one out of every two hundred women had experienced a rape or attempted rape during the twelve months preceding the survey (Walker 1993). Many of the survivors who wrote in describing their victimisation felt that this number is far too conservative.

What is it about Australia, aside from the false myths already enumerated, that contributes to a particularly high incidence of sexual assault and low reporting?

Societal beliefs about rape are in large part a by-product of the plethora of misinformation and mythology about sexual assault. They are also the result of other values and behaviours in the culture. For instance, cross-cultural studies have found that rape is most prevalent in cultures with low female power and authority and where masculinity is expressed with violence (Chappell 1989). In this vein some authors have described Australia as one of the most misogynist countries in the world (Westbury 1991). Historically, female convicts were released to fulfil the 'needs' of the male inmates (Gilmore 1990). Thus, Australia's history and the persistence of certain values and gender roles in the culture would conform to the highest risk-type environment for rape.

Misogyny is also derived from the emphasis upon aggression in the enculturation of males which is manifested in the type of sports which are popular. Males are more

9

comfortable with males; they tend to socialise and communicate at a non-intimate level with other men; and they are apt to have a low regard for females. The latter is evidenced by both the type of verbal comments directed at women and the high frequency of physical violence toward female partners.

Reasons for Non-Reporting

There are a variety of reasons why survivors do not report the assault. It is abundantly clear from numerous reports that rape by a stranger is more likely to be reported than sexual assaults by other perpetrators. Fear, dislike of going to the police, or a belief that 'it was not serious enough for the police' were the two main reasons cited in the last national crime victim survey (Walker 1993). Two-thirds of Victorian callers believed that the police would not believe them, while a half thought that it would do no good (Corbett 1993). Fear of being blamed and having their families find out have also been found to stop victims from going to authorities (*Criminal Justice Newsletter* 1992).

If a victim believes that the police will treat her supportively she is more apt to report (Feldman-Summers & Norris 1984). Those survivors who have suffered injuries that required medical attention and have family or friends with strong values about reporting are most likely to go to the police.

However, as the National Committee on Violence Against Women (1991) has stressed, women within Aboriginal communities, rural areas, and migrant women may be particularly reluctant to report the attack. This reluctance stems from lack of confidentiality, cultural norms, and in the latter case, lack of English. Further, the intellectually disabled may be at particularly high risk for victimisation.

Either there has been an increase in rape in this country or an increase in its reporting to authorities. For example, in

Queensland, sexual assaults reported to the police increased 160 per cent from 1980 to 1990 (Westbury 1991) and throughout Australia reported rape had steadily increased from 1973 to 1987 (Wilson 1989). However, the increase may be attributable to legislative changes or police behaviour rather than actual incidence. In New South Wales reported rapes increased from 27.5 per 100,000 in 1981 to 70.3 per 100,000 in 1987-88. It is speculated that this increase was a by-product of the legal changes in that state and education of police which has resulted in their increased sensitivity (Weatherburn & Devery 1991).

A NATIONAL SURVEY

Even if it is true that more victims are reporting, we have a long way to go in encouraging disclosure and narrowing the chasm between what is perceived as a 'real' rape and what is seen as non bona fide sexual assault. As a means of promoting that process and dispelling some of the attitudes which are conducive to high frequency of sexual victimisation, the Australian Institute of Criminology ran a national survey on rape. It is the responses to that questionnaire that are found in the following pages.

On Sunday, 13 September 1992, the survey appeared in all Murdoch newspapers of News Limited (every state). The following two Wednesdays, an ABC TV documentary 'Without Consent' was aired. Each broadcast was followed by an announcement of the survey with a toll free number to call to request participation in the study. Over the course of the subsequent weeks 2,852 surveys were received. These were not sent in by 2,852 individuals since numerous respondents were multiple survivors and submitted more than one form. However, if raped by the same person more than once, such as in marital rape, these assaults were counted as one response.

Many of the senders included lengthy comments, some in the form of letters. Thus, aside from the quantifiable data,

11

much qualitative or anecdotal material became available. Several months after initial receipt, all of those who had signed their letters were sent permission slips requesting permission to use their comments in *Voices of the Survivors*. Everyone who was asked, agreed! To me, this was further validation that the book needed to be written.

The quantifiable responses were coded by a team who were instructed on interpretation in order to ensure inter-coder reliability. Following data entry, these data were analysed for significant variation by several variables using the SPSSX software package. The results of this analysis appear as tables and figures in Appendix I.

The respondents in this survey, whose letters and comments appear in the pages that follow, were self-selected. Hence their experiences may not be typical of a randomly derived sample of survivors. It is possible that the results may be biased by those who had particularly negative experiences with reporting parties and were therefore more eager to participate in order to 'vent their spleen'. Further, it is possible that individuals who had not been raped could have responded to the survey as a prank. On the latter point, however, it should be noted that the veracity of one's informants can never be entirely ascertained. Although it is always a potential risk, survey methodologies continue to be used, probably since the risk is understood but the advantages of the method are also apparent.

No method is without its weaknesses and biases. For example, much of the study of rapists has employed samples of imprisoned perpetrators. As will be shown in the following, there is strong reason to believe that such a data source would not be representative of rapists in general, but only perhaps of those reported, arrested, and imprisoned. Although data from a self-selected survey of survivors has potential unreliability, the same could be true for studies based upon victims who have disclosed to a sexual assault service. Again, the question of being able to generalise would be pertinent since such a sample might not be reflective of those who chose not to report.

THE VOICES

None of the letters is reproduced in its original form. In varying degrees, the content was edited in order to ensure the privacy of the writer. Any potential identifiers, names of people, places, ages, occupations and in some cases the particular dates, were eliminated. Sections which could be regarded by some as 'pornographic' due to detail concerning the assault were also deleted. The only such descriptions that remain are necessary in order to convey the breadth and range of offenders' inhumanity and savagery. This is especially important to understand in the context of appreciating why many victims do not report; how these abominable crimes can boomerang back on to the survivor, both internally and from the reactions of friends, families and the criminal justice system.

What value is there in editing and reproducing the letters and comments of some rape survivors? This has been answered in part above. However, let me reiterate. First, there is potential gain for all members of our culture who continue to subscribe to beliefs about rape that are not only false but also highly inflammatory and conducive to rape and the blaming of the victims. If we read, over and over again about the pain which the survivor experienced, perhaps we can learn that no one wants to be raped. Indeed this is what happened for many of those hired on a casual basis to code the respondents' answers. Included in this group were several teenage males:

For those boys, it was an extraordinarily enlightening experience. They realised rape is not something to joke about; that it has a serious impact on the survivor's life ... the boys no longer speak to one of their acquaintances who has committed rape (Easteal quoted in Kissane 1993).

And what about the value for the survivors? As one wrote: 'Scared silent. Let us finally be heard.' For many of these women, writing about their experiences was cleansing and empowering:

This is the first time I have 'seen' all six assaults written down. I am outraged, for so many, many years I was 'INRAGED' turned back on myself. I have, to the greater extent, through guts, determination and HARD WORK, healed from my past abuse and made a clear choice of my sexuality—claimed it FOR myself.

I have had the support of counsellors and friends in my recovery, not only from the assault/rapes but also my alcoholism and drug addiction [number] YEARS clean and sober. I believe the fact that I was raped and assaulted so many times, and also raped in relationships where my 'no' seemed to say 'yes' so sex happened anyway, in some way left me vulnerable for it to happen over and over.

For those who dared to open up it would be further violation not to use their words to help others. As we will see, the process of healing from sexual assault first requires awareness; shame can keep us locked into the darkness of secrecy not only from the rest of the world but also from ourselves. If someone can pick up this book and identify with one of the voices and know that she was not bad or responsible, then the pain which the writer endured in writing out her story has been worth it. There were many who wrote about their feelings of aloneness, of not even seeing someone with their story on the documentary 'Without Consent'. Hopefully, the heterogeneity of experiences detailed in this book will provide others, who believe that they are alone and different, with some support and validation, albeit in words on pages. This identification can be the beginning of a healing process.

There may be some who choose to regard the stories told within as voyeuristic, or even, if there is explicit reference to body parts or the assault, as pornographic. Perhaps any form of literature that reflects the pain of human experience could be construed as voyeuristic. The *Diary of Anne Frank* took us inside the heart of a young Jewish girl in Nazi-occupied Holland. Through her eyes we were able to understand that horror and hell better, perhaps, than we could through reading a hundred history books. One wonders how much impact that book had upon reducing prejudice and bigotry in order to ensure that there would never be another holocaust.

Perhaps the difference between voyeurism and reading about another's experiences in order to understand lies in the motivation of the writer, if not the reader. For this writer the intent of *Voices of the Survivors* is to assist survivors: those already in some recovery from their pain; those whose secrets lie within, festering and insidiously impacting on their lives; and those who, in the future, may be saved some of the self doubts and recriminations. One survivor put the value of sharing in this way.

I believe no woman asks to be raped. I blamed myself for many, many years. My pattern of abuse started at the age of seven. I was too scared to tell anyone. I believe men sense it more with people who are insecure within themselves. I feel rapists choose their victims well before they rape. I was petrified of the man who raped me as he was strong and threatened to kill me. I saw the madness in his cold calculating eyes at the time and knew that I had to run for my life, though he was faster. After the rape he let me go though he was waiting at the other end of the park. He got out of the car and asked me if I wanted a lift, as if nothing had happened. The rage I felt inside at that split second, if I had a gun I would have shot him dead without a second thought.

It took me three years to share this awful, shameful experience and I lost trust in all men as I didn't ever want to be a victim again. I've sorted 90 per cent of this out today. Though I feel we need to make public statements to parents concerning abuse to children. To let children know that it's OKAY to tell their parents of any abuse which might be occurring or have telephone numbers children can ring or encourage them to talk to a teacher. It is the silence that creates abuse on all levels, this has been my biggest downfall. If I told

15

someone when I was seven there is a chance I wouldn't have been raped. What I'm saying is it would be interesting to see how many rape victims were abused as children. I hope any of my comments could help in this survey as I feel there is still a lot of silent sufferers, who may need something to give them courage to tell someone. So they may get help and start healing.

TWO POSTSCRIPTS

Some of those who read this manuscript prior to publication were concerned that the emphasis and tone of the book are negative and that not enough physical space has been provided documenting the progress which women and rape victims have achieved in Australia. It is indeed important for the reader to remember that a mere twenty or so years ago there were no services for rape victims to turn to. Appendix II lists over 100 services now in existence throughout this country. However, as we will see in the following pages, these services are often under-funded and do not have the resources to meet the critical needs of women and children who have been sexually assaulted.

Less than a decade ago in some Australian states a man could not be charged or tried for raping his wife. Today, all states and territories no longer exclude ex-husbands from rape. Other legislative changes to ameliorate the revictimisation of women in the courtroom (discussed in Chapter 9) have also been enacted. These laws have reduced the difficulties for survivors but they have not eliminated them. Legislation is only as effective as the attitudes of the practitioners allow.

So, what does this mean? That there have not been any improvements in rape services and prevention? No, on the contrary there has been a lot of improvement. However, it is important not to focus too much on the improvement since complacency may set in, followed by inertia. Is the glass half empty or is it half full? The risk in perceiving it as half full is that we settle for the status quo instead of working to fill the glass to the brim. Until the incidence of sexual assaults radically decreases, the glass is not full. Until attitudes about sexual assault within the community dramatically change and shift from placing any responsibility or blame on the survivor, the glass is not full. And, until a survivor can go through the criminal justice system and receive both support and justice then that glass is still only partially full.

As it may be clear by now, this writer has also been a victim of sexual assault. It would not have been possible to have done this work and kept one's own secrets. The pain of such hypocrisy would have far exceeded the pain of reading the letters and comments, editing them, writing bits and pieces, and coming out publicly as a survivor. However, as some say, 'No pain, no gain.' It is only through experiencing the feelings from long ago—the sadness, the anger, and maybe most of all the fear—that we can go beyond and proceed from awareness through to anger, to action and empowerment. The tears have had to fall again before the wounds can reach another stage of healing. To all whose voices are encapsulated within and all of those who need to share, this book is dedicated to you with gratitude and a promise of a new tomorrow.

2
INCEST

From a very early age I thought that this was the done thing
by all males. Then as I grew older I just thought it must have
been my fault. It just seemed as though everywhere I turned
there was some male wanting to touch me. (Raped by
stepfather and brother aged six onwards)

Rape was a reality for all age groups in the 'Without Consent'
survivor sample. Well over a half of the respondents (61.8 per
cent) had experienced sexual assault prior to their twenties.
Other family members either living with the survivor or apart
were the perpetrators in 13.5 per cent of the total cases with
young children at the highest risk from someone in the family
with whom they lived. Thus it is no surprise to find that in
response to another question on the survey, over a third
(34.6 per cent) stated that they were also survivors of incest.
However, of these, only 35 per cent actually filled out a survey
describing the incest—the remainder were describing other
rapes.

WHO WAS THE PERPETRATOR?
Fathers
Although they were not the most common relative-offender,
biological fathers were the rapists in quite a few of the incest
cases involving female victims.

The first time my biological father started sexually harassing me was
when I was nine. He played with my tiny young breasts. I felt
uncomfortable and tried to move away but his power as a father
won. I knew that he knew that it was wrong because he spoke with a
guilty tone in his voice. I told my mother and she just laughed, she
said laughingly 'Oh, he was just after those tiny breasts . . . never
mind'. She treated it as if it was cute.

The sexual harassment increased, through one of his attacks on me, because I did not give him what he wanted he punched me in the nose and broke it. A pool of blood ran onto his bedspread, he ordered me to wash it and to tell my mother he had spilt paint on it. After this attack I had nose bleeds nearly every day and this in turn affected my tonsils. Through surgery my nose and tonsils were operated on years later plus the blood vessels.

Later on it led to him creating situations where I'd be alone with him, and he rubbed his finger around and almost into my anus, he would poke me with his erect penis, he would touch me between the legs and come into my bed. I HATED IT. I ended up hating him.

My mother's attitude was at times that because we were the 'same blood' he couldn't possibly have these feelings for me. I dressed poorly so I would not attract him and tried to look ugly. Yet other times she would accept my explanation and her comments were, 'He wants to kiss you because he loves you', but I knew it was a different type of kiss. Other times she said, 'Don't fight him, let him and see if he'll really rape you'. I used my 12 year old brains and ignored my mother's advice thank God.

I now feel free for the first time in my life. He also knocked me out when I was 18 years old and laid me on the floor and held my head in an open fire, at the same time he was choking me.

I struggled with him many times when I got older and he beat me so much I could hardly walk, then he had what he wanted and left me lying on the floor or bed like a lump of dirt. Why should women have to put with that?

He was never put in jail for the crimes he committed against my sisters and I. He ruined our lives. I have never had any help as I feel OK but have sisters here who are receiving help as they are in a bad way with nerves. I did my best to help them but I was never believed.

Thank you so much for letting me have my say. It is very much appreciated. (Female raped from aged 8 through 16)

•

My father sexually molested me. My grandfather never quite got that far, so I guess that was OK!! (Female raped at age 14)

•

When I was young, 11 through 14, I was abused by my father, emotionally, physically and sexually. It wasn't till several years later that I revealed this fact initially to my brother who gave me little support. I was under threat from my father that he would do something far worse to me and said if I told someone it would split up their marriage, which is what he knew I wouldn't want.

His excuse for what he did to me was 'he didn't want me to be frigid like your mother', and wanted to teach me how to have sex.

Stepfathers
In the 'Without Consent' sample, as will become evident in this chapter, stepfathers were most frequently named as rapists.

My stepfather used to take me fishing or taught me driving lessons. On these occasions, we would drink a few beers which was a 'treat' as I was still at school. He coerced me into sexual relations with him and performed oral sex on me regularly. One time at home in the pool, whilst everyone was out he performed sexual intercourse on me.

I was never attracted to him (especially as he was married to my adoptive mother) and was repulsed by the whole ordeal. The most I could bring myself to do about it was telling him after the sexual intercourse it shouldn't happen any more and, as a small recompense, 'traded' with him to allow me to smoke at home! How pitiful.

I believed I would be judged as a willing partner and I also did not want to destroy the family unit. I initially told my de-facto but he blackmailed my family and myself with that information, along with previous sexual experiences and assaults. Thus I was loathe to tell anyone for several years until I confided in my good friend. She was very understanding and supportive and prompted me to tell my husband who was also the same.

•

I was about 7 years old when my stepfather started fondling me.

At the age of 9-10 he made me do things to him, then at the age of 10-11 he would have intercourse with me, mainly when my Mum was at work or in hospital; she spent a lot of time in hospital.

For punishment he would send me outside to the garage then he would come down close the door and get me in the back of the car. He would make me go for drives with him, he would park at the side of the road, make me go down on him.

He would sneak into my room at night, even if my Mum was home. And believe me I always heard him coming down the hall. At one stage of my childhood I had a man across the road, and an uncle feeling me any chance they got.

I used to think my real Dad was crazy; I didn't think he loved me at all because all he expected from me was a kiss and a cuddle; he wasn't like the others. My stepfather would tell me he loved me and say he would never do anything to hurt me. As a child I didn't know any better and of course, 'It's our secret, don't tell anybody. If you tell your mother it will kill her.'

I have been in touch with the police officer to see if anything can be done but because no dates, times, witnesses I can't do anything.

I would like to see him rot in hell. But because I was so scared and silly to say anything, he walks away unscathed ... but I will always protect my children from any harm.

•

My stepfather liked to play mental games with me. There is a lot more incest out there than what you think. I hope this helps because it has started to help me.

•

Although in the generally accepted sense I have not been raped as an adult, I was repeatedly raped or sexually abused as a child. My perpetrators were my mother and my stepfather and I am still coming to terms with the horror of those years.

Although suffering bouts of depression through my life, I actually started to 'remember' the incest about five years ago. The actual memories I can only describe as horrendous and [illegible] the pain, fear, guilt and anger that came with them.

I survive and I slowly heal. Life is becoming bearable and even dare I say enjoyable at times. For my survival I thank God and two wonderful people: firstly a lady [in a sexual assault centre] and secondly, a man [from a victim assistance organisation] where we moved to earlier this year. Without the [two organisations] life would have been very grim indeed. These agencies and ones like them throughout the country are invaluable and must be allowed to remain and continue their wonderful work.

Throughout the years I have sought help from various psychiatrists and doctors and with the exception of one marvellous lady doctor in [name of place] I have found them to be fairly hopeless. I also at one time had very helpful assistance from the Domestic Violence and Incest Centre in [name of city]. The assaults were so long ago but my pain is still so great I feel I must speak out.

Children mainly do not and cannot report sexual abuse at the time because the only way they survive the horror is to forget straight away. I could not have reported these things. I believe this defence mechanism automatically operates after each attack—otherwise how could a young child possibly survive? (Raped by stepfather and mother at the age of 3)

Grandfather

My grandfather sexually abused me. Because of who he was and my age I did not feel I could tell anyone with authority. My brother helped by ensuring I was never alone with my grandfather. He then tormented me for most of my life with subtly implied comments on my sexuality. He also interfered with cousins of mine. None reported it to an adult because of our relationship.

MALE VICTIMS

Overall, females are the more likely victims of sexual assault. However, for those males who had been raped and sent in surveys and/or letters, the risk for young boys was particularly high with 70.1 per cent of the males' victimisation taking place prior to the age of seventeen. Females were significantly more likely than males to disclose. Less than half (47.4 per cent) of the male respondents had ever told anyone in contrast to almost two-thirds (63 per cent) of the females in the whole sample. This is undoubtedly a reflection of the age distribution by gender.

Father also allowed his male friends to rape me. (Raped by father from age 4 through 13)

•

Two to three times a week for eight years. I was in constant fear of the so-called scum of a father. I was always sent to school with that many cracked ribs it was not funny. I was also made to go and steal from the market gardens. If I was five minutes late a hiding and straight up to bed the same with coal. If I was back 10 minutes late I would not be allowed back in and would have to sleep in the laundry with my dog.

•

I am still a virgin, growing up being told that sex is a type of crime—still have nightmares and depression, often think of suicide. No amount of water will ever make me feel clean. (Raped by father at age 8)

•

Nine years of age: My natural father got into my bed and placed my hands on his penis. I recoiled, hated him from that day on and had no compassion at his death bed.

•

My mother sexually and physically abused me all of my childhood. I had no idea it could be reported or even that her behaviour was wrong or bad. I wanted to respond to the survey so people would be aware that rape is not the only sexual crime. I was continually bashed and sexually abused by my mother for most of my childhood. She used to 'torture' my penis by squeezing it in her fingers. She also used to force her little finger into my anus when she caught me touching my penis at all.

This was her 'anger' response to having been raped continuously by her father when she was sixteen through twenty years old. She chose me, her first male child, to release her anger on, and also to totally repress my sexuality, presumably so I would not be like her father. (Raped from age 3 through 10)

THE EFFECTS OF INCEST

Although the following poem actually refers to molestation by a stranger and not a relative, the feelings that accompanied the assault and the consequences for the survivor/author will be found as common threads in the many stories which follow.

I don't want to
Can't you hear me?
can't you tell?
I know I have to do
What you tell me to,
Because you're an adult
and I'm just a child
So I have to
Besides, you scare me
with your threats,
How can this give you
pleasure?
Touching a small, scared
defenceless child
You're a sick man.
Even though my body
screams no
My mouth won't work,
No words come out
And I mustn't tell anyone,
No, I never tell
My heart's beating fast
and my muscles are tense,
No one will come
to this small girl's defence
You know you are safe,
To do what you will.
Ten years later, it's coming
back to haunt me.
You're still my nightmare,
Even though I don't know
your name, or remember your face,
Even though I can
remember the place.
I realise now, what I didn't

know then,
That the only reason I
couldn't tell
was so that you wouldn't
get into trouble.
I'm in a private hell,
Everytime I remember.
Did you ever think, what this
would do to me?
I know I'm not to blame myself
by thinking.
Your selfishness has damaged
my life.
What right did you have
to do that to me?
You took my childhood
innocence and naivety.
You took what was not
yours to take.
Insecurity, frustration.
Why me? No one should
have to go through
that pain, or the
punishment.
Sex should be a
beautiful thing,
Not a time to remember
what you've done to me.

Several survivors write about the general consequences of their victimisation.

The intensity of pain as a result is at a level I could <u>never</u> have envisaged. (Raped by cohabiting family member aged 3 through 8)

●

The bastard is dead now. He tried to rape me vaginally at six months. He oral raped me from [number] months on. Had many dislocated jaws. Now lost marriage, lost work, lost health and life totally stuffed up trying to sort out the mess now.

•

In a group of seven close acquaintances, all respectable middle class so called 'normal' women only one has not been molested; all unreported. I think you will find your statistics (1 in 4) are much higher than you realise unfortunately. We don't ever discuss it among ourselves and the one lucky unmolested friend has no idea that she is the only 'clean' one amongst us. HELP US!

I was cheated out of my childhood; my innocence was stolen; my life was shattered by men. I chose to be a single mum—I'm happy now. (Raped by cohabiting family member at age 5 and 6)

•

I would like to take this opportunity to share my story of how I was sexually assaulted by my stepfather when I was 17 years old.

At the time I thought I was pregnant and I confided in my stepfather. He sexually abused me. I find it extremely difficult to talk or even think about this incidence, it is just so painful.

At the time I felt emotionally confused and upset and I felt life was not worth living any more. I made two suicide attempts with Bex tablets. I admitted myself to a mental hospital. I received drug and ECT treatment and was put in lock up wards with insane people. I had told everyone about the assault but nobody seemed to listen.

My mother was never informed about the assault or the ECT treatment and I have only told her recently. My mother took me from [name of hospital] and we went to [overseas]. For years I suffered terrible anxiety feelings. I had problems communicating with men who were in authority to me.

I never sought any help. I did not want to become anybody's patient.

I have now come to terms with everything, which took a long time and it was all through the help of the [name of a church denomination]. Two ministers saved my life and even my anxiety feelings have completely disappeared.

I have since requested and am in possession of my case notes. I found I had been diagnosed with schizoid depression, pre-psychosis, endogenous depression, schizophrenia, etc. I feel quite angry about this. I sent the hospital a letter and they sent a reply without much content. It is also recorded in the doctor's notes that my stepfather was to be interviewed. He could have possibly said things to damage me and protect himself.

I feel so helpless. I have suffered unjustly and I am disabled with a diagnosis that was never true and is really only there to protect certain people and cover up their errors.

The Cycle of Abuse

Many victims of incest are also adult survivors of sexual abuse; they may 'shut down' their emotions and bodies at the onset of a rape and therefore, for that reason and others such as low self-esteem, might be more vulnerable to relationships with abusive men. This could be the principal contributor to another major finding in the survey: not only were many survivors children or teenagers at the time of the rape but about 60 per cent had been raped more than once during their lives to date; 13 per cent reported that they had been sexually assaulted 'too many times to count.'

Thus, many of the letters and comments described lifetimes of sexual and physical violence victimisation which started with some type of incest. (This statement and section in no way imputes the blame or responsibility for their victimisation upon the survivors.)

As I had abuse in my childhood, sexual and physical, I blamed myself in marriage because I was used to it and also scared. So it was worse in marriage—sexual, physical, emotional, mental, verbal. (Female raped as child by family member living in the house)

•

I was (late thirties) years old before I remembered an incident when I was 12 years old in which my father violated me sexually. I had completely blocked it OUT of my consciousness.

I had been working on my low self-esteem for many years— doing courses, having therapy and it took six years for this memory to surface and along with it other incidents of sexual abuse. Only when I was reading a special book did I even admit that I had been raped by my then fiancee.

Most of the sexual abuse I received in my childhood was covert —it was verbally directed at myself and the women in my family by my father. There was also violent physical abuse of women in my household as a child which I perceive as a form of sexual abuse. As I came in the same physical package as my mother—when she was beaten and I saw it—I felt that I too was punished for being a female. I thought that it was ok for a woman to be treated like that. It hurt like hell inside me when my fiance raped me and at the same time a part of my mind told me that it was his right. I thought I belonged to him and I could be treated as he wished and I didn't even question it at the time.

This is how I thought—this was my learned behaviour. I knew that what my fiance had done felt wrong inside of me but I didn't know what was wrong about it. I felt the pain of being violated and my right to say 'no' to sex was not respected but I didn't know it was appropriate to do something about it.

I went on to marry this man and years later when I was being physically beaten I broke free. The work I've done on myself since then has broken the cycle. I now have a relationship in which I respect myself and my partner respects me.

●

The abuser may have been abused as a child too.

My father constantly molested all his daughters; he held me against an erection and jerked off into my stomach, rupturing my intestines, leading to surgery in hospital when I was [age]. He threatened me with being responsible for 'breaking up the family and having no food, drink or shelter' if I told my mother. Innumerable other assaults —penetration of mouth by penis from 3 to 10 years. It stopped when I threatened to tell the police and get him put in jail. He then moved on to the younger kids. It wasn't so much the taste for young flesh as looking for a victim too young to report him.

My paternal grandfather raped my aunt, his daughter, when she was 12-13 'to teach her a lesson'. My father was 16 and 'was forced by the old man to join in the rape'. Another brother enjoyed it so much that he went twice, 'had another go'. A third brother cried and refused to take part. The fourth and fifth brothers were too young. My grandmother was away with the other two daughters (9 children). My grandfather thrashed my aunt afterwards to prevent her telling anyone.

When I was [age] my father was aware he'd die soon, so he admitted all the above and said all the siblings feared their father who was very violent and dictatorial. He admitted raping my youngest sister when she was 12 at the same time.

I was a virgin when I was raped. Although I had been sexually assaulted before, intercourse had never taken place. In this incident I was raped 'fully', all three ways.

Capital Punishment should be brought back and it should be applicable to rapists and paedophiles. Rape/incest is worst than murder, the victim has to live with it forever, you never really get 'over' it, you learn to cope but it's always there. It affects your whole personality even if you're not consciously aware of it at times. You tend to build walls around yourself because it's safer that way.

Question: Why is the innocent victim the one who receives the death sentence?

No Memories

Another consequence of incest, as frequently mentioned by its survivors, is the loss of childhood memories:

I regard incest as rape. Mine was vaginal and anal. Memories have only recently returned . I was 3 through 7 as far as I'm aware. I totally blocked it out. Skilful counsellor has helped. I do not trust the legal system for victims—it's a male system.!!

•

I repressed these memories for decades but I was (as a child and teenager) depressed and tried to kill myself more than once. I sought help for years. Working at a Women's Refuge was the first time 'incest' was labelled as serious violence and I was finally able to get help and then regain memories. (Raped by father as a toddler)

•

I had no memory of the childhood incest until I was in my thirties. As you would appreciate children under four years old aren't able to

29

carry memories and it is common for people to block out incestual rape even if it happened when they were, for instance, ten.

My first inkling was when I tried to have a surgical procedure. The practitioner [description of procedure] and said 'This will feel a little peculiar'. For the first two seconds peculiar is all it felt, then my body went into deep shock. My skin went—literally—white as a sheet. I felt deep-body nausea. I fainted. We couldn't proceed with it. The practitioner said, 'I've done thousands of (these) and no one's ever done this to me'. My body had remembered something which I couldn't.

Some months later I began to recover memories of it during rebirths. (I have found rebirthing to have been of benefit to many survivors of childhood interference.) The first memory was of my father sticking his finger in my anus and then into my mouth. Then it went on to anal and oral rape. This all happened under the age of about two-and-a-half.

As I became verbal, my father got scared of continuing. Recently, my elder brother who is [medical condition] has also begun to recover memories of these sorts.

Having done a lot of deep-level consciousness work in groups, the official estimates on sexual interference of children are very, very conservative. Not all of it is as horrible as my experience. But many, many adults who do deep consciousness work recover memories of having been 'disrespectfully handled' as young children—handled by adults for their own sexual pleasure or perhaps masturbated over or, of course, outright rape. I wish you all the best with your research. (Raped by father, from age 6 months through 4)

•

I blocked my incest for most of my life (only remembered in the last year). I still don't have 'picture' memories but I do have body memories (eg phantom hands on the body) sensory memories (reactions to smell of alcohol etc).

•

I have no real memory of my childhood. Feels like a big black hole, have one memory however of trying to run away from home when I was about 5 or 6, feared for my life was caught in the act don't remember what happened though. I believe I may have suffered sexual abuse, possibly from my father, I just don't know. I have a brother who saw him as abusive, I saw him as very loving.

The incest probably started before I was one year old and continued for several years, at least six or seven years old, probably much older. My perpetrator is my father. There is a sense of trying to tell my mother at some time and being told that I imagine things. One very common issue with incest survivors is lack of memory of most/all parts of childhood.

Relationship and Personal Problems

When the child whose trust was violated grows up, she has learned the rule of 'Don't trust' well. She has also probably acquired a deep sense of all encompassing shame which is antithetical to self-esteem, self-acceptance or even self-identity . . . all helpful personal qualities in maintaining functional relationships.

After I married it caused major marital difficulties for some years but my husband saw me through with great love. (Female raped by father at age 17)

•

As my life was threatened this rape was repressed from conscious memory. Hereafter I was very depressed, suicidal, lots and lots of fears, nightmares, phobias. Bottom of the class at school. Barely even spoke. Memories became fully conscious during nine years of psychotherapy. There are more assaults I know, from the fragments of memory, dreams I haven't placed. I do not want to remember any more.

I would not pursue legal action even if it were possible. I would not want to be victimised again in the court/legal system. I want to heal my emotional wounds, learn how to have relationships and live.

For women and children who have been assaulted there needs to be much more support. Looking back on my childhood I wish another adult had intervened to help me. Removing my father from the house appears to have been the best option. Mother physically and psychologically abused me too, but I was so emotionally dependent upon her for protection from rape and murder I don't think I would have tolerated being removed from her.

My greatest need in adult life has been for money for counselling. I have chosen professional psychologists in private practice to help me and they cost. There have been times I have been very depressed and it has been hard to remain in employment to earn the money. For the past ten years I have managed, just, to earn enough to pay rent, food, pills and counselling. Counselling has saved my life—living has become bearable now. (Female raped by father at age 9)

•

Yes. I have been in and out of the mental health system on and off since [number] years old—tried suicide several times as a teenager and twice as adult. Marriage failed. My three children believe the mother to be 'off the planet' as I have continual severed mood swings —too happy one minute, screaming uncontrollably the next. I can't find any normality in my life. I have numerous vaginal problems— severe pain, uncontrolled bleeding, discharge, etc which the doctors tell me there is no cause for and severe headaches also for no reason. These problems have plagued me on and off my entire adult and teenage life.

I feel I am being eaten alive by an evil blackness that consumes me and all that is or was good about me. I feel used and abused.

That is what rape and incest have done for me. I am so sad every time I hear or read about another child who has joined this sad fate of mine and too many others.

I pray for their souls, victims all.

•

This has affected my whole life. I have [number] children. I am scared to death of something happening to one of them. I find it very hard to trust anyone. Ever since I was first molested I built a wall around myself and find it hard to make friends, except for my ex husband.

I even find it hard to leave the kids anywhere. I have a baby sitter who comes to my house. I only go out when I want to go shopping and pick the kids up from school, it's a [number] minute walk to school, so I drive them. I don't know what age would be acceptable to let them walk to school by themselves. (Female raped by cohabiting family member at age 9)

•

I consider this to be incest as I looked to this man as my father. It also happened to my brother by the same man, my brother was [number] years younger. I do not know when it happened to him. I have trouble dealing with anything affecting the sexual parts of the body, including bathing my little girls. Sex is not good with my husband.

•

Grandfather had incestuous contact with [number] grand-daughters; outcomes for all of us were different. We have all reacted in different ways, i.e. promiscuity, withdrawal, low self esteem, etc. When I was older I learnt that my grandmother and grandfather had not been intimate for many years.

If I smell alcohol or cigarettes on someone's breath it makes me feel sick as that was how my grandfather smelled. My husband smokes and he has to scrub his mouth before he makes love to me. The other grand-daughters experience different traumas. One even ended up in a mental hospital.

WHY THEY DID NOT DISCLOSE OR REPORT

More than a third (37 per cent) of those raped by cohabiting family members had never told anyone; 43 per cent of those assaulted by family members who lived in a different household had never shared their story until they sent in a survey or letter.

Some were warned that they or their mother would be killed if they told.

I have only remembered the above in the last four months. It was extremely brutal and my father had threatened to kill me if I told anyone. I've talked to lots of people, many who have never told anyone else about their own sexual abuse. The fear of telling anyone is pure HELL! (Female raped by father and grandfather at age of 4 onwards)

•

I was only 9½ years of age, when my then future stepfather, introduced me to 'THE GAME'. I do not recall how or why it all started. It started out as what seemed to be a game, tickling, playing, fonderling! [sic] This was all before he said 'I DO', to my mother!

I did not inform my mum of the game, as he played with me in front of her as well as in bed (in private). So to a nine year old child, all was thought to be natural.

After the marriage, approximately [number] months after, was the first time for the game to stop, and 'GROWN UPS FUN' started. I cried and cried, but he threatened me from the very first time he touched me. 'You tell your mother about our fun, and I'll just have a little accident, while we are out Roo shooting.'

He insisted, that I always go with him. The excuse was, 'I need her to hold the spot light.'

Rubbish. He wanted me there not only to hold the spot light, but also for his own pleasures.

My mother finally caught him out, after years. He was trying to awaken me, by rubbing his hands all over my upper and lower areas of my body. This was being done very gently, as not to arouse me instantly with a fright. (So I would not make any sudden noises, as my mother was in the kitchen.) My mother faced him within hours of being caught out. She made arrangements to be moved out and have family help. He became extremely aggravated and came close to shooting my mother. My mother stood in the centre of the room, he stood in the doorway, with the rifle by his side. His eyes looked like the pits of hell, his face like a . . . Devil, mean, angered, bitter. I stood at the other end of the room, near another doorway.

My mother asked, 'Did he touch you?' I looked at her. She asked again, 'Did he have sex with you?' I looked at him with extreme fear running through my whole body, my heart seemed to pump 10,000 times faster, than normal. I replied 'Yes' and ran like the wind was carrying me out of that house. I could hear them arguing, as I ran.

Next thing I know, he was behind me with the rifle. He stared me straight in the eyes and said, 'I warned you'. He lifted to sight it up. I ran, he called my name. I stopped and turned around. He pulled the trigger. The bullet hit the tree, just inches from my head, it ricocheted off the tree and skimmed off behind me. It seemed like slow motion, through this whole five minute episode. Five minutes of my life like a deep scar!

After we got off the property, we were taken to my grandmother's house, in a little country town. Within days, I was taken to a doctor for an examination, and total physical check-up. From there we went to [place] to charge him for what he did to me. I couldn't face the questioning, as always in the back of my mind, was that rifle being fired at me, and his continuous threats. I feared for my life, as well as my family's, I could not testify on those grounds. Court officials informed my mother, that he would have been sentenced, if I could of given evidence.

To this day I truly regret not having that . . . person sentenced for what he did to me! But you cannot turn back the hands of time. Because of him my internals (tubes etc) were badly damaged, and I had to have a [name of surgical procedure] at the age of [early twenties]. This has devastated my life.

I am fortunate to have one child, a beautiful daughter, whom I watch with eagle eyes! I fear for my daughter, as she is now [number] years old and all the memories have come flooding back.

Others were simply afraid that they would not be believed.

Did not report it—fear of not being believed, especially by Mum. I knew it was wrong but did not know it was rape as I did not know anything about the body. (Female raped by father at age 11)

Some were afraid of the parent's anger:

My father used to take me outside a mental asylum threatening me if I told anyone. I would be put in this place and my face would become ugly and distorted. I was constantly bashed from the age of [number] to [number], also my sister and mother. I was in and out of hospital because I couldn't think. Headaches and vomiting especially after my head was kicked and bashed. No one did anything.

I can remember as far back as [number] years the violence in my home. Watching my mother being beaten until she lost conscious. Myself on top of the stairs being kicked and falling, hitting my head on the slate floor. Apparently I was unconscious.

I had trouble at school because I could not concentrate. I was worse if my head and body had been kicked and bashed the night before. If anyone noticed the bruises no one said or did anything. After all I lived in the poor part of town; nice people didn't want to get involved.

I can remember being brought home by an ambulance from the cinema. I had a violent headache and I was vomiting. I was given an injection. Dad came to the bedroom to see how I was. I can remember the glazed blue eyes, Dad taking his clothes off and came into the single bed. Daddy started to kiss me, his tongue in my mouth. I was frightened but felt limp, then Daddy came on top of me and kept putting this hard thing between my legs and kept at it until there was a pain, a terrible, terrible pain. I started to scream but Daddy put the pillow over my face then everything went black. I was 10 years old. Sexual abuse continued until I was 14 years when my sister came in. She tried to kill him with a knife. I stood between her and him, not to protect him, but her and myself.

Dad took me so many times to a mental institution where we looked through these heavy iron locked gate. In the yard were all sorts of deformed people jerking, frothing at the mouth. Dad told me if ever I told anyone I would be put in this place and my face would turn like the people we were watching. My sister was very beautiful. I didn't want to see her being put in this place so I stopped her from killing Dad.

One day the Pandora box opened, every time I read or saw on TV about a child being violated I became a different person. The urge to kill these monsters, kill the do-gooders, judges who seem to be on the rapist side, especially where children are concerned. I would actually kill the rapist slowly and painfully. Then I would come out of this trance. I am shocked when I think of what I'm like. I vomit and get terrible headaches.

I don't care if I die hitting back at these so-called justice, but when we start and the result is seen all over the world this country will become safe again. Everyone can feel secure in their home, walking the streets instead of making ourselves prisoners in our own home. Now I feel sick, drained, after writing this letter.

Another concern expressed was the effect on the family of breaking the silence.

I feel OK. Hate my stepfather and haven't reported it to authorities because I feel it would be hard on me and my family. (Female raped by stepfather from age 5 through 14)

•

The punishment for him was not worth the pain and humiliation I would have had to put the family through. I did not tell anyone until my mother was divorced for other reasons. (Raped by stepfather, at age 8 through 12)

And of course they were also children with children's restricted awareness of what is and is not appropriate behaviour.

I knew all my perpetrators. They were supposed to love and care for me. I could not comprehend that it was a crime, they were my family. I had been emotionally manipulated to such an extent I accepted life as it was, as my lot in life and that I was worthy of nothing better. They also ensured that I carried the guilt and responsibility for their actions.

Because my abuse started at such a young age I was never given any choices, I had an inability to make any decisions 1. as I was a child and 2. because they had always been made for me. The threat of violence was always there.

The police were always made out to be the 'Gestapo'. There was no way I could contemplate trusting them. I couldn't even trust my own family.

Please excuse the writing as this had been very difficult—I hope with the women who break their silence and contribute to this survey some very much needed changes will be able to take place. God knows we need them. (Female raped by grandfather and brother from the age of 3 onwards)

THE RESPONSE OF FAMILY MEMBERS

The reactions of family members varied according to the nature of the relationship between the offender and the survivor; and the age of the survivor when she was assaulted. Fifty-nine per cent of relatives were supportive if the offender was a stranger, 63 per cent if the offender was a boyfriend; however if disclosing about another family member living in the same house, only 32 per cent received support. Difference by age (the older the victim was when assaulted the more likely she was to receive support) was undoubtedly a correlate of the preceding finding on relationship since the younger-aged victims were more likely to have been assaulted by a cohabiting family member.

Those who did not Believe

Family members—for me—have been the least supportive and will not believe nor listen re anything to do with sexual assault or incest. My sister died last month—suicide from 20 years of incest/assault by a family member.

•

Most of my family are unsupportive of me and some are openly supportive of the rapist.

I feel a great sense of anger and betrayal towards my family and towards the abuser. Most of them either disbelieved me or totally disregarded my feelings. (Female raped by cohabiting family member from age 7 onwards)

Those who Allowed it

I kept telling my family what was happening. One sister said I was making it up and looking for attention, the other sister said she'd fix it up but she didn't. Brother said he felt helpless. I eventually retaliated when he attacked me with a knife and rang neighbours for help who I then told the whole story to. My brother and I moved out of home the next day and I haven't seen my father since and I can't wait for the day he rots in hell. (Female raped by father from age 12 through 17)

•

Speak out. I was continuously assaulted by father from the age of five. I attempted to tell my mother but she was horrified of him [sic], so therefore couldn't or wouldn't do anything.

At the age of [number] I had an illegitimate baby to him.

The police laughed at me and took me home and I had to stay there until I was 18 years old.

•

Dad just thought he had the right to get sexual gratification and it was cheaper to do so in the family. Mum was no protection and was often brutal to us. Myself and my two sisters were always used like this. Mum was not likely to trade minimal physical comfort for morality. All of this led me to doubting my ability to be a parent. Dad used to play 'mind games' to control 'our little secret'. We were scared. (Female raped by father from age 10 through 16)

•

I was raped by my father with my mother's prior knowledge and consent at age 15. I confided in my mother and was begged by both parents never to tell anyone about it. Until [early thirties] I was a psychological mess—at that time I saw a psychiatrist who helped me get over it.

Those Who Blamed the Victim
I did tell my mother. She said I lied and named me a slut. What was the use of authority?

So many deep blocked memories came flooding back. Yes, I was one of many that wasn't raped but fondled, poked, inspected and felt up and told never to tell. The first was my own brother and somehow when that nightmare ended, my stepfather decided to 'show me the facts of life' (no rape, but so much damage can be done to the mind and innocence of children).

When my stepfather decided I was a prime target, I told my mother which is what they advertise and she called me a liar and jealous of her new relationship! He was sleeping with her and trying to use me! A barrier went up. Authorities?? Like hell if your own mother doesn't believe you, who else would!!

•

I had never understood my mother's dislike of me. When I was [forties], my mother 'confessed' that my father was 'fooling' around with me, when I was 18 months old. My mother treated me as the 'trollop' or 'slut'. Under the patriarchal system what else could she do?

THE RESPONSE OF NON-FAMILY
For the following survivors, people had been less than supportive, perhaps finding another's incest story too threatening or uncomfortable.

It is great that something is finally being done and that survivors are now being encouraged to speak out. My experience has been the opposite. Society has had a need to enforce the secret to maintain the myth of 'happy nice families'. One way people have maintained the silence is by immediately changing the subject as if I had not even spoken. No acknowledgment at all that I had mentioned the incest would certainly test anyone's ability to continue to speak out against sexual assault. You may help give us a voice that will be heard in the hope of keeping others safe in the future from any form of sexual abuse. Thanks. (Female raped by father, grandfather, older brother from 2 through 12)

•

I did not tell anyone 'til I was 18 and the counsellor I saw told me I had survived for eight years and I was lucky to forget it and to get on with my life.

At [age] I left home and was too scared to go back to see my mother and family. All I could do was move away so that I had an excuse not to see them.

RESPONSE OF THE CRIMINAL JUSTICE SYSTEM

Police response was perceived as supportive by only 30 per cent if the rapist was a family member living in the same house as the complainant.

My stepfather used to try to ask me to let him explain sex and facts of life to me. I said no, but I mistrusted him and was scared of him and didn't want him to tell me those things which I knew little of. He used to say he would show etc.

One day I was taken to the beach at (place) for a swim etc. Mum said it would do me good, she was working. After the swim he said he had to go and see someone before we went home, and we walked for a long time.

I kept asking, Where are we going? Where does this man live?'

We ended up off the road going through some paddocks, he said he has a farm through here. I didn't know where I was at all. But I got suspicious of him, and was walking behind him, and just kept picking up small stones and putting them in my pocket. I kept thinking if he tries anything with me I'll throw the stones at him. As I must state here that my sister five years older than me didn't know but I had seen him with her having sex. At the time I didn't know if it was willing on her behalf or rape.

He kept calling me to keep up to him. Finally waiting for me to catch up, we were in the middle of nowhere as I thought. When he knocked me to the ground and jumped [sic] his body over the top of me and said he was going to have sex with me it was time I learnt how to do it, and he could introduce me to men who would pay me to have sex with me. I was scared, didn't want sex or men paying me etc. As I just tried to wriggle and fight him off me. But wasn't getting far only he relaxed his grip over me to undo his trousers and his fly. I managed to get enough strength to push him hard in the chest and push him off me. And I ran and ran and cried and cried. He kept running after me and calling me. I kept throwing the stones at him. Finally I found my way out of the paddock and into the street. He kept calling me and saying he was sorry, not to tell anyone and he won't do it again.

I came up to a man watering his yard and asked where I was etc and he said I think it was [name of place] I forget which place it was now I think it was so long ago. He asked me,' Was I alright?'

By now [Name] had caught up to me and said, 'My daughter panicked as we were lost. We were looking for a friend or something.'

The man said,' Are you sure you are all right?'

I said, 'I just want to go home.'

The man told us where the station was and my stepfather said, 'Now don't tell your Mother she will be upset etc I'm sorry.'

And I was always brought up not to pimp or tell tales. My mother always drummed that into me so I said all right. I was working and I was very upset still and one morning a few days later I packed a small bag with a few items and went to work. But I let them all think that I was off to work and I went down to see my father and asked him if I could stay with him and my brother. He said, 'Of course you can. Is anything wrong?'

I said 'No, I just don't like [name of stepfather] and don't want to live with Mum any more.'

My mother got worried when I didn't come home and rang my boss and he said I didn't go to work. So she rang the hospitals and no I wasn't there. She rang my Auntie and I wasn't there. So she rang the policeman where my father was and sent him down to see if I was with my Dad. When he came and found me he asked me why I went to my Dad's and why I didn't tell my mother where I was going.

I said I didn't as I wanted to live with Dad. So he told Dad he wanted to talk to me privately and would take me under the house to talk to me. He kept on why did I leave and he said I'd have to go home to my Mother's. I said, 'No I won't go I'm staying with my Dad.'

'Do you know your Mother can make you go and live with her as you are under age,' he said to me. 'So you will have to have a good reason for not going to your mother's or the courts will make you to go back to her.' He said, 'Did anything happen to make you run away?' I said, 'I won't say'. He kept asking me nicely and I said, 'I don't pimp or tell tales'. He said, 'Look, did your stepfather do or say anything to you to make you want to leave home?'

'I won't pimp,' I said to him again.

'Look I'm going to tell you straight you'll have to tell me what he did to you or you'll have to go back,' he said. 'I can tell he did by what you have said to me. He will only do it again if you go back.'

So I told him and he said, 'Why did you say you won't pimp?'

I said he told me not to, and Mum always told me not to pimp on anyone. He said this man had been in trouble before. So he said come up to your father. He told Dad and told Dad to get me ready for the police to come. I was taken and interviewed by a detective and a police lady and I told them what I told you.

So therefore I was lucky. Rape didn't occur then just assault. He was interviewed and told that if he ever did anything to me again he would go to jail.

So a few months later I saw my mother in town and she said to come out and see her in the day when [name] would be at work. I went and was waiting on Mum to come home. As my sister said she was cleaning the offices in town and would be back in around an hour. [Name] came home and found me there. We all had an argument and he punched me in the face. The neighbour rang the police and the policeman said it was my fault for going there. Mum still wasn't home. So the policeman got me out of there and said you were told to keep away from him etc.

So I never seen my Mother or stepfather for years after that, and I wrote to my Mother when I was nearly 23 and told her I was pregnant and my boyfriend was away and I would like to be with her to have my baby. I asked was [name] there. I got a letter from her briefly which said, 'I've paid for an aeroplane ticket for you to come up to [place] from [place] as I'm working and living up here.' No mention of [stepfather] so I thought its ok he is not there so I'll go.

When I got off the bus from the plane ride, I saw him with Mum and didn't know what to do being pregnant etc and nearly having my baby. So I thought well I'll have to stay. I'll get out if I have to.

... so he found me on the beach walking and paddling. No one else was around and he pushed me over and raped me. I didn't want to cause a stink on the island and waited till we got back to town and told him and Mum I was leaving I was not going to have him rape me again. I didn't go to the police as I still today think I was at fault as I should have left when I found him still with Mum.

•

I found on the whole no-one believed me except for my pastor. The police tried to get me to say I had made it up so it would not have to go to court. I ended up being kicked out because mum said if it was true I couldn't stay there and if it wasn't true she didn't want me there. (Female raped by stepfather)

•

I would still like to kill him.

Because there were so many children in my family, my parents often farmed us out to relatives. He was a relative and regardless of our obvious fear of physical abuse, our mother would not believe what was happening and forced us to stay with him, sometimes for six months at a time.

My father went to the police when he found out, but my [relative's] father was in charge of the country station and blackmailed my father into not going any further with it by threatening to prove that it was my father doing this (my father had a criminal record) and it would put him back in jail.

My father committed suicide not long after. My mother had an affair with her son-in-law and her son-in-law raped, buggered and beat all her children and any other children that he had access to— even in front of other children and some other adults, including his father and brothers.

For some, the cases went to court where, for all but one, the process and/or the outcome were unsatisfactory.

I was sexually assaulted for three years from 12-15 years old. I was told it was my fault that it happened. I believed this and just accepted that I did deserve it, I put up with this for three years until my grandfather started on my sister. I told my mum about a month after this. To accept what was happening, I blocked everything out of my head. When I made my statement I still couldn't remember everything.

After it was reported, I felt disgusted and ashamed of myself. I felt weak because I let it continue for so long, I also felt dirty because my mother and sisters now knew that my body had been touched.

I would like to say to other victims that it is never too late to speak up, It is your body and you have the right to say no! If that person doesn't do as you wish then it is wrong! Even if you're a child and are too scared to say anything, that person shouldn't be touching you. I'm proud to say I'm a survivor and I'm trying to live my life.

Also I don't agree with the sentence length he received, only three years. He will be out soon and I will be a nervous wreck! Scared to go anywhere! The sentence lengths should be longer, take a page from America's book, their sentence lengths are much harder over there.

•

Even though the court case was a nightmare it was worth it to tell everyone what Mum's father done to me. I think all rapists should have their balls cut off so they bleed to death. It might only take an hour to rape but it takes the victim the rest of their lives to try and deal with what happens. (Female raped by grandfather when she was 14)

HEALING

As many of the writers have already indicated, they have begun a process of healing. For some, this is at an incipient stage, for others, it has been a long journey. As the stories disclose, the first step is breaking the silence and the 'Don't talk' rule which perpetuates incest and other dysfunctional family behaviours.

My sexual abuse is so horrific it would shock many people out there. I would not go into detail here at all. In short, I lived with almost daily sexual abuse for 10-11 years from the age of 4-15, by then I still did not understand what this was called, all I know is I was a daily victim for 10 years of my life.

Fortunately I have just begun to talk about it and have finally found counselling which I found extremely hard to get into. I would like to emphasise one thing, although people are supposedly available, when I rang, all the Crisis Centres said I was out of their areas. I was almost distraught by the tenth phone call, then I went to my doctor and asked for a referral. Thankfully, these people have taken me on as the anger within me can be so destructive and I find this quite frightening.

I think that my sexual assault will be with me forever. It has contributed to many problems I have i.e. I have no close friends; lack of trust; never had a sexual relationship or boyfriend (male as a friend) I struggle with anorexia/bulimia; and after five years psychiatric treatment I'm slowly improving. (Female raped by cohabiting family member aged 4 onwards)

Even after one thinks the healing is complete, another assault or incident may trigger a recycling of feelings and hidden memories:

I was subjected to five years of incest/rape between the age of five to 10 from my father. I consider myself healed from that now, however, the incident (rape) in my last relationship triggered some unfinished issues for me.

PREVENTION SUGGESTIONS FROM THE SURVIVORS

Numerous letter writers and comments referred to the inadequate response of the criminal justice system and the need for much more severe sentencing.

I also found that due to the lack of evidence and difficulty in prosecuting a case like mine the police were not interested at all in what happened. I strongly believe there needs to be a lot more research into these cases and the laws changed accordingly. (Female raped by father at age 13)

•

The perpetrator should not be seated so that the victim has to see him when answering questions to his lawyer. There should be some kind of law that the perpetrator is punished somehow when he admits doing it to the victim, even if it was a long time ago, because the victim could not report at the time of the rape. Our lives are wrecked for the rest of our lives while they get off scot free. (Raped by summer-time cohabiting relative at age 15)

An attempted rape by her stepfather when she was twelve culminated in the next letter writer's own incarceration. She speaks both about prevention for other children advising them to scream and of the tacit role played by some mothers.

Some years ago at the age of twelve I was attacked and almost raped by my stepfather. When I say 'almost' I mean that he entered my bedroom, threw me on to the bed and was actually lying on top of me with a red face and heavy breathing, when I managed to really yell and make a whole lot of noise. Noise is one thing paedophiles are very averse to, I discovered that night and my advise to all kids if finding themselves in such a situation (in the home) don't just say 'No', yell it at the top of your voice! You can't believe how quickly he loses the urge. Paedophiles can only operate in secret.

In my own case my stepfather backed away towards the door. He said terrible things to me such as (quote) 'You are only here on sufferance' and (quote) 'Do you think I am going to feed and clothe you for nothing?' (unquote). I heard him return to his own room.

Just the same, I didn't trust that he might not return and try it again, as we were alone in the house, my mother having gone on a holiday and left me with him. So I counted up what money I had and praying it was enough for my fare to [name of city] I set off through the bedroom window and took a [form of transportation] to the station and took the train to [name of city] and then another one to [another city] to my real father.

My stepfather was only questioned by police concerning my charge of attempted rape. In the end they decided not to believe me on the evidence from my mother that I was always highly imaginative and a habitual liar and that her husband was a very kind and gentle man who could not possibly commit that kind of offence.

I was brought into the children's court and exactly what the charge was I really don't know because there were a whole lot of adults talking about me in front of me as though I didn't really exist except by nuisance value. But I knew that God knew I was there and

I was my witness [*sic*]. My sentence of being the victim of a crime of violence was [number] years in a State Institution.

I almost lost my faith in God during those years of absolute sheer hell in that place. At this point I must add that the hell was some of my own making because of my rage and hate of all adults and my total refusal to cooperate with anyone.

Just to illustrate how insensitive some social workers are. On the day of the court hearing my mother was in Court saying all these things about me and I was placed in the care of this social worker who was to escort me to that place and as we were standing there, my mother was seen to approach us. I, of course, ignored her. And this lady actually said to me, 'Aren't you going to say goodbye to your mother?'

I really felt, and still do, that this was the most deplorably insensitive attitude that one could ever imagine! Of course I didn't say goodbye or anything else to my mother and neither have I spoken a word to her from that day to this.

I could have come out of this maternal betrayal very badly indeed except that I was feeling very low in spirit and I met a beautiful lady who became my real mother. The mother I never had. There was this instant bonding. Unbelievable! She had a son and I became the daughter she never had.

Back to this other woman, my biological mother. I believe that just as she knew all along that I had been telling the truth, eighty percent of mothers are aware that their child is being molested sexually. And if not, they ought to show cause as to why not!

I understood that some States in America have passed a law which states that when a family member (father, uncle, stepfather, family friend) is arrested and charged with sexual abuse of a child, the mother is also arrested and has to show cause as to her failure to protect the child.

I firmly believe that were our Government to pass a similar law the incident of child abuse would decrease by about eighty percent. Because, of course, the mother must know if something major, as serious, as sexual abuse is happening to her child. Apart from all of the physical signs there is also maternal bonding which is the instinct.

I suggest that many mothers (such as my own) submerge all of this in the cause of her own economic survival. My own (biological) mother admitted that she had known I was telling the truth (to a relative of mine) but that she was afraid that if my stepfather got into trouble she would lose the roof over her head. In other words there are women who are prepared to act as 'pimps' by selling out their children just in order to keep the roof over their head!

I repeat my earlier advice in the campaign to protect our children entitled It Is All right To Say No. Tell them it is even better if they yell it, real loud. In the case of my stepfather, although we were alone in the house, he was afraid the neighbours would hear me! So tell them to yell!

The following two women stressed the need for sex education in schools and community information programs so that children feel safe in saying 'no' and in breaking the silence.

A woman never ever recovers. Never can trust again either. The man is always, in rape cases, seen as the victim. The woman always has to prove her innocence. I would never ever report rape. Why should you have to go through hell again after something like that has already happened? But for the very brave who do they should be treated with so much respect and dignity for what they have been through yet still have the guts to go for justice. I say justice, but we all know it doesn't exist. The law does not provide for these victims. They are punished again by the system, then again by society.

I truly believe if a man is a repeat sexual offender he should be castrated, then let free. He can live a normal life without being a threat to society. It's not out of anger I say this. It would be better for someone who has his behaviour out of control. With drugs they can always eventually refuse to have them. Rapes would drop because potential rapers [sic] would fear the loss of power they think they have. If they carry on anyway eventually they will get caught and be treated anyway.

Although I would never go to the police it is common knowledge how women are treated if they report a rape. How accepted physical domestic violence is. I know the laws are about to change on that, but how about trying to change attitudes? Laws do not change attitudes that has to be done by education. (Female raped by cohabiting family member)

•

Due to insufficient sex education I did not know what was happening. Education in schools does not breed promiscuity but rather understanding!!!! (Female raped by cohabiting family member at age 12)

A recurrent theme that has appeared in many of the preceding pages, either directly or indirectly, is the tragic consequences of not heeding the advice to believe the children.

Children are the most precious beings on earth. They should never be dismissed and they shouldn't be treated as second class citizens. We need to cherish and look out for our children or we will have no future. (Female raped by stepfather from age 10 through 14)

•

I harbour a lot of resentment about the fact that what happened to me remains (still) a family secret. If it had been a stranger the likelihood of it being brought out in the open would have been much stronger. I think the community still needs to be made aware that most survivors of sexual assault knew the perpetrator. (Female raped by family member living apart, aged 7 through 12)

•

Though the molesting stopped at fourteen years, the beating and verbal abuse escalated until I could leave home at eighteen years. Verbal abuse and threats via the telephone continued for about six months.

Obviously my self-esteem and self worth was totally negligible and I ended up marrying a violent man. I have been separated [number] months and been in counselling since. I hope no other child has to go through what I and my sisters and brother went through. Education of children and mothers is essential. Believe the children.

The final suggestion offered by many who have been through the pain, self-doubt and denial was to report the crime.

Any woman or man who has been a victim of rape or incest should report it. I know it's hard to do for sometimes the person who has done it you trusted, especially a brother or sister you loved and didn't want to hurt them, that's only if they didn't hurt you at the time the crime happened. (Female raped by foster-father when she was aged 11-14)

•

I reported it twenty-two years later to collaborate [sic] incest charges laid by two other family members—no action taken [number] months later.

After seeking counselling years afterwards I realise my silence has 'let it happen' to many other little girls at this predator's hands. (Female raped by family member at age 10 and another relative at age 14)

The following letter includes all of the above and adds some warning signs to watch for in a child that may be masking her sexual abuse.

Until we can change judges, jurors and police attitudes towards incest and rape, men will still continue to rape and walk free. Society's attitude of the difference in boys and girls must be changed firstly in the house and school. Some examples are that when a boy reaches his teens usually his father and mates will say, 'Son go sow your wild oats as often as you can', yet at the same he says to his daughter, 'Don't do it or you will be a slut'.

There was an example recently where the judge threw a case out of court because he didn't believe a poor little eight year old girl. My heart goes out to that poor little girl because of what she has physically gone through and her future emotions.

When I was nine, I was raped on a regular basis by my father. This continued until I was eleven, when finally I ran away from home. I knew it would be tough, scary and dangerous but then I thought it cannot be any worse than at home. Unfortunately I didn't get too far. I was caught by police in [name of place]. I told them why I had run away from home and that I didn't want to go home. I even asked to be put in a foster home.

This was years ago and no one wanted to know about it, so they rang my parents to come and collect me. The rapes stopped then because I kept threatening to run away again and a few suicide attempts.

As soon as I told my mother she yelled at me for telling lies. So where does one go—mothers, teachers and police won't believe me, because my father was a so-called respected member of the community.

Over years of counselling I have learned to live with the horror and get on with my life. I am a survivor but I do have a big grudge against any molesters and rapists—a bullet is not good enough for them—do to them as they do to others; then kill them—GET RID OF VERMIN.

My life always has been totally free of drugs and very little alcohol, was well in control, then I met a man who I trusted and loved. We finally got married, had several children and then disaster struck, he found out about my childhood. His reaction was the worst any one could cop. It was worse than what happened. He resented me, didn't want any sexual relations with me, and was very negative, such as if I yelled at the kids, got upset over anything at all—his response was that it was all because of what happened. Our marriage has broken down and divorce is on the way. I didn't expect a lot of sympathy, all I wanted was a little understanding and support but all I got was abuse and blame.

My advise to any children suffering as I did, just be strong and keep telling (as hard as it is) until someone does believe you. Tell the family, neighbours, teachers, friends even strangers at community centres etc until it stops. Thank God things have changed a lot now and people do believe but there is still a lot who don't want to know, so they ignore it.

No child (male or female) dreams up specific events, places and times and claims, or has the courage or guts to stand up and say this is happening or has happened, if it is not true. When judges and others won't believe a child, then it just gives the perpetrator a free ticket to go and do more damage as they think, 'Well I can do it, I won't get caught because no-one will believe the child or do anything about it.

A message for all parents, if your child is usually a well behaved child, good grades at school, sports etc then suddenly the child becomes bad mannered, trouble at school, grades slip, lose interest in their favourite sports etc, there is a very good chance that your child is not 'just going through a silly phase or fad'. Ask many questions and keep asking until you get the real truth.

3

HUSBANDS

> If your husband rapes you, you think that it's not really rape. He considers you're his property and you usually believe that but a rapist is a rapist and other women have been raped by this man and done nothing.

Legally, in Australia, a woman is no longer supposed to abdicate her sexual rights in marriage; a wife's consent is no longer to be implied. However, the reality is that few rapes by cohabiting spouse/rapists are either reported or tried. Even estrangement has proven problematic. Certainly the change in legislation has not resulted in a flow of marital rape cases through the courts. In September 1991, a man in Tasmania was sentenced for the rape of his wife. This was the first marital rape trial in that state although immunity was abolished in 1987. The couple were estranged.

Extreme violence appears to be a necessary component in the marital rape for it to be deemed a criminal act. For example, in January 1993, the Australian public, or segments of it, were shocked by the revelation of a judge's remarks during the trial of a rapist in South Australia. The perpetrator had raped his wife and had admittedly used force. The judge remarked that some force was a necessary adjunct to sex with one's wife if she did not readily agree to intercourse. This comment is indicative of the gap between substantive legal change and its implementation, interpretation, or practice.

When I went to court I was the only woman there and I came away feeling that I was in the wrong and it was all right to strangle and rape your wife—even though I was admitted to hospital.

OTHER VIOLENCE IN THE MARRIAGE

For over three-quarters (77 per cent) of the women who had been raped by a cohabiting partner, the sexual assault was part of a general pattern of physical violence:

My husband threatened me as my brother did. While married my husband often used fists and mental cruelty as a weapon, as well as rape.

•

Rape, hits and slaps experienced as part of marriage breakdown after [number] years I was afraid until I found courage (after [number]) years to walk out on everything I owned and had worked for and started a new life all over again. My husband refused to undergo any form of counselling. (Raped for five years during her mid-forties)

Physical force could be accompanied with threats to kill:

I have been the victim of various bashings and forced sex for years, not knowing how to get out of the relationship (he threatened to shoot myself and the kids—he would have, I have no doubt). All I could do was protect and love the kids. We are slowly building a new and better life. To those who are suffering like I was, don't hesitate like I did, get out.

•

In 19XX rape in marriage was not considered a crime. The police regarded my assault as a simple domestic argument and asked my husband what I'd done to deserve two black eyes and two broken front teeth. He raped me by threatening to hurt my daughter. After this I left him, and have had successful relationships since and consider I am a fortunate survivor.

In some of the letters, such as the following, the physical violence described is so extreme that one might be tempted to question its veracity; too much pain to comprehend.

Shortly after I married, my husband and I went out socialising at a hotel. On our return we went to bed. He was angry that I had danced with another man. We argued and he pinned me to the bed. He began raping me saying things like 'You want it, don't you bitch? Say that you're a whore and that you like my cock'.

He then began to hit my face with a closed fist but in slapping motion. I don't know how many times he hit me, I may have blacked out. The next morning he denied all knowledge of the night's events. I was [early twenties] years old.

On another occasion my husband thrust a bottle into my vagina. On other occasions he placed a cucumber and many other objects into my vagina. Another occasion he placed a vacuum cleaner hose into my vagina and joked that one day he would make it come out of my mouth. On another occasion he 'made me' have sex with the knob of the couch we were sitting on.

Me and my husband were having sex one night and he removed his penis from my vagina and thrust it in my anus. I was extremely sore and could not walk properly for several days.

My husband would rape me at will during our marriage. Once he came up behind me while I was washing dishes. He pulled my pants down and entered me from behind. My son was in the room.

I was about to leave my husband due to his abusive behaviour. We were holidaying and I made the mistake of telling him my plans. I drove home and began packing clothes in my son's room. I looked up and saw my husband's boots in the doorway. I didn't want my son to be alarmed so I pushed past my husband to the lounge room. He then slapped my head into the sliding glass door, then threw me on the bean bag and raped me. Afterwards he laughed and said 'You'll be back when you find out you're pregnant'. We were using the rhythm method of contraception and he knew my fertile days.

I returned to him six weeks later after testing positive to a pregnancy test. Ironically he then wanted me to have an abortion.

The violence in the marital relationship which accompanied the sexual assault(s) was not always physical:

I was not physically battered because I always submitted. Mostly my husband jumped on me when I was asleep, pinned my arms down and clutched my legs with his so that I could not move. I was threatened and abused for thirteen years and finally left. Then he continued to intimidate me by driving backwards and forwards in front of my house and laughing at me. It took me years to realise that what my husband did was rape.

•

I personally experienced sexual harassment and was made to comply to the sexual wishes of my husband against my will. The point to note is that there was never the threat of physical violence. My husband would psychologically and mentally abuse me to the point that I began bellowing at him and from then on it was so easy for him to take from me what he wanted. This abuse would begin with him telling me how sexually dissatisfying I was, that I was frigid if we didn't engage in sex seven to ten times a day or whenever he wanted it. He would discuss the finer points of our sex life with his mates and make me listen to their lurid comments etc and ultimately I was made to comply to his perverted ideas.

The reason he was able to turn a healthy, self assertive woman into an insecure, low self opinionated one was because (1) he was my husband and I was raised with the belief that a wife was to obey her husband and (2) I didn't think there was any help out there for me. I still don't know who to contact now to help me deal with that part of my relationship and I have been separated for [number] months now. The worst thing I find even now is that I feel because I wasn't in a physical violent situation I had no right to leave my husband.

Other forms of coercion were used.

My husband raped me after my child was born—threatened to kill the baby unless I consented on a few occasions after the first time he raped me.

•

I consider having to do it just to keep the peace in the home as rape. In my younger years it was violent rape. Often now it's not so often and rarely violent. I've left my husband [number] times in order to improve things which they have. Fear of him doesn't go away just because I live in a different house. I have three children.

•

He would continue to get very sexually excited and did not take into account my feelings. I wanted to make love even less and this caused more resentment. He started to put me down frequently and call me frigid etc. On numerous occasions he 'needed' to have sex that much that he ended up raping me. He never hurt me physically but the incidents had a lasting effect on me emotionally.

There was no violence (bruises, etc) because my children were in the house. But the feelings of disgust, filth, nausea and repulsion are indescribable. I have since had the courage to get an intervention order.

LOW LEVELS OF REPORTING

We know that marital rape has been found to be a component in a high number of marriages that involve physical battering (Bowker 1983). Finkelhor (1985, p. 204) estimates that 10 to 14 per cent of all married women have or will be raped by their spouse. In the 'Without Consent' survey husbands were the offenders for 10.4 per cent of the survivors. For women in their thirties and forties, the husband or the de facto spouse was the most likely perpetrator.

Although marital rape involves more violence and physical injuries than acquaintance rape, the lower rate of reporting can be attributed to both the isolation of the battered woman and to the assumption indicated by those below, that husbands are immune from sexual assault charges.

This is a case of rape in marriage: abusive sexual intercourse, forced against my repeated opposition, unambiguously without my consent and during a menstrual cycle. It was a one off incident but in a background of occasional physical abuse (marginally violent) and on-going psychological harassment. This is not reportable to the police, but rape nevertheless.

At the time you think it is an aberration. Give him the benefit of the doubt and live with a positive outlook. But it became evident, over the subsequent months, there was no basis for the relationship to continue. So I lodged divorce proceedings against him on the grounds of 'irreconcilable breakdown' after [number] years of marriage. With the benefit of hindsight years later and the public articulation of such violations, only now are we given a 'voice' for this experience. I may have appeared complicit [sic] with my lack of a more vehement denunciation of his actions. But there was no real alternative.

•

He raped me a lot. He said he owned me. I had no rights.

My husband thought it his legal right to insist on sex at any time. He felt I had no right to refuse and would just use force. He also became more and more perverted and sick and would entertain perverted fantasies (with male, female or animals!).

He also admitted to having bi-sexual relationships. He also tried to force me to have oral and anal sex.

•

During my five years of marriage I was raped, belted and abused to the point of being pushed to the limit. He came home in the middle of the day one day and began belting into me for no reason—at that point I thought 'that's it! I can't take any more'. My parents were oblivious to the nightmare of a marriage, in those days women just didn't leave their husbands. I have never hated anyone as I hated that man. I have a truly beautiful, extremely soft hearted, loving, kind daughter as a result of that rape. I left with my daughter and our clothes and left everything else.

Financial dependency was another factor that contributed to staying in the violent marriage and not reporting the rapes.

I stayed in the marital situation until I was in the position of supporting my children and providing them with a home, despite being assaulted and raped on an almost nightly basis over a period of [number] years.

•

That's the way it was—one kept it all to oneself. New divorce laws are a Godsend. Children and access to money were the main deterrents from any action. Never married again and probably won't—too scared.

Being protective toward the spouse kept some from reporting.

He forced me to have sexual intercourse many times—he thought I liked it that way. I loved him in spite of it, so would not report it because of the consequences on him.

The survivors' own feelings of shame played a major role in their reluctance to report the assaults.

I felt so worthless and humiliated that I couldn't bring myself to tell anyone. I am a mother of two small children, both extremely bright and talented. To report the assault (by my husband) would have spelled the end of my marriage. The end of my marriage would have meant facing a future on the breadline with my kids, unable to give them the education and the start in life that they should have. My health won't stand up to full-time work.

If he hurt me again, I would have to leave, but right now I just don't have the courage to face life alone. There is no real equality for women, especially mothers, and rarely any justice. He said afterwards that he was ashamed, but I'm not at all sure that he meant it. At the time it was obvious that he enjoyed the big power kick.

Becoming a mother was one of the highlights of my life, but you don't realise at the time that you are usually giving up your career, your independence and what little bargaining power you had in life. Of course, you can go straight back out to work, but there is still the 'second shift' at the end of the day, and if your husband 'won't do women's work', and many won't, either the kids miss out, or as usual, good old Mum. And if you do give up work to have children and care for your family, your options, if your marriage falls over, are piss-poor compared to a man's—and again, it's Mum and the kids who end up paying the price.

Daddy, you sold me out!

As the following letter shows, even the survivor of marital rape does not always see the extent of her victimisation. The woman focuses upon one rape incident in her marriage but refers to many times when her husband would not accept her 'no' and would 'keep on at her' . . .

One New Years Eve, I had, for the first time in my life more than two drinks (that was my limit). I had four which made me dizzy, my responses were lethargic, slow, made me dizzy, felt immobilised, but still registered everything going on. But I was unable to stop what went on. I was drunk and my husband raped me.

I repeatedly said no. There was no way I could push him away. He said horrible obscenities, he raped vaginally and then rolled me onto my front and I was so scared. I felt numb. I think he raped me anally. I couldn't believe he was doing this. When he finished raping me, I said again 'I said no'. I yelled it repeatedly.

Next morning he said he was sorry. I was going to leave. I was disgusted, never trusted him again. I didn't speak to him. It took me several days to decide what really to do. He cried, carried on, what could he do to make it up to me etc. So I stayed for the famous reason 'for the sake of the children'. I devoted myself to them. To me, my love for my children was what marriage is all about.

We went to a psychologist counsellor. I said what upset me about him, my complaints, my anger, his lack of motivation, his lack of pride in himself, his tantrums when things went wrong and he'd leave it half finished. He never finished any project he started. It was so frustrating. I couldn't stand not to finish what I started. He would humiliate me in front of my family and think it was so funny.

I said everything but the rape. The counsellor wasn't much help. He said either put up or split up. I couldn't at that time picture how I would cope splitting up, so I made my children my focus, and tried to block the rape from my memory. Tried to rationalise the rape, and tried to feel sorry for him.

I have never drunk like that again. Memories are horrible, keep on flashing. After that the only reason I had sex was to have children. I did not enjoy it, it made me feel dirty. I didn't want it. (Sometimes in the years before he had raped me, I felt uneasy having sex with him, because he did hurt when he entered me—no circumcision and the foreskin pinched.) I thought there must have been something wrong with me. While I was pregnant he didn't touch me. I was safe.

I never initiated sex. I would say no and he would keep on at me and persist and I would have to give in. I was so stupid. I should have left him. He made me into an angry, unhappy person, low self esteem, no self-respect. He would put me down and ridicule me in front of my family and friends and embarrass them.

The memories were nightmares, he disgusted me, by the rape, the countless times I didn't want sex and he forced me and every time it hurt on entry. He wanted a vasectomy so he could have more sex. I was very unhappy. The rape and everything else flooded my mind so I said straight out my anger, how unhappy I was, didn't love him,

59

brought up the rape, told him I never wanted him to touch me ever again.

He said 'Do you want me to leave?'

I said 'yes'.

Took him two weeks of crying, yelling, tantrums, saying his boss didn't want us to split up, that he'd kill himself, before he left.

Some, like the next woman have stayed because they blocked out the rape experience for years from their conscious mind.

I have been married for [number] years and for the last [number] I have been very miserable and unhappy. I have felt trapped in this marriage. My husband is a pleasant man, easy to talk to and fun to be with, however I have not wanted him to touch me in a sexual way and have felt cornered every night when he approached me sexually. I thought for a long time that my reactions were rather normal—the available research indicates that the sexual desires of women are quite different to those of men, however only recently have I become conscious that there is a far more sinister explanation for my own reactions.

Early this year I spent a weekend doing a course. During this course I became aware of a very heavy feeling in my stomach and in my throat. I was unaware of the cause of this however I recognised that it had been there for some time and was at its worst when I had sex with my husband.

It took a further two months for me to observe this feeling and to work with it. One day I worked with the feeling and concentrated on it. I nearly gave up because the sensation in my throat was so strong I nearly choked, or at least it felt as if I would. Suddenly I was aware of the first occasion I had experienced this feeling. It was a memory which had somehow been forgotten for eight years and had been buried deep in my subconscious.

[Number] years ago my son was born. The birth was very difficult. He was a very large baby. I had an episiotomy and suction was used—that brought his head into the birth canal and he was finally delivered by forceps. Once this was all over I was a mess—I had torn in many places and it took a long time for the doctor to stitch me up.

After the birth the doctor spoke to both of us (my husband and I) and told us that my vagina had been badly stretched and I would need reconstructive surgery in the future. I was exhausted but ecstatic about my beautiful new baby.

When my son was [number] days old we came home. I was still very shaky and needed to rest often. I had another small child as well. The day after arriving home [several days after the birth] I went to bed very early. My husband cooked tea and sat up to watch a movie on T.V. The baby woke up to be fed at 10 pm. I fed him and put him back in his bassinette. Shortly after that my husband came to bed. I was glad to see him and snuggled up in his arms; however it was soon obvious that he wanted sexual intercourse. It was something I could not face—my vagina was swollen and sore and I had many stitches there—it hurt to move and to walk—in my mind sex was totally out of the question.

I told him, 'No, it's too sore.'

'Come on, I know about stitches—it's all healed up now, with new skin and everything.' He sounded loving but the idea of intercourse was something I could not face.

'No.' I offered him other alternatives, but he was insistent.

'I will be gentle—shush' and with that he went ahead with it.

I felt his penis as it entered. It was very hard and felt very big. As it entered, my vagina felt if it had caught fire—each stitch was stretching and pulling with each thrust. His weight pinned me down and I felt the word 'NO' deep down in my throat. I can't remember how long it took but the pain was excruciating. When he had finished he pulled out and went straight to sleep.

I lay there. I felt semen stinging the stitches and the pain in my soul was intense. My husband did not love me. How could he do this to me if he loved me? Why did he do this? I needed his support and love. I had two small children and I was on an emotional see saw with the hormones which were circulating in my body after the birth. I didn't know how to handle this. Somehow I kept going, looking after the children and coping with household chores.

The episode was repeated in two days and again two days after that. Each time the pain was intense. It was during this time that I learned to depend on my own inner resources. I thought that I needed support and love—however that was only available through sex and sex hurt. I went to visit my parents when my son was [several] weeks old.

When I returned, sex no longer hurt and my husband was needing my emotional support as he was facing a nervous breakdown. Gradually what had happened after my son's birth faded into a place where I no longer remembered or thought of it.

Somehow during the next few years I learned to steel myself whenever my husband approached me sexually. However I was unable to hide my lack of enjoyment and participation from him. This has been the source of many bitter moments. He has told me on a number of occasions that I was frigid and had problems with intimacy. We had had a number of financial and legal problems and my husband felt that if we had a more enjoyable sex life we would have been in a better position to cope with these. Probably this was true. I was puzzled about myself and tried very hard to understand what was happening.

I told my husband of what I had remembered and how it had affected my body reactions; he said he was sorry but he had been immature, ignorant and not in a normal frame of mind at the time.

Later I discovered that he has been having a sexual relationship with another woman since April this year. He told me that he had conveyed my memory to her and she had said that she had had the same experience after the births of her children. All her girlfriends had also 'been screwed' by their husbands soon after the baby was born. His implication was that it was NORMAL. If this is the case there must be many, many women who have had the experience I have had and stay silent because they love their husbands.

It seems to me that there is a general lack of perception in the community as to the humanity of women—even on the part of women themselves.

To use a woman in such a way within what is supposedly a loving situation is to treat her as an object, a source of comfort and relief—she is not a person with needs of her own.

THE POLICE

Only 13 per cent of the women who were raped by their husband reported it to the police. For those who did go to police, the response was generally non-supportive.

He is [another nationality] but I am Australian. I used to be very independent, self reliant and confident. After [number] years of marriage I seemed to slowly lose reality especially when I had my first child and stopped work then he did totally believe he had total control of me physically and mentally.

On three occasions I phoned the police. On all occasions he seemed to convince them that I was overreacting and crazy. They actually believed him and in his most violent attack on me said if he promised to stay downstairs it would be all right. The gloating, winning look on his face some ten years ago still haunts me. See he could fool the police—see there was nothing wrong with him, it had to be me. I told my family only small pieces of what my life was like but they only said, 'You made your bed, you lie in it'.

•

I was raped on numerous occasions by my first husband. I was bashed, kicked and had food thrown in my face. I was forced to have oral and anal sex.

After finally separating (I had [number] kids) we were trying to maintain his contact with the children. On one of his visits I accompanied him and the children to the park. They were [young] so he needed help to look after them. He wanted us to see where he was living, we went with him there in his car. When we arrived he locked the kids in the kitchen and proceeded to bash me and then raped me. The kids started screaming and so he left me to attend to them.

I escaped and took his car and drove straight to the police and asked for help (he had the kids). I was bleeding and bruised about the face. I was told to be sensible and go home, they did not want to know.

A friend of mine went back to the police station and threatened to contact [a television program] if they did not help in getting the children. Only then did they go and get the kids. No charges were made.

•

The number of assaults are too numerous to mention them all. One time I was tied to the bed and a bucket of water thrown over me. I was punched, scratched, bitten and slapped, then raped, untied and told to put the kettle on. Another time I was beaten with a broom into submission.

I have had my clothes ripped off, raped, then locked outside in broad daylight.

These three times I have reported to the police at three different police stations. Twice with a male officer, then once to a female officer. I was told 'not to worry he is your husband, it will make the violence worse'. I have heard it all.

Many, many times I just laid there. I know I would be beaten if I struggled, even uttered the word 'no', so I just laid there while I was raped.

Several women had more positive experiences with the police to relate. It should be noted however that the assistance was centred around the other physical violence and not the sexual assault.

This man scarred me for life and I still have nightmares years later. I would like to explain my case a bit clearer. At the time it wasn't the rape that I felt so wronged against but the fact that he, my de facto wanted to kill me and had a loaded gun which he aimed at me to shoot. How lucky I am not to be dead, which in tough times I think of this.

I reported what happened to the police and the domestic violence unit at the police station stepped in and provided counselling straight away, at midnight this was.

Even though he forced me to have sex when I didn't want to and caused a lot of pain I didn't consider it rape then, but now I know different.

A number of the husbands, like the next, were police officers:

My husband raped me in anger—he mainly used to use violence against me in the form of hitting, pushing, throwing things at me. He was then a senior policeman, therefore I could do nothing but leave the marriage.

I feel that police themselves often, not all of course, have the same attitudes and behaviour of other males—in fact because of their close associations with violence and the fact that most could be classified as being attracted to the job because of their authoritarian attitudes, they are often worse than the un-hardened member of society.

RISK FACTORS

Pregnancy

Those who work in the field of domestic violence know that pregnancy is a high risk time for battering victimisation. It can also be a time of rape:

I was seven months pregnant with my second child and my husband wanted to have sex with me. I didn't want to so he kicked me several times and I landed on the floor on my stomach. The baby kicked and I was in pain. My husband lunged for me but I was able to get away and outside the front door sobbing. He caught me and said that if I gave him a 'head job' he'd leave it at that. We ended up having sex because I was crying too much to give him a 'head job'.

Afterwards I had to stay in bed for a day due to severe abdominal pain. I did not seek medical assistance. I was [number] years old. I left him [period of time] prior to the birth of my second child.

•

In the marriage I was raped forcibly or else I would submit for fear of what might happen. Handcuffs, guns, knives were used for intimidation. The worst incidents occurred while I was pregnant the last time. I was seven months pregnant. I was handcuffed and violently raped—he threatened to cut the baby from me. I went into premature labour and had the baby. It has taken me years to remember all the details. No-one even asked if I was OK.

•

I was so horrified that my husband didn't care enough for the health of our unborn child. He kicked me in the stomach while I was lying on the floor. I went and slept in the spare room. He came in while I was asleep and attacked me. Fortunately he didn't rape me as I head butted him—he had my legs pinned down and my hands pinned above my head. My husband ripped my nightie to my waist. If I hadn't hit him with my head, I do believe I would have been raped and lost my baby.

My husband was in a bad mood because of the problems I was having with my pregnancy which meant he couldn't have sex for weeks at a time (Doctor's orders). He still does not believe he did wrong.

Alcohol
As should be apparent from many of the 'voices', alcohol abuse played a role in a substantial proportion of the marital rapes.

My alcoholic husband raped me countless times during 11 years of marriage. He used to say, 'What do you think I married you for?'

•

On one occasion in his drunken state he made me have sex with him all night against my will, and other times for about three hours. I will not stand to have that same event happen again. Other times he would not allow me to sleep until he had an orgasm. (Fourteen years of rape)

EFFECTS OF THE RAPES

The effects of marital rape can be worse than with other perpetrators. The low level of reporting has already been discussed at length. Aside from that exacerbating factor, feelings of betrayal and the isolation for marital rape victims are variables which produce even more feelings of shame and aloneness.

I could not contact anyone, I was watched all the time. He woke easily, I could not do anything. I was never alone, he questioned me incessantly, he kept me in a state of fatigue. Interrupted all thought processes. I was imprisoned mentally, physically and emotionally. (Raped for five years of marriage in her thirties)

•

Worse than the actual rapes was the shattering of my trust in this person I loved.

In addition, as one woman eloquently wrote, the effects upon the children can be tragic.

At times the pain in my children's eyes haunts me. We don't often talk about those years but there are occasions when we do, because we have to. He has caused so much damage to the children. I feel as if, especially the eldest child, they were robbed of their childhood. Through his violence they lost the ability to trust and love him and that flowed on. He had no excuse, not even the excuse of being drunk.

The irony of it all is that in our home where we should have been safest, where we should have been cared for, protected and grow as human beings [*sic*], yet our home was a living nightmare, a place of torment, a prison. And I am told there is nothing you can do about it legally. Why not???—again I ask you. I would live every one of those years day by day again if I thought it could in some way <u>stop</u> the violence against women and children. Get the laws changed on rape. Educate the public that it happens <u>everyday</u> and by ignoring it is condoning rape and violence.

I would have murdered my husband, if I had not left. God knows I thought about it over and over. Our bodies are beaten, raped, our minds nearly destroyed and when we lash out to protect our children and ourselves, we get put behind bars. Don't you think those kids need their Mums more than ever now??

•

The on-going violence throughout my years of marriage was mental and sexual. My urethra was so battered I became incontinent, my psyche was so battered I became a mental cripple. I finally got out and changed name and city, and found myself again.

He is the most charming man you could meet! (Raped during a fifteen year period commencing in her early twenties)

RECOMMENDATIONS FROM THE SURVIVORS

Many of the women whose letters and comments have appeared in this chapter included a few lines on prevention or requisite change. Below, are a number of others who made specific suggestions on how Australian society can better assist the victims of marital rape and/or prevent such crimes in the future. Some focused on the importance of early socialisation for boys.

When I had a nervous breakdown I went to a psychiatrist who helped me see what was happening. [Some] years later I left my husband as he continued to believe he had a right to sex with me as his wife, and he 'could not change', so I had to be 'patient with him'.

I believe boys are still socialised into the attitudes that they are entitled to use women, and respect should be taught in schools and homes from babyhood.

•

We need strong, gentle role models in educators, TV heroes and much more emphasis on kindness, caring, patience and closeness and cut down macho, violent aggressive role models.

•

I think that boys should be taught at an early age to have respect for women even when they're married, and when you say 'no', you mean 'no'!

The depiction of females in the media was also talked about by several letter writers such as the following:

I believe that as long as our society allows women to be depicted as second class citizens, bimbos and sex objects in the media—be it literature, newsprint, movies, TV or in something as innocuous as an advertisement for detergent. Then there will always be men who see us as sex objects for their use, rather than the whole human beings that we are.

The inadequacies of the courts to punish rapists severely were also discussed and one woman discussed the implications of the judiciary's lack of awareness about rape in marriage.

He has custody of our three girls. The courts don't care about rape in marriage. I was forced to have sex many times, 'It was his right'. Despite continued pleading with him he always continued, with me in tears and often vomiting. To cope with what was done to me for many years I saw a psychiatrist. This was used against me in the Family Court, whereas his violence was ignored by the judge, also possible sexual abuse of our oldest daughter. He has custody of our daughters now.

Rape in domestic violence situations is more prevalent than we care to acknowledge and very subtle, e.g. under the guise of 'making up'.

Another letter writer was concerned with having people made aware of the cycle of sexual assault; the role that her husband's own incest background played in his own sexual violence.

Yesterday I wrote a full report re the sexual abuse I had experienced in my marriage. I had been raped by my husband, and the sexual abuse had been high, particularly for about [number] years of the marriage, about [number] years ago.

My own naivety in these matters caused me not to know what constituted sexual abuse. I relied heavily on the church (Catholic) for my own decisions.

Had I more knowledge at the time these things were happening, I would have pressed harder on charges. I can see that were I to proceed with charges now so much 'old mud' would be raked up, it would not be gotten over for the rest of my life. There would be too much to try to clarify at this stage.

Having been a virgin and no sexual experience before marriage in this situation, caused me to be taken advantage of by my husband. Of course, being in a Catholic family in the 1950s-60s when I was at school, nobody discussed sex. My sexual education was from nuns, one of whom caused me a great deal of trouble in this area. I used to get very bad periods. She had, in a lesson, told the class that girls who got bad periods were promiscuous. Imagine, how that affected me, as one of the top students in the class. She also had 'bawled' me out in front of the class over medication my doctor was giving me at the time.

My friends wanted me to tell my mother, but I couldn't for shame. Anyway, mum was 'hot on my heels' when I missed my periods—'Had I been mucking around with the boys?'

What I'm saying is this. Sex education and personal human relationship classes for teenagers is vital. (Also having the proper people to teach them.) Had I had more education in these areas, I would not have been as vulnerable as I was with this man.

Also, if I had known how to handle him I most probably would have been able to get him to the help he needed, and our marriage would have been corrected. He certainly was not a 'bad man'. He had many redeeming qualities and attributes, and when things were going well he was absolutely beautiful.

I experienced everything those women who had been attacked said, the heavy guilt, the feeling of being 'dirty', ostracism by some people in the community, the 'doubting' of my sanity by myself and others, the disbelief by police, etc.

My husband always said his mother didn't molest him (only battered him at times). She seemed to like him the best. But we always felt there was an 'emotional block' somewhere with him. I believe like the rest of his family he has been sexually abused. My counsellors thought likewise. Having seen the television reports I can see the parallels in my marriage problems.

I have had a great deal of counselling—a marriage guidance counsellor, an excellent doctor specialising in family counselling, an excellent psychiatrist—who was the first person to take me through all of my husband's behavioural symptoms, my children's school counsellors. I also have read extensively myself as a person who must have the 'reasons' for it all—I have them now.

I did not want to accuse him falsely about what happened in our marriage. Now I know I haven't.

Our children have come through this with remarkable balance. One thing through all of this, we both loved our kids very much.

I had not been told before we were married about the incest problem in the family. I found out after I was married. But it was told to me in an awful way. Then I was never told the 'full' story. It was always in a confused piecemeal way that I heard about it.

I am writing this in hope to give a full picture of how incest affected 3 generations of a family.

I have always only had one good friend I could tell who believed me. When I tried to tell others my husband had had a bad childhood, they did not believe me, nor listen. Of course I never mentioned incest—especially by the mother.

For some like the following woman, her acceptance of her husband's violence derived in part from what the author describes as unawareness of her rights in the marriage or naivety which needs to be addressed for future women and wives.

When I married my husband my mother told me, 'It may seem a bed of roses but you have to lie on it no matter how many thorns'.

I was given no formal education about sex. I was told earlier about menstruating but not much more. As a child I asked, 'What about boys, men, what do they have?'

My mother's answer was, 'They have their problems, too'. She did not elaborate any further. I was ten years old at the time.

The man I married, to me, seemed the perfect man. After some months he started to change. Sexually he was never satisfied. He was not satisfied with what I regarded as normal. He forced me to submit to him anally and orally. When some nights I fled to the toilet to get away from him, he locked me out and as I would be so tired I lay on the cement or paving to get rest. Just before dawn he would let me in to the house, usually his words were, 'Now, will you do as I want?' It was revolting.

After children were born he told me to ask the doctor to sew up part of my vagina. Stupidly I asked the doctor and he assured me there was no need for it.

I married my husband at [a young] age. He was considerably older than I and therefore had an overpowering influence over me. When I was pregnant with our third baby he ordered me to get rid of it. I was told an old woman's method to do so. I used the method and after some time the doctor sent me to a leading women's hospital. The baby was dragged out of my body by the doctor. I remember my screaming with pain. No drugs were given me for the medical people could not get me to admit and tell them what I had done or taken. It was a crime in those days. My husband and grandfather were told I was dying with septicaemia and would live perhaps twenty-four hours longer.

Yet the horror of my marriage has stayed with me all these years. I stayed with my husband just to get my children through education and in my younger son's final year at high school I was struck down with sickness and landed in hospital for months.

My doctor at the time told me 'No more. When you go from this hospital, do not go near your husband. He is mad.' My husband divorced me.

I had the same nightmare for many years. I'd look out the window and see my husband walking towards the homestead on my last property and I would run with my little dog terrified, over the rise at the back of my house to try to reach my neighbour's. Sometimes I would awaken on my feet in the kitchen, sometimes still in my bed and the sweat would be pouring out of me.

I believe there has been and still is a gross miscarriage of justice in the courts, in our parliament where our laws are made in this country in regard to the woman.

Politicians and others have regarded abortion as abhorrent and illegal till lately. Never have I ever heard the question asked if the woman who seeks abortion is doing it because as in my case, she was ordered to.

Several women addressed the need for reaching the survivor, isolated in her own shame.

My rapes occurred in a marriage, over a period of years. I told no-one for a couple of years. I got counselling from a Rape Crisis Centre but I stayed with my husband until it became too unbelievable and I thought I would end up dead. I felt so isolated and alone through all of it. Maybe if I had had a book to pick up I would not have felt so alone. If I can help then that helps me.

●

Let women out there know they don't have to live like that. Despite women's liberation many women still believe that this type of thing is just part of being a woman.

(NOTE: Appendix II lists agencies and self-help groups in each state and territory)

4

ESTRANGED PARTNERS

> The man that raped me was once jailed for a gang rape. I
> didn't report it to the police because he now had a wife and
> children, and he was an old lover, and to start with I blamed
> myself. I realise now that I was not to blame at all, but
> looking back I should have reported it and regret not doing
> so. (Raped by ex-boyfriend when she was 17)

One might think, or hope, that battering in a marital or other
intimate relationship ceases upon estrangement. In fact, this is
far from true. For example, in looking at homicide between
adult sexual intimates (these homicides may be seen as the 'tip
of the iceberg' of domestic violence), the opposite has been
found (Easteal 1993) with the covert impact of a battering
prehistory most apparent in those cases where the couple are
estranged. The physical violence may no longer be taking
place. However, perhaps its legacy and the male's perception
of his loss of power and control over the woman does live on
and ends in the woman's death.

Given this type of obsessive possessiveness and exertion of
domination or power, it is hardly surprising that jealousy
emerged as an even more common contributory variable in the
killings of ex-wives than cohabiting partners: in over one-third
of this sub-group of homicides, jealousy played an important
role.

Further, in at least one of the homicides, rape or the threat
of such an assault appeared in the background.

'Ross' and 'Rosemary' had been in an intense relationship for about a
year when Rosemary decided to break it off. She felt that it was not
getting anywhere and she did not desire permanency although Ross
did want to get married.

Two months later, Ross came to Rosemary's flat overtly to get his
flat key back from her. When she gave it to him, he grabbed her

around the throat telling her that he wanted to get back together and that if they did not, he didn't know what he was going to do. He also at that time held a knife to her face and threatened to rape her. Rosemary was able to calm him down and convince him to leave. She then called the police who consequently warned Ross to stay away from Rosemary's apartment.

About six weeks after this incident, Ross entered Rosemary's flat and hid in the wardrobe. When she returned from her date and went into her room alone, he came out of the closet and stabbed her over forty times. (Easteal 1993)

If one defines rape as an act of violence and if one attributes much of male violence to a need for the maintenance of control over females, then Ross's sexual violence can be seen as part of the general motif of domination. His particular abuse ended, as it does for about sixty women a year, in the death of the woman. For sixty-five estranged women who sent in 'Without Consent' surveys, and numerous other survivors of rape by an ex-boyfriend, the sexual violence (thus far) was the finale.

Penetration did not occur. He wasn't prepared to kill me. I fought hard. (25-year-old raped by her estranged husband)

The presence of rape or threat of rape after separation is not surprising given the history of battering in the relationship and/or the persistence of physical violence as the male struggles to regain control.

Although I did not suffer any physical abuse within the relationship or during the rape—I suffered extremely from emotional abuse. I finally managed to leave him in a very abrupt manner and I believe the emotional trauma of my leaving him so callously, caused him to rape me. This is why I felt to blame. My mother reinforced this feeling in me as well. I have not seen him since that day and I don't know how I'd feel if I did. (Raped by her estranged husband, when she was aged 19)

In the 'Without Consent' sample, of those raped by estranged partners, other types of violence had occurred in 65 per cent of the relationships. The following letter illustrates both the antecedents of physical abuse and the theme of control that seems to play an important role in these cases.

I was not physically battered because I always submitted. Mostly my husband jumped on me when I was asleep, pinned my arms down and clutched my legs with his so that I could not move. I was threatened and abused for thirteen years and finally left. Then he continued to intimidate me by driving backwards and forwards in front of my house and laughing at me. It took me years to realise that what my husband did was rape.

We were married for a very short period: the third week after our wedding, we were travelling up North. I had been married before and we had my son and a friend with us. We had an argument in the car. He pulled the car up and told the children to go and play. We walked for awhile and started to have a fight. I called him an 'ass hole'. He back handed me and pushed me down and then walked away.

I was cut and bruised. The children came over. I told them to go to the car. After further discussions he held a knife to my throat and I ended up grabbing the boys, flagging a car down and trying to make our way back to my mother's. When she collected us from the station, during a conversation with my mother, she told me 'I made my bed, now I had to lie in it'.

This was not the last time he belted me. We were separated when he raped me.

I remember my mother being belted by my father when I was young. The strange thing is that I have a problem even talking to my mother now.

Indeed, rape by an estranged partner, just as by a partner, comes only second to strangers as far as the amount of violence and physical injuries inflicted.

To this day I will never know whether my back problem was actually caused by the force of the rape or me trying to push him off me. I have permanent damage to my back. (Raped by her estranged husband, when she was aged 33)

OTHER FORMS OF COERCION

However, not all the rapes involved physical violence beside the rape. Other forms of control were used just as in other perpetrator rapes. As the comments below show, emotional coercion can be brutal for the victim and effective for the rapist.

I worked for [an occupation] and knew the police could do nothing unless I was hurt. My [estranged] husband came after me with a butcher knife. I stayed calm and wasn't hurt physically. I never let him in my home again nor do I trust him. I always made sure his access to the children was with supervision.

•

Mine is the culmination of a [number] year, [number] children marriage. The threat was 'sex or the children will be told and it will wreck them'. A subtle pressure—I gave in, HATING it, but it is not a notable case. It is worth documenting because the force of the male was the overriding factor. I feel I had no choice and was at the point of announcing the divorce. (Raped by her estranged husband during her forties)

For some, the lack of physical force with its overt bruises and scars resulted in the survivors taking on the responsibility for the rape.

In both instances I felt that it was my fault because I didn't fight or object strongly enough, even though I had made it clear that I didn't want sex prior to the assault. Even now it is confusing—it is difficult for me to see that I was assaulted or 'attacked' even though I did feel I was violated. (Raped by her ex-boyfriend when she was 20)

Once again, we learn that survival of childhood sexual assault can play a major role in the response of the woman to an adult rape.

As regards number of times, I have deliberately singled out an incident of rape which occurred when I was nineteen, as after much healing it seems easiest.

The perpetrator, as I have indicated, was an estranged de facto, however I feel I should say that before the separation rape was a common extension of his physical violence against me. I told no one out of shame and self-blame. I have also had many experiences of sexual assault by various (non-related) perpetrators in my childhood, and on occasions (not all) when I did tell, I learned that I was not important, that what happened to me was not important and in fact believed it was my fault.

I am currently undergoing some powerful but painful healing from these experiences and I feel that I have had to set the boundary of responding to your questionnaire with just the one experience as to detail everything in my life is at this point a little too difficult and traumatic to think of in terms of how many and whom.

I believe, as is the case with many survivors of child sexual abuse who remained unaided at the time, that such experience and subsequent non-caring reactions in the childhood, can be a strong determinant factor in how a woman will react to sexual violence in her adulthood. In my own healing, it causes me great pain to see other women failing to see their violations for the crimes that they are, just because they happen to live with (or have done so) their rapists. It is so soul-corroding to accept rape, and further believe that one is not worthy of justice. However, with the humiliating conditions that still exist (however much the government lets us think they are changing things) for victims of rape in the legal system, I am today still half-glad I did not report what happened to me.

EFFECTS OF THE RAPE

One woman wrote about her feeling of dirtiness and the recycling of feelings which she is not sure have been resolved.

I initially thought it was not rape as it was oral—severe beating. Happened in 1984. Still feel unclean and have worn away the enamel on my teeth with continual brushing.

Had AIDS test and tests for other STDs. Have not dealt with the issue and feel as though I should have worked through the feelings. Not sure now whether it has been resolved or not.

Police took me to hospital and photographed the bruising. Also had to take my [young] son with me. At court his lawyer said it could not have been traumatic because he had previously been my lover.

I said it was more traumatic as I had trusted him. He was jailed for [number] years and expected to be out in [number] months. He did plead guilty. He also visited me after the attack to ask me not to go to court 'as it would ruin his life'. He apologised for what he had done. (Raped by her ex-lover when she was 32)

For some there was obviously still a great deal of emotion, for some anger and for others, fear.

I would rather be dead than ever be raped again, maybe that way something will be done as the crime will be murder and not rape—or I'll try to kill him. (Raped by estranged de facto when aged 33)

•

I still fear him, e.g. I don't want my photo in the paper. This was physically scary. I thought he was going to kill me. (Raped by her ex-boyfriend when she was 17)

For at least two of the survivors one of the effects of the sexual assaults was physiological: for one venereal disease and the other became pregnant.

I contracted herpes as a result of the assault. He obtained my new address via Telecom. (Raped by her estranged husband when she was 26)

•

I think another thing that rape has direct relevance to is pregnancy from rape. I fell pregnant from the rape which added more disturbed feelings to my situation. Abortion was my only alternative and considering it is illegal in my State, it brought up a lot of problems considering I was under the age of consent. I think it is important for you also to inquire about pregnancy from rape. (Raped by ex-boyfriend when she was 14)

Many comments concerned the amount of time that must elapse before any sort of real healing can take place. During this process, difficulties with relationships may be apparent.

I still live with it every day. I have a few problems in my relationship I am in now and wonder whether it is a result of my last experience. I now wish I had contacted the police because he is still free to do it to other women. (Raped by ex-boyfriend when she was 16)

•

I can't stand men. I live alone and don't go out. I hate them. You don't have to believe me though. But it's true. I wish I was dead. (Raped by estranged husband when she was 36)

DISCLOSING

As we will see in Chapter 8 those raped by a stranger were the most apt to talk to someone; those assaulted by estranged partners were the next most likely to disclose, over two-thirds, 69 per cent. As the following indicates, reaction varied although on the whole was not particularly sympathetic.

My parents could not cope and chose to ignore what had happened. My ex-husband's comment during the rape was 'I don't know when I'll get this again so I may as well get it now'. The marriage guidance counsellor said it was my fault as I must have deprived him and that I should ask for his forgiveness. I only went to the counsellor under immense pressure. I did not forgive my ex-husband. My mother-in-law said I should forget the rape and stay married because she was raped for fourteen years and if she could put up with it then I should put up with it this time. I did not wait for a next time and remained separated. (Raped by her estranged husband when she was 26)

•

I was living apart from my spouse (now divorced) [aged in mid-thirties]. A neighbour turned up her stereo so she couldn't hear my screams and ruin her overseas trip by having to testify in court. The detective left behind vital evidence and then complained I wasn't beaten enough to make a strong court case. The doctor treated me with contempt. The family law court and my solicitor allowed the rape to happen in the first place. My ex-spouse had a long criminal record for sexual deviant [sic] against the public and had to have access to the children. (Raped by her estranged husband when she was 35)

Reporting to the Police

Those raped by estranged partners were also the second most likely to report the assault to the police (29 per cent). It is apparent from the majority of those who wrote about their experiences with the police that their encounter had been at the best ambivalent. Some felt that although they had come forth, the police were neither encouraging nor did they try to arrest the perpetrator.

I was emotionally distraught, but was made to feel it was unimportant by male police. I am heterosexual. (Raped by her estranged husband when she was 30)

•

I reported the rape to the police and they told me it would be devastating to go to court. Almost impossible to prove—'I would be better not charging him even though he had a knife'. (Raped by her estranged husband when she was in her mid-twenties)

•

The police did not keep any evidence which allowed the offender to be released at the trial. Police are hopeless. (Raped by estranged husband when she was 17)

On to the Courts

For the few whose offender was charged and a trial took place, the results were less than satisfactory.

I was too upset to find out that ten out of the thirteen charges were dropped even though he said that everything in my statement was true. How can this happen? I was given no say about it. A few charges carried a life sentence. He got five years—two years bottom. (Raped by her ex-boyfriend)

•

If I was ever attacked again in a similar way I would be inclined to attempt to kill or maim my attacker during or after the incident.

The trauma of the court case itself was degrading and humiliating to the victim and I doubt I would ever put myself through that again.

As it is I have no intimate contact with any other male person and have not done so since the attack. (Raped by her estranged husband when she was 35)

THOSE WHO DID NOT GO TO THE POLICE

As noted above, almost three-quarters of those raped by an estranged partner did not make a formal report. Unlike the other victims, shame was not the principal reason cited by those raped by a husband or an estranged partner; fear of the perpetrator and the belief that the police would not act were the major factors given by survivors of estranged husband rape.

I was friendly with my ex-boyfriend's sisters. I was waiting for them to come home when this happened. If I had reported it, I would have my ex-boyfriend and his friends after me for life. (Raped at the age of 18 by her ex-boyfriend plus four of his friends)

Shame or a feeling of responsibility still played a role for some.

At that time there was no support centre that I knew of. Also there was the attitude that if boys did these things the girl had led him astray. I felt ridiculous for getting into the situation and strangely enough feel that my own feelings of responsibility have stopped me feeling I was a victim. (Raped by her ex-boyfriend when she was 18)

The next woman had feelings of loyalty and the need to protect her rapist/estranged husband.

I did not want to cause problems for my estranged husband in the community or at work or damage his career.

The last comment comes from a woman who did not want to protect the rapist but did want to protect the child who was born as a consequence of the rape.

Did not report as I fell pregnant. Wanted to keep the child—figured she needn't know how she was conceived.

I have helped others deal with rape and sexual assault and could not bring myself to go through the police, courts and publicity. I feel ashamed that I didn't speak up but as a single mum in a high profile position, could not afford to. When police treat women better, I will. (Raped by her estranged de facto when she was in her 30s)

SUGGESTIONS

The following letter speaks for itself; the writer tells about why she could not disclose, the painful consequences and the deep and pervasive fear. She concludes with a series of recommendations to help other survivors.

I spent [number] years in small country community working with [type of occupation]. Do not want to destroy my respectability or reputation with their pity and gossip. There is no privacy in small country towns. It is only a matter of time. What can anyone do to me again? I died ages ago.

I thought rape was having sex and saying 'No' at the same time. I didn't realise it could hurt so much, the pain would have nothing to do with any sexual feelings. That the price of penetration could rip you more than any baby could, and the wound would bleed for days afterwards. That I'd be too scared to see the doctor because he was male and I'd have to show him my private parts.

I didn't know I could go round and be normal with family and friends while I was nothing inside. I doubt whether any person, no matter who they are or what degrees they have, would ever know the fear and pain of the act and the anguish suffered afterwards.

I always thought I'd wake up if someone broke into my home—I didn't. I always thought I'd know if someone was in the room—I didn't. I'm too scared to sleep now. I drop to the floor if a car goes by at night for fear it is him with his gun pointed at the window.

This loving father, upstanding member of the community whose wife has thrown him out of home and denied him the right to family life. He is so nice and polite and friendly—who would believe that he causes so much fear in me. How can you tell your children their father is a rapist. Don't fight in front of the children; be amicable in your separation; don't be seen to be the vindictive wife and passively refuse his advances in front of the children and in public.

If I kill him it is murder. If he kills me I drove him to it. How can I stand up to him without losing my dignity and self-respect with other people? I've already lost that with him, why lose it with other people as well.

Men know it is wrong, that it is unlawful and they are inflicting pain on someone else. It is premeditated and meant to hurt. Mothers need to educate their sons to respect women as individuals and not as servants or chattels.

More funding should be given to marriage guidance agencies so that people don't have to wait to be on a pension, e.g. sole parent, before they can afford to attend. Just because they are on an income, doesn't mean they can afford $35 twice a week for counselling. More than half of stress in marriage is due to financial difficulties.

I hope you find some answers and someone there is strong enough to do something about it. Rape is a crime—it hurts, but at the moment it only hurts me.

The last writer in this chapter explains that prison is not necessarily the answer when the offender is someone with whom the survivor has had a relationship.

Prison does not 'cure' a rapist and sometimes the victim may not get any comfort from the rapist going to prison i.e. does twenty years help the victim? Would mandatory sentences make a victim reluctant to report the crime. Who can believe in the prison/legal system anyway? Yes, a rapist must pay for his crime but the survivor must not in anyway feel responsible (or end up feeling guilty) for the punishment. It would be really difficult if you know the rapist. (Raped by ex-boyfriend when she was 18)

5

DATES AND BOYFRIENDS

[Some] years later I had contact with him and asked him
why. He said he had never been refused by a woman before.
He was tall, very good looking, very well educated and
upper class. Now a high profile wealthy public business
man. (Raped by a date when she was 16)

Boyfriends or dates were the perpetrators in 13 per cent of the
survivor sample, 383 individuals. As the following chapter
illustrates this was of course a heterogeneous group
differentiated by age, experience, consequences and other
variables such as the presence of other violence in the
relationship.

OTHER VIOLENCE

If the rapist was a boyfriend, there was a 30 per cent chance
that other violence had taken place within the relationship.

Violence was a part of my family life—sexual violence seemed
normal particularly when combined with low self-esteem. Sexual and
physical assault were part of this relationship. (Raped by her
boyfriend when she was 15)

•

I went out with my boyfriend for [number] years and I kept letting
him force himself on me. I consider myself a reasonably intelligent
woman yet I kept going back to him. The final straw was when he
resorted to physical violence after I refused him anal sex. I truly
feared for my life that night and had nothing more to do with him.
He had a drinking problem.

SELF-DOUBT—WAS IT RAPE?

However, in other ways, this sub-set of survivors sounds
almost remarkably homogeneous; but the reason for that sense

of commonality is tragic. Almost all victims blamed themselves to some degree; some continue to do so. Coupled with these inner qualms was the underlying question of whether they had actually been raped. Let us therefore look at some of the reasons why sexual assault by a date or a boyfriend can be particularly problematic for its survivors to define as 'real' and legitimate.

Several 'date rape' studies have shown that people are more likely to label such an act as rape if the victim protested both verbally and physically early in the scenario, and if the male arranged the date but the female paid her own way (Shotland & Goodstein 1983; Muehlenhard 1989). The victim has been socialised with these fallacious concepts and others which contribute to her own sense of responsibility for the crime.

I had believed rape to be forced intercourse. This incident involved my soon-to-be ex-boyfriend. We were making love, when he withdrew and picked up an empty coke bottle and shoved it in 'to see how big you can take it!' Small incident but bad results and feelings.

•

In my instance, there was a string of verbal and emotional coercion, although no real physical force. This is the main reason I did not report it as I somewhat blamed myself for being manipulated and ultimately allowing him to anally penetrate me. Initially, however, I had said, emphatically, no. (Raped by her boyfriend when she was 22)

•

I did not want or consent to the sex but was shocked by the quickness of his action. I was naive enough to believe that I must have been 'asking for it' or that it was his 'right' after we'd gone out. (Raped by a date when she was 18)

A number of the victims were quite young, in their early teens at the time of the rape. This further exacerbated their confusion and doubts.

I didn't tell anyone and I could never tell anyone. I don't think anyone would have believed me as I was so young. Sometimes I still think about what's happened to me but I have managed to overcome it but I certainly won't forget it. (Raped by her boyfriend when she was 12)

•

I was forced to perform fellatio as a trade off to vaginal rape (I was a virgin) but now know it was sexual assault. (Raped by a date when she was 14)

In the date or boyfriend context the victim may have willingly kissed or hugged. Or she may have willingly gone to his flat or elsewhere. Then, when the perpetrator continued without her consent, she was unsure about her responsibility for the act and felt (misguidedly) that what she had done was sexually provocative. If only she and others in our society could accept that there is no provocation for rape.

I liked him. We kissed. I touched his penis and allowed him to touch my breasts, then I told him to stop and he didn't. (Raped by a date when she was 20)

•

The perpetrator had taken me for an evening meal and then took me to his home against my will for a period of hours. Then drove me home dropping me at the kerb before my parents could confront him. (Raped by a date when she was 21)

The issue of consent, which continues to change within the legal statutes, may also be a source of ambiguity and ambivalence for the survivor. Is not saying, 'yes' sufficient? Or should she have said, 'No', wonders the next woman.

I'm not sure that it was rape/assault because I didn't actually say 'no'. I never said 'yes' either. I believed that I was emotionally blackmailed by a pushy boyfriend who in the end didn't give a stuff about me. To top it off I found out that he taped us having sex. (Raped by her boyfriend when she was 17)

If the victim was drinking alcohol before the assault, she was also likely to feel some blame or responsibility for the subsequent rape.

It was a case of 'date rape' as they call it. Very difficult to prove as I was seen drinking and yes, actually flirting with the man at a local bar. My God; was I asking for it???? (Raped by her date when she was 21)

•

I was a virgin, and he knew I didn't want sex before marriage. He was eleven years older. We were at a camping ground. I got drunk and went to bed (he was still drinking). I woke up at some time in the early hours of the morning and he was on top of me, screwing me, and I couldn't push him off.

The self-doubt may also be a consequence of how the culture, and the woman raised in that environment, defines 'real rape' as requiring brute force and physical resistance. 'Date' or acquaintance rapes are more likely to involve verbal threats than either a weapon or physical injuries.

I sneaked out to a club with a friend. Met a 'nice guy' and went back to a party at his house. He tricked me into going in to a room alone with him. He told me if I did not have sex with him he would call his friends in to rape me as well.

•

He told me that if I didn't do it with him and cooperate then I would have to do it with his mates too, so I had a choice in the end of one or five and I took one. (Raped by her boyfriend when she was 15)

•

He was a twenty year old 'yuppie', very smooth and successful. [I was fourteen]. I had wagged school to have lunch with him. He took me to his house and when he took off my clothes I was too terrified to move. I knew he'd go to jail if anyone found out, but afterwards he pretended to be sorry and I didn't think anyone would believe me anyway. Thinking about it now I'd love to prosecute, but I have no evidence. It was years ago; there's nothing I can do. (Raped by her date when she was 14)

Some, like the next writer, did in fact meet the false criterion of resistance but still felt ashamed.

I was a virgin and he kept saying that to me and that I was a lesbian and I was going to get it really good. I struggled but it was useless. I felt numb. He dumped me at the corner when it was over and he said, 'Next time we'll try it with some rubber things'.

I felt really stupid and ashamed—it is not until now that I'm strong enough to cope with it and my incest. I blocked it out for years. I'm applying for compensation for the rape. (Raped by a date when she was 16)

KEEPING THE SECRET

About one-half of those who were raped by a boyfriend or a date had never told anyone about the assault. This proportion was only second to those raped by a non-cohabiting family member. Why did so few disclose? The main reason appears to derive from the self-doubt, self-responsibility, and the shame discussed above.

After being sexually assaulted against my will I felt stupid. I didn't tell anyone because I thought they'd think I was stupid to have got into that situation. Lack of self-esteem of the victim is a BIG problem with wide ranging ramifications. (Raped by a date when she was 20)

•

I originally agreed, being a virgin and my boyfriend knew this. But when I said 'no', he ripped off my underwear and did it anyway. I bit his shoulder but could not get him off me. Believing it was my fault I stayed with him until after the second time at the age of sixteen. When it happened again I was too scared to tell anyone until many years later. My own father's comment was 'she probably deserved it, any woman can fight a man off'. Even though he was much larger than me, and they wonder why you don't tell them.

Fear kept some, like the next writer, from telling anyone.

I was a virgin and completely inexperienced. The 'date' was an outing to the [name of activity] with a friend from the country. We stopped at his brother's house for a coffee—they were drinking beer. They were both involved in the rape. I was too scared afterwards to tell anyone, e.g. in case they hurt my Dad or something. At that time rape was not talked about and I had no idea about Rape Crisis Centres etc. (Raped by a date when she was 15)

Other factors that contributed to survivors' silence included the machinations of the perpetrator.

Two days after the rape my boyfriend visited my parents and told them that I was a slut and a whore and slept with every man in town. He was, in fact, my first real boyfriend. My parents believed him and so I couldn't tell them I had been raped by him. (Raped by her boyfriend when she was 17)

One woman was afraid of upsetting her mother.

I was raped when I was eleven by a friend and his friends. After, his friends continued to sexually assault me over six months. Then a couple of years later my boyfriend raped me and him and his friends sexually assaulted me over a few months. I couldn't tell anyone close as I didn't want my Mum to hurt over [sic] what happened to me. In both cases I had no choice but to wait until they got tired of beating and sexually assaulting me.

Another survivor simply felt that no one would believe her.

The incident occurred in his bedroom at his family home with both his respectable middle class parents sitting in the lounge room! Who would believe it? (Raped by a date when she was 14)

The last writer in this section psychologically repressed the rape (as many do). Thus, there was nothing to tell.

I blocked the incident out of my memory entirely until two years ago. It is only in the last year I've told anyone. I felt very angry but still feel that nothing can be done about it. (Raped by a date when she was 14)

DISCLOSURE

What about those assaulted by a boyfriend or a date who did disclose to someone? The overwhelming response described by the following survivors was unsympathetic and non-supportive. It would appear that one's family often acted to validate the victim's own sense of shame instead of affirming her victimisation.

In the 1950s when this happened the only word for it was 'shame'. It was shameful to happen; it was your fault and it was never discussed with anyone! NO support from the family as it added <u>shame</u> to the family. (Raped by a date when she was 17)

•

He really had pre-conceived this rape, planned it with his friend and <u>tricked</u> me into going to his friend's house. He set it up in such a way no-one would believe that I had not consented I am sure. My parents did not believe! I hated men after this experience but luckily soon afterwards I met my husband who is a 'model' man and a feminist and he helped me feel OK again. I <u>trust</u> <u>no</u> man. (Raped by a date when she was 17)

•

About six months after the rape I told my mother about it. She slapped my face and told me I was a slut. It is little wonder that I never went to the police when my own mother was conditioned to think/react this way. It compounds the victimisation of women. I believe my sex life has been affected by the rape and indeed my very loving marriage ended because of sex related problems. (Raped by a date when she was 15)

Friends and work mates could be equally unempathetic.

I became pregnant and had a termination. I was told by two friends, 'Oh, it's rape is it if you get pregnant'. I could not have a baby with those eyes—I did not go to a doctor as I had cut off 90 per cent of my pubic hair in an attempt to cut it out of my life. I am still missing bits of my life at that time.

I was studying at that time and everyone expected me to top the class. I continually failed. A woman [in the course] told others of my termination and so I was rejected by the group—was talked about in front of me. Looking back, I feel ashamed I worked in a so-called caring profession.

•

The perpetrator was not only known to me, he was a close friend of my brother as well. When I attempted (years later) to tell a friend of his, he made me feel like a whore as if it had been bandied about in the locker room. The outcome was it was my fault. I never told my brother who thought he was a 'great bloke'. (Raped by a date when she was 15)

Professionals to whom women had gone for counselling were also not necessarily supportive or affirming.

The psychiatrist said it was normal dating behaviour for the man to be sexually pushy. (Raped by a date when she was 19)

NOT REPORTING TO THE POLICE

The rate of reporting to the police by those raped by dates or boyfriends was extremely low, 6.6 per cent and 9.1 per cent respectively. Over one-quarter of those who did not go to the police did not believe, or were unsure, that what they experienced had been rape or sexual assault. For example, one writer felt that since penetration had not taken place she could not go to the police.

I was not actually raped—I managed to get out of the room before he could go any further than feeling me up and down. Because of that I didn't think I had any grounds to report it. (Assaulted by a date when she was 18)

Date rapists are also more likely to threaten the victim about disclosing to the police (Bownes et al. 1991).

I was threatened with a knife. I was also threatened that photos taken during the attack would be sent to my parents if anything was said or reported. (Raped by a boyfriend when she was 18)

Further, if the perpetrator was significantly older than a teenaged victim, this age differential could be intimidating.

My case was very difficult because I was seeing the person by choice and therefore thought no-one would believe me. My rapist was [a number of] years older than me and, as a child, I felt he had all the power. Finally, he was a close family friend and I felt that any official reports would bring my parents into question. I knew people would ask how they could knowingly allow me, so young, to be involved with this grown man.

By the time I realised I had been raped and could have done something about it, I think too many years had passed and there would never have been enough evidence to get into court. People must be educated to speak out about rape. (Raped by her boyfriend when she was 14-15)

The lack of injuries seemed to exemplify the survivors' own doubt about the rape and their projection concerning police scepticism.

At the end of the evening my date drove me to an area I didn't know and I was given the ultimatum to have sex or be left in the middle of nowhere. Because I complied out of fear, but I didn't physically resist, I thought that it would not be considered rape if reported. I know from his attitude after the incident that the perpetrator did not consider that he had raped me. (Raped by a date when she was 21)

In some cases, however, the violence was extreme yet the survivor did not report to the police, concerned that she would not be believed.

The sexual assaults were part of the relationship so I haven't listed number of times. Also I did not report the rape because my family would not understand and as I had been involved with the man before, I believed at the time I would not be believed, despite my injuries.

My boyfriend raped me and physically kept me hostage in a bedroom and when I tried to get out he physically bashed me and threw me around the room. (Raped by her boyfriend when she was 15)

Even if the survivor did label the act as a rape she could be reluctant to go to the police since she might either believe in her own partial responsibility or believe that the police would blame her.

I had been going out with the man for some months and we had a good sexual relationship. This night we went back to his place after dinner—I was a bit drunk. He wanted sex and I didn't so he bashed me up and raped me.

There is no way under these circumstances I would have reported it to the police. A few days later the man rang me to see me again and was very surprised when I said that I did not want to see him again! (Raped by a date when she was 38)

•

Partly believed I consented/blamed myself for getting very drunk and therefore unable to get myself out of the situation. (Raped by her date when she was 25)

•

I didn't report it because I felt sorry for him (he broke down and cried when I cried). The way I felt then it was my fault because I let him kiss me. I don't feel that way now. (Raped by her date when she was 14)

As with the other perpetrator rapes, shame was the main reason given for not reporting.

Not reported to police. I did not want my children to know I had been injured. I was ashamed I had allowed the relationship to continue for years despite constant smaller injuries. I attended group therapy at the Rape Crisis Centre at [name] Hospital for several months.

Protecting her girlfriend kept the next writer from disclosing the rape to the police.

The rape occurred at my girlfriend's home in her backyard whilst her parents were out on New Year's Eve. I didn't raise the alarm because I didn't want my girlfriend to get into trouble for inviting boys to her house without her parents' permission.

I was a virgin and I resisted as much as I could without screaming, but his physical strength won out in the end. I was looking at the sky, crying and thinking so this is what intercourse feels like, so painful, rough and unromantic!

Working in an almost all male occupation acted as a deterrent to reporting for this survivor.

I was a member of the defence force—I would have ruined my career and self-respect from colleagues if I had reported the incident. Women have a hard enough time in the forces without trying to win rape cases. (Raped by her boyfriend when she was 20)

Some women did not feel that they could go to the police since the rapist/date was a police officer.

I did not report the rape to police because it was done by a policeman! (Raped by her date when she was 19)

•

First time when he took me out. Other times he came to my house at night. My children were sleeping inside so I was very quiet. His police friend was in police car outside. He was a policeman. (Raped by her date when she was 36)

And what can be the outcome of not reporting to the police?

I did not report the rape because I had gone with this man in a group of 'friends' to a picnic. A week later this man raped a little girl—he was caught and sent to prison—perhaps if I had reported my rape this little girl may have been saved. (Raped by her date when she was 16)

RESPONSE OF THE POLICE

For those who did go to the police (n=32) there was little satisfaction with the criminal justice system. Only eight perpetrators were arrested. Of these, two were found guilty and imprisoned. The outcomes did not compensate the victims for the arduous process of going through the police and the courts.

I complained to the Crown Prosecutor that the sentence was too lenient. He replied that if the attacker was unknown to me he would have received twice the sentence! Where is the justice in our society? There isn't any real justice for the survivors of violent sexual acts in our society. I choose to speak out about child sexual abuse, domestic violence and rape. If you're not part of the solution, you are part of the problem. Please continue to release details to the media and the general public. Perhaps in the future people may open their eyes to this 'poison' in our society.

To a large extent I believe the 'system' works against the survivors. The police who I first encountered didn't want to lay charges because the attacker was my boyfriend. Half-way through my police statement, the sex offenders squad were called and they were far more empathetic. Since then I have spoken to police groups about rape and how to deal with survivors. Victims of Crime groups provide the greatest amount of support to survivors. Their support includes liaising with police, counselling, support groups, 24-hour phone lines and so much more.

With regard to appearing in court, this is a very enduring and horrible experience. Defence lawyers virtually get free range to say anything they like, no matter how disgusting. For me this included suggestions that I had venereal disease and other lies. The fact that I had to endure these lies made me feel sick. My view of defence lawyers has greatly changed. If I encountered that particular defence lawyer and he was 'on fire' I wouldn't even spit on him.

For most of the women who went to the police there was to be no appearance in court. Many of these survivors were dissuaded by the police from going ahead with the rape case.

My boyfriend raped me twice (week apart) in own home. I did not want to tell anyone—told a girl friend. She urged me to report to police. I did so and they were good. They told my parents and family not to put me through ordeal of court system. I stopped my relationship with my boyfriend and his family.

Bit angry 'he got away with it' and feel it was my right to charge him, but don't feel he would have even gone to jail. (Raped by her boyfriend when she was 15)

•

The policeman who dealt with me had a hangover and was in a bad mood. He was not sympathetic at all. I was on holidays at the time and even though I said I wanted to file a complaint the sergeant told me to wait until I got back home in four days and do the paperwork there. I was referred to the CIB who took a statement and arranged photos (which were bungled) of my injuries, but eventually the detective talked me out of signing because there was no proof of the actual rape by then! He didn't think I'd win the case and it would have been traumatic. (Raped by her boyfriend when she was 32)

•

Twenty years ago, it's hard to believe it was so long ago, I was advised by police not to bother pressing charges as I probably wouldn't win. But this was after I had been through hours of interrogation and been physically checked and it had been confirmed I had been physically bashed and penetrated by force. I was scared and totally intimidated. (Raped by her boyfriend when she was 17)

Even in instances with additional violence police allegedly refused to charge the perpetrator. Some justified their lack of action overtly on the grounds that the case would never make it in court given the relationship between the couple.

In this case there had not been any hint of violence. The violence erupted because I wanted to break the relationship because of bizarre possessiveness. My 'boyfriend' then kept me from leaving by use of tacit threat with a rifle for an entire weekend; only letting me return to work because I told him that a friend from work would become suspicious because she knew I wanted to leave and had fears for my safety if he were to find out.

Once at work I did not return except to collect what belongings he allowed me to take. When I reported all of this to the police I was told that unless I actually had broken limbs it would be difficult to make anything 'stick' because we were living together and therefore it would be treated as 'just another domestic'. I hate this man because he has done it before. I've since found out he owns an unlicensed rifle and is quite frightening in his instability. (Raped by her boyfriend when she was 28)

•

The attack by a date was repeated—he having at one time stolen my keys and taken me from my flat, had beat me up etc. Several times I lodged complaints with police. Several times, one just after I escaped abduction. They never believed me. (I'd been out with this guy once!) He'd come and bashed my door. I lived down the road from [name] Police!!! I ended up in hospital, with four subsequent operations for a broken wrist. Generally the police are good. Not on sexual assault. (Raped by her date when she was 36)

•

Although I knew two names and one address I was told 'forget it' as I wasn't a virgin and therefore I wouldn't be believed. Required sutures/hospitalised and fell pregnant! (Raped by her date plus two males when she was 20)

Some women ended up feeling not only disbelieved but humiliated and ridiculed.

The police told me that even though I had complained they wouldn't charge the chap as I had voluntarily given my knickers to him—this I did under threat of having my head crushed with a rock.

I was further embarrassed by the police who confronted me at my place of employment with the rapist. They were all laughing together, they also told a member of staff why they wanted to see me. They suggested in future that I keep my knickers on and apologised to the rapist for inconveniencing him. As well as my knickers the rapist asked me to give my walking shoes, necklace, glasses and purse. I escaped leaving all my belongings which were handed to the police as the rapist said, 'She trusted me with her things to mind'. (Raped by her date when she was 24)

Another survivor was also very negative about her experience with the police.

All throughout the rape, he kept on calling me a prostitute and saying, over and over again, 'You love it, don't you!' When I said, 'No I don't!' he seemed not to hear me and just kept saying it again.

His parting shot was 'I wouldn't bother calling the police if I was you, they're more likely to believe me'. I slowly got dressed, shaking, sobbing, feeling like a dirty, used piece of rag. And feeling angry, angry and impotent.

Than I rang the police. About six of them came over a few minutes later. I had to repeat my statement to each of them, in extreme detail. They even asked me, 'What did he say, then what did you say?' The detective who came in at the end and read my statement said there was many holes in it; it wouldn't stand up in Court.

For God's sake! I was upset by the whole experience of the rape and already felt like blocking it out of my mind.

Then two officers accompanied me to the medical centre for a physical examination. A neighbour stayed at my house to check on my child. After the examination a woman from the rape crisis centre showed up briefly. She said she'd ring me the next day to arrange counselling. I never heard from her again. So much for community concern.

When I went to the police station the next day to make a formal statement, I decided that my chances were hopeless. The police woman I spoke to was very bitchy, sceptical; kept asking me if I knew what rape was. One of the senior police officers who'd been to my house rung me a week later to tell me that he'd given [name] an informal warning to behave himself in future and to consider himself lucky that charges hadn't been pressed.

Verbal abuse continued to be hurled at me unrelentingly for almost a year. The police said there was nothing they could do about it. I have found it a lot harder to form friendships with males since this incident.

EFFECTS OF THE RAPE

How can one convey how devastating rape is for its victims. Although words do not seem adequate, the following comments does describe the horror quite eloquently.

Rape is not just physical violence, it is also mental violence. It is not easily forgotten. (Raped by her boyfriend when she was 22)

•

The system must get its priorities right. Even me and my current boyfriend agree that rape is worse than murder, even though death is terrible, but only family and friends suffer and get on with their lives. Rape lasts forever. The pain is always there. It is like a long agonising killing that continues till either you wipe it out or you die. (Raped by her boyfriend when she was 17)

Although many rapes by boyfriends and dates did not involve additional violence and injuries, for some there were physical injuries.

This was a 'date' at the drive-in, resulting in forced intercourse and damage to my clothing. My lip was split and resulted in scarring to my face, even to this day. (Raped by her date when she was 15)

•

I bled for weeks and future sexual experiences were extremely painful and caused more bleeding. (Raped by her date when she was 16)

Among other physical consequences of rape may be venereal disease.

My date set me up for a pack rape of six. I was beaten, stripped, old branches thrown over me and a match dropped on it. Then one of them urinated on me to put out the fire. I was then left in the bush with no clothes on. I just lay there. One of them came back much later and drove me home.

I have only just been able to talk about it thirty years later. One of them had gonorrhoea which I then contracted. I lost my job as the police came to see me about spreading the disease, even though I didn't say anything.

•

I was in severe shock after the incident and was unable to speak. I was a virgin prior to the rape. I had extensive bruising and was unable to urinate for about four hours. My face was extensively swollen and grotesque. My attacker tried to suffocate me as I tried to fight him off and scream for help. In hindsight I realise I was close to being murdered.

I later discovered I had a [medical ailment] and sought medical attention after a week but was unable to tell my doctor what had happened and was in fear of him being critical and unsupportive. I suffered severe depression for several years after the incident as in those days there was no supporting nor sympathetic institutions to help victims of rape. The assault has affected my relationships with people. (Raped by her date when she was 22)

•

I did not know this man very well before the date. I did know, however that he was a [prestigious occupation] and I therefore did not feel threatened by a date with this man. I put my trust in him because of his profession and thought he would not force himself upon me against my wishes. But I was very wrong. I was a virgin when this happened and I was very scared and frightened.

I became very ill after the attack with a venereal disease which my doctor felt would clear up, which it did, but some months later I had another attack of the same disease in my vaginal area. This I caught from my rapist. I only wished that the doctors had diagnosed it when I had my major attack after the rape. If it had been diagnosed then I most probably would have taken the perpetrator to court. But at the time the doctor (my local GP) said it would clear up with antibiotics. And therefore I felt that I would cope with this experience better without more friends and family finding out and that time would eventually heal my wounds and sadness. But now I have something I must live with for the rest of my life. It was an awful experience but to end up with a disease I'll always have just does not let you ever forget it.

But it is now years later and I have a very understanding boyfriend and think the emotional upset has gone. I'm now just very angry and bitter. Hopefully, with more time my anger will go. (Raped by her date when she was 17)

Another physical by-product of rape may be pregnancy. For some survivors this meant having to deal with abortion.

I was widowed at the time. I also became pregnant out of this and had an abortion after telling my friend, who arranged it. It left me scarred for life with guilt. I left the church. The date was a married man. I did not know that at the time. Met his parents who invited me out as well. I rang the wife later to tell her. He then raped me as a punishment. (Raped by her date when she was 30)

•

I conceived a child as a result of the assault. I had great difficulty in getting an abortion and had to wait until I was 3½ months pregnant before I obtained one. I was very ill afterwards. (Raped by her boyfriend when she was 22)

•

One incident happened the day I came out of hospital after having an abortion. Aborting the foetus that was the result of an earlier rape by the same boyfriend. (Raped by her boyfriend when she was 17)

Others, such as the next woman gave birth to the baby but gave it up for adoption.

Became pregnant. The baby was adopted quietly at birth and the birth certificate states 'father unknown'. No trace since, but wouldn't refuse contact if requested by the child. (Raped by a date when she was 18)

For some, the baby was kept which could act as a constant reminder.

I was taken to hospital, put on nerve pills, sleeping pills etc. So my rape was blocked out. I have a child from this and spent the next [number] years on pills till the doctor weaned me off and sent me to the Rape Crisis Centre where I spoke it all out. (Raped by a date when she was 26)

•

I have tried talking about it, but there's always doubt on their faces. I can't face that, too. I had a child as a result. (Raped by a boyfriend when she was 15)

An effect of sexual assault which was described by many of the survivors was the emotional legacy of the rape within their relationships and sex lives. For some this has contributed to estrangement in a primary relationship.

I think what happened to me really affected my sex life with my husband. (We are separated.) When I had that reminder [of the rape] I couldn't sleep with my husband without remembering what happened to me. My husband didn't understand what was happening to me and I couldn't tell him. I felt like it was my fault and my responsibility to sort it out myself. My husband was violent sometimes and I didn't know if I could trust him.

I've been separated [some] months. I still don't know if I'm over what happened. Sometimes I feel like going for counselling. Sometimes I still cry and feel bad about it. But other days I feel okay. (Raped by her date when she was 20)

As a result of the rape, the following writers spent many years without a sexual intimate relationship.

Even though there were almost no physical injuries this assault affected me. I was fearful of being alone with a man in a car or a room and didn't have another boyfriend for many years. I had lost my virginity so I considered no good man would want me.

My boyfriend was shocked by my shocked response and my immediately breaking off the relationship. I didn't want him punished, just a program to teach him that not everyone thinks like him. (Raped by her boyfriend when she was 19)

•

This physical attack was accompanied by devastating verbal abuse—lasted one hour or more. Over the years since, I have become increasingly unwilling to have intimate relationships, and I have had no sexual penetration since the rape. (Raped by her date when she was 30)

The impact on one's sexuality may be direct as described above in celibacy or it may be more covert, contributing to the survivor's 'submission' in other sexual encounters.

102

Although I knew at the time it was 'rape' because I was aggressively forced to take part in a sexual act against my will, I did not fully understand the implications of the assault, maybe due to my youth and naivety. I didn't think I'd be taken seriously as I was in a 'relationship' with the offender and had consented on other occasions. I always believed up till this time that I could control my sexuality, but in the end, I wasn't physically strong enough to 'fight off' my attacker.

I now feel that this experience had a very negative impact upon my early relationships with men, making me 'submit' more readily . . . for fear? To avoid violence? To maintain control? (Raped by her boyfriend when she was 17)

HEALING

As related by a few of the voices in the sections above, the effects of rape by boyfriends or dates can be ameliorated over time. This process involves disclosure and usually working through the experience and its radiating issues with counsellors trained in this field.

Earlier this year I went to a Women's Health day organised by the [name]. The assertiveness class confirmed for me my emotional inability, lack of direction and my right to do something about it. Not long after that I heard a segment on the radio on sexual assault about clinics and counselling.

Anyway when she talked about seeking help, even if it was twenty years ago she seemed to be talking right to me. So one day when my child was asleep I looked in the phone book and found myself crying on the phone to someone at [name of agency]. I felt so stupid after so many years but that was quickly replaced by the feeling of sheer relief of letting the monster out. I had counselling sessions that turned my life around.

It's hard to know which is worse, to be pack raped in the summer before you turn seventeen or holding on to it for all that time. The counsellor took me back to that sixteen year old girl and beyond. It was like being jettisoned back through time, to me. I started to remember things about the rape and about what I used to be like and liked doing.

As for prevention—in my case if I had followed my gut reaction of dislike and not accepted the date . . . I now teach my daughter to trust her feelings about people.

I needed the assistance to come out and get me as it's done these days. Now I feel less like an accomplice to a crime and more like one of many who have been wronged. I now have support to face the pain and dare to be open and tender and vulnerable again and enjoy the sexuality we all have a right to.

The next account highlights the concept that 'we are only as sick as the secrets we keep'. The writer sought counselling but did not begin to heal until she was able to fully disclose.

At the time I was assaulted by my boyfriend I knew there was something wrong about what had happened, but didn't know what. I then literally blocked the event out.

In the proceeding [sic] months the perpetrator, who had since been diagnosed with [a psychiatric disorder], rang me, wrote to me, showed up at my house and generally pestered me. I was scared of him but did not know why.

Some weeks after the assault I was hospitalised with depression. I had been taken by a friend to the nearest public hospital. I underwent extensive counselling with this counsellor and with a psychiatrist but still did not talk about what had happened.

The problem which had led to my depression dawned on me when I was walking on the beach. Images came to me in flashes. It was then that I went through the feelings of shame, guilt, dirtiness etc. Well at least that's when I realised why I felt that way.

Eleven months after the initial assault I told the counsellor what had happened. It was the hardest conversation I have ever had.

Now, years later I've learned to like who I am. I am beginning to learn to trust people (especially men). I'm probably one of the lucky ones—the only residual problems are those which still stop me being raped again. But I was very ill for some time, all because I thought being raped was my fault and people wouldn't respect me any more. The only other fear I have is of bumping into the man involved in the street one day—I'm still terrified on him!! (Raped by her boyfriend when she was 18)

Although the following comment does not discuss the survivor's healing per se, it is included in this section since the message conveyed is one of empowerment. One can read it and believe that this is one survivor who has taken steps to validate herself. It should be noted, however, that the research on fighting the rapist is mixed. *See* Reekie and Wilson (1993) for a discussion of the literature on this subject.

I took up martial arts because of the attack. If I ever get attacked again I will not hesitate in fighting hard and hurting him back. What he did still can upset me.

Good luck with this work. It's important that someone listens to us!! (Raped by her date when she was 19)

The next writer in this section indicates that for her to understand and heal from the many date rapes she has experienced, she first has had to work through the issues of her childhood sexual assault. (Note: The fact that she believes that her incest history rendered her passive during other sexual assaults should in no way be construed as placing the blame on the victim. Rape does not require physical resistance nor is the victim in any way responsible for the assault.)

From when I started dating at the age of fifteen years until I married and in the years since I left my husband until this year I have been 'date' raped on a number of occasions. When it comes to sex and consenting to it I have been, up until now, very passive. This is because of my history of sexual abuse starting at an early age.

I never reported these 'date' rapes. In one way I have been lucky because, except for once when a guy I was going out with raped me, had anal sex and punched me, violence has not been involved in my 'date' rapes, probably because I have been so passive.

Since last year I have been working on my history of sexual abuse. First in a group using the book entitled *Why Me?* as a guide and now on a one to one basis I am working with a Social worker using the book entitled *The Courage to Heal, A Guide for Women survivors of Child Sexual Abuse* as a guide.

SUGGESTIONS FROM SURVIVORS

Again, the main theme iterated by several women was the need to increase the public's awareness and education about sexual assault and precautions and preventative methods.

More needs to be said about date rape. When it happened to me eleven years ago I had never heard of date rape. I didn't report it because I thought the police would say, 'So what, he's your boyfriend'. Besides that, the criminal justice system seems to favour the criminal not the victim.

I'm still not over what happened to me. Several weeks ago while watching a story on child sexual abuse I finally realised what happened to me and for the very first time I cried and told my husband what happened. My husband is very caring. We met a couple of months after the rape and for nearly twelve months we couldn't have sex because I couldn't relax, at that stage he didn't know about the rape neither did anyone else.

Please do something about the system. It's not fair that the victim is made to feel guilty. We have male friends (who don't know about my rape) who think that a woman begs to be raped.

I'm terrified that it's going to happen again one day and I get scared when I'm home alone day or night.

•

I too am another silent victim. I was incredibly emotionally scarred. It wasn't until I saw the program that I realised how lucky I was to escape from being assaulted further. It is the victim's choice to speak out. I happened to know my attacker. I never thought what he did would lead to much. But at least he knows he did wrong and hopefully regrets it.

The problem that upsets me is how to let people know when they are pushing the limit and breaking the law, how to get help and how to deal with it and recognising a crime when it has occurred. I was assaulted over a period of hours in broad daylight and trying to get help, I was in a crowded city at midday and no one helped me. Those who saw I was in trouble ignored me and no one interfered. That was the scariest part of my whole experience.

I was out of harm finally when I fled out of my aggressor's grasp and onto a moving train leaving a station, with a conductor running after me, who happened to see me attempt to catch a moving train. Sure it was foolish, but I was desperate.

My situation was becoming more tense. At first I tried to talk sense into him. At the end I wouldn't have cared what I did. My main aim was to escape from him and not have to look back. I never told my family or my mother (and we are so close). Two girlfriends know a little but not every detail. They made me feel guilty as though it was my fault and that crushed any ideas of mine to 'blow the whistle' on this attacker.

People need to be made aware. There is a lack of knowledge about precautions. They can be taken if people are educated in assault awareness and prevention. If I had been previously given a mild awareness education, my nightmare date may not have had such a horrible ending and I may have received the help I needed at the time.

This happened to me months ago. Since then I have been able to cope and recover, but the fear remains as does the mistrust and I feel sick when I ever return to the city because the memory is revived. Somewhere there has to be more help and guidance. We want help and want to fight for protection.

•

I didn't report my rape because I was scared of disbelief. Encourage others to charge their rapists. Advertise this widely. (Raped by her boyfriend when she was 17)

Specifically, the following writers believe that education programming should include a sexual etiquette component for males to be taught some basic truths such as 'no' means 'no'.

I dated a man to whom I had been 'properly introduced' by a friend. I did not believe that such a person would pull a knife and demand sex. I was wrong!

I was an unmarried mother, therefore I would not have had any importance. I would have asked for it—wouldn't I?

There should be more education of young men about date rape. A dinner etc does not mean they are owed anything.

I think I felt shame because apart from struggling, kicking and screaming there came a point where I realised the inevitability of the act and 'went along with it'—I let myself go limp.

107

The man rang me again to ask for a second date and when I accused him of rape he said 'I thought you must have liked it like that!' What? Screaming and kicking and saying 'No', continually?? (Raped by her date when she was 22)

•

At least 50 per cent of my friends have been raped. We need to change men and young boys' attitudes. I have a baby daughter now and live in fear it will happen to her later.

Societal values need to shift away from blaming the women victims.

You are made to feel like it's your fault. It boils down to the fact that it is unfair. Males are allowed to do what they like and get away with it. If women were to act like males (e.g. one night stands) they are labelled sluts but it is OK for the men to do so. Where is the justice in that?? It's unfair!! What is good enough for one should be good enough for the other whatever the sex or colour. There is no excuse for rape!

Further, according to the following survivor, other values and roles about males and females need to be changed.

As far as I'm concerned I was raped. However I would have a pretty hard time proving it.

I was out for dinner for a not so close friend's birthday and all of her friends were there. We had decided early on that I would stay at her friend's house (two girls, one guy) since I was drinking. We went out to a club after dinner and I got pretty drunk. It was pretty late and I was dancing with the guy whose house I was staying at. He said we were all going and I was so drunk that I just believed him. I got into a cab with him and I told the cab driver to go to [a certain place] because I think it's beautiful down there and this guy had just moved from [another city].

He didn't seem interested in the view at all so I went over and sat next to him and tried to, I guess, 'sell' it to him. Next thing I knew my pants were down and he was on top of me. It was just a spilt second. I was so shocked but I was so drunk that (I'm so angry that I could possibly believe this next line) somewhere deep inside I believed I should submit. That scares me so much—that somewhere inside me I've subtly learnt that that's the way it is, that a woman should submit. Don't get me wrong—I love sex (with people I choose), but if I had been sober I would've realised the aggression in his actions and also I wouldn't have been even vaguely interested and (I think) I would've said no.

It was over and he got up and left. I was so confused. I chased him and he tolerated me until we found a cab. In the cab I realised how drunk I was. I felt really ill. We got to his place and I said I was going to crash on the floor. He said to just crash in his bed, it would be OK. So I went upstairs and just crashed out fully clothed. Last thing I remember I'd woken up and he'd just finished ripping all my clothes off. I passed out again but I suspect he went ahead anyway.

The next morning I felt really strange so I just left. I would never have even thought about rape except that I felt so violated. At the time it happened I believed it was OK—The 'right' thing to do. (That makes me so angry. It disgusts me.) But the next day I felt so . . . strange. It really was a helpless feeling of having been stripped of something.

I'm just so angry that such primitive, sexist, degrading, worthless beliefs were ingrained in me somewhere. I'm very aware of women's rights and I'm just so damn angry. I spoke about this to one friend and she told me a similar story. That's scary.

As much as we all know that rape is wrong, I think deep down (unless we have made a conscious decision to change) we will all have a certain tolerance (albeit unconscious) for this kind of abuse while women in Australia are presented and treated the way we are. We are merely objects, vessels, second-class citizens.

To me the women's movement as presented in the media (in real life could be vastly different) is merely a token effort. As the cliche goes 'pushing shit uphill'. There seems to be no true recognition of us as equals. It's scary and frustrating to think that we are still being controlled by narrow-minded insecure men. I would really like to do something, in some way, to help change the subtle education we receive through the media and the education system and especially our parents and grandparents, etc.

I realise that my story is not especially shocking or unusual but I think that that is exactly the frightening part. For some reason rape is never really considered 'unacceptable' unless the victim is killed.

According to survivors, females also need more education about sex. They must know what their rights are, learn some skills such as assertiveness and be encouraged to develop a better or greater sense of self-worth.

It was the custom to push sex on girls in those days. We girls knew nothing. At least this working one didn't. If only I had talks at school about self-esteem; self-worth; assertiveness; sex education; the difference between love and sex. I would have been better able to cope with male/female relationships.

I thank God for the 'sexual revolution' and I strongly agree with sex/relationship education in schools. The way rape crimes are investigated must be changed. The way rape trials are conducted must be changed now.

A number of recommendations concerned the criminal justice system.

Prison does not improve them, only makes it worse. They should get hormonal treatment as well as prison. Special training for the police; there should be [a] rape squad available for each case, and specially trained officers only to handle the reporting. (Raped by her date when she was 18)

Several women stressed their belief that the courts need to stop their lenient sentencing of rapists.

Stiffer penalties are needed before women will feel confident about reporting rape. Also the victim should be allowed a legal defence in the court to ensure her character is not on trial, just the crime perpetrated against her. (Raped by her date when she was 22)

•

Rape and murder should get a harder sentence than fraud and white collar crimes. The law is male! (Raped by her date when she was 18)

One writer narrowed the focus of law reform onto pornography.

110

I believe we need stronger laws against selling and possession of videos and magazines. Not only those depicting sexual violence but also those that demean and devalue women and present them as merely sexual objects. I appreciate people facilitating this sort of change in our society. Thank you. (Raped by her date when she was 18)

Another mentioned the need for laws about stalking to be changed.

I'm a survivor only because I made myself strong. We need new laws especially for stalking. This man is still annoying me stating that 'he loves me'. The police do nothing. (Raped by her boyfriend when she was 16)

The next letter writer has been waiting for more than two decades to see some change in the judiciary's attitudes. After telling us the story of her victimisation, she concludes that no real change may occur until more women occupy roles of judges and lawyers.

It happened over twenty years ago. I knew or thought I knew the man. He asked me out lots of times but I had always refused, but eventually accepted. We had a good evening out at a club, only a couple of drinks and supper. He offered to give me a lift home in his car which I accepted; I didn't have a car then. On the way to my home he said we were just around the corner from his place so we should go for coffee. I accepted, something that I had never usually done on a first or second date.

We never had coffee. I struggled with this man for almost an hour before someone threw a brick or something at his door and said to keep the noise down. Afterwards he refused to take me home and very reluctantly loaned me money for a taxi. I didn't know where I was. I was terrified, but found a phone box and inside an advertisement for a taxi firm. I rang and asked for a taxi. I was crying, but the taxi firm seemed nice and kind and said he would talk to me until the taxi cab arrived at the phone box address. Fifteen minutes later the taxi arrived and I felt safe at last. Whilst driving in the taxi cab I was once again humiliated when I found out that the man who had spoken to me at the taxi cab firm, who I thought to be nice and kind, had broadcast our conversation to the whole taxi cab fleet. They kept calling the taxi cab with ribald remarks and laughing.

Once home, everyone was asleep. It broke my heart. I was so angry with myself for putting myself into a position I couldn't handle. I was feeling so humiliated, frightened and shocked. I told no one in my family. I would have got into so much trouble from my parents and siblings. I know my friends would have thought me cheap for allowing myself to get into such a situation, and certainly would have disowned me, and mostly it would have given them something to gossip about. Nice girls just didn't allow this kind of thing to happen to them. I was just so full of shame.

I have never told my husband or another being except my friend of years ago. My husband wouldn't be able to handle it I know, but the feeling of shame still persists, and that alone is enough for me to be persuaded to keep quiet.

It would never have dawned on me to report it. Twenty years ago, it was never discussed, kept quiet and swept under the carpet. I get emotional about rape when I hear of it, only now is something starting to be done about it. I've waited twenty years for hope of new laws, meanwhile lots of women still live in dread, and fear.

The years ago attitudes for men haven't really changed one jot. The men who slept around regularly were always patted on the back and thought of as some kind of hero, especially if they had had lots of sexual partners. The girls with whom they had sex were treated as social prostitutes and outcasts and certainly were only good for one thing, you didn't go out with them, they were treated like dirt.

To this day I hate that man—I always will. He had seemed so nice and friendly, but what an animal he turned out to be.

I can't imagine I would ever have written this down but there you go, times change, hopefully the system will change. We need to have more women judiciary to lend an empathetic ear to women's sexual harassment or rape cases. Men do not seem to want to understand. I get the impression even now we're all a bit of a joke and a nuisance to the law and courts, and will have to wait a long time yet before the punishment fits the crime. How do you punish a man for touching you, defiling your body, hurting you, embarrassing, humiliating you, and taking away all your self-esteem and confidence in one powerful moment of male dominance, and for what! I still don't understand and I still get angry.

The need for more improvement in the services for survivors, particularly those adults attempting to deal with child sexual assault, is advised by the next writer who recognises the importance of counselling.

There is a serious lack of facilities available for abuse victims. Most services only take what they call 'fresh rape' cases. What happens to those people who were assaulted as children and are only facing it now? Or those people who were too afraid in the past to tell anyone? Also people need to be educated about their rights (sexually etc). It is amazing how many women still believe that men can't control their sexual urges and are thus compelled to rape.

A lot of people don't understand the difference between a bad sexual experience that involved mutual consent and rape/assault which does not involve consent. As a result a lot of people think that it is possible to just forget about it. But the effects of being overpowered, of being denied control over your own body and the shame and humiliation that results from it influence all areas of a victim's life. For example, throughout the time that I have been moving through the effects of both assaults, I have had a fear of wearing skirts! I wear baggy clothes to hide my figure. Until this year I have either avoided sex or 'switched off' mentally during sex so that it just became an issue of going through the motions. Often I would think 'when is this going to finish', or else I would think of other things e.g. study, shopping list etc. This year I have developed a fear of going to pubs, parties etc, anywhere where there are a lot of people, even if my boyfriend accompanies me. Mostly I overreact to things, become very emotional (cry a lot) blame myself for everything that goes wrong etc.

It is very important that the government admit that there is a serious problem in relation to sexual assault in Australia. Counselling services should be free; a person does not ask to be assaulted and as a result should not have to pay for counselling. But it is absolutely essential that survivors receive counselling to move through the far reaching effects of assault. It is possible to recover to a certain extent but it takes a lot of time and a lot of help.

Finally, there was a suggestion for future research needs.

Can I suggest that instead of pouring money into the victims of rape, that money be poured into looking at why men perpetrate crimes against women, because only then can we be safe from men and their power games. (Raped by her date when she was 15)

Note: A part of the difficulty in accessing assistance is lack of knowledge about the existing resources—although more services are desperately needed. It is hoped that Appendix II will provide some assistance.

6

ACQUAINTANCES

> After the rape the thing that most often goes through one's mind is—'How Ostupid of me, how could I have been so naive—how did I get myself into this—how come I was so trusting?' It is as though in one moment the trust goes and thereafter you can only see yourself as stupid for not realising that all men cannot be trusted.

In the 'Without Consent' survey one-quarter of the survivors stated that they had been raped by an acquaintance. In fact, the proportion was higher since many of those who wrote in a specific person, eg. doctor, for 'other' (perpetrator relationship) were actually describing an acquaintance.

CHILDREN

Although the most likely perpetrator of children under the age of eleven was a relative, for those raped from the age of eleven through their teens, acquaintances were the highest risk. For some children these offenders were older males such as neighbours or friends of the family. In the next two cases, such men assaulted without penetration.

About six years of age. A male friend of my parents, placed his foot in my crutch, whilst we were travelling in the back of a 'ute'. He hurt me. I screamed out to my mother and she told me to 'shut up, you dirty little trollop'. The man leered at me and continued moving his foot around.

•

Again I was only young and blamed myself because I used to go to his place to play with toys that he had there. He used to touch my hair and hold me close but the last time I went there he had been drinking as I can remember the smell of beer on his breath. That night he trapped me in the kitchen of his house and lay on me kissing me and rubbing up against me. He wouldn't let me go until I cried. The smell of beer on my husband's breath gives me the same sick feelings thirty-six years on.

For two thirteen year olds, the rape was their first experience sexually.

I had never heard of oral sex and was totally horrified and thought I must be the most disgusting human being on earth. I thought nobody would ever accept me if they ever knew what a terribly revolting thing I had been forced to do. It destroyed all my self-esteem for years and I spent years trying to prove to myself that I wasn't a 'slut'. (Female raped when she was 13 by three males)

•

I was a virgin and was held down by the two men in their late teens while a third person raped me! Then they changed places and the second one raped me. The third person could see how distressed I was and decided not to rape me. (Female, raped when she was 13)

A 'pack' rape as described by the preceding survivor is also recounted in detail by the next writer. Her voice enables one to feel her humiliation and pain.

The other experience I wish to relate to you occurred when I was thirteen. I was raped by a seventeen year old boy that I knew, and held down by his two elder brothers and one of their friends. One of the brothers was in his late 20's. No one can tell me that they didn't know that they were doing wrong.

I was out [activity] with a girlfriend. We called into the house where this boy lived. I was very sweet on him. He was everything that my parents saw as being bad. To me, this was attraction enough. My girlfriend split her jeans, and as she only lived down the road, I stayed at the house while she went home to change.

Just after she left, the men started whispering to each other and there was lots of laughter. The four of them grabbed me and I knew that I was in trouble. They told me that they were going to help me to 'lose my cherry'. I struggled for a while but I didn't have a hope in hell. I didn't scream. I don't even remember the thoughts crossing my mind. I guess that with all the secrets that I already had and the silence that I had been forced into, screaming just wasn't in my thought patterning.

I had my periods. I told them this, and asked could I go to the toilet to take out my med. I thought that if I looked like I was going along with them I would have a chance to get away. The toilet was in the back yard and I had every intention of running for my life. At this stage, terror isn't a strong enough word. They knew what I was up to. Somebody said, 'You're not going anywhere because you'll run away'. The four of them carried me into the bedroom. I was kicking and struggling quite strongly. They thought that this was hilarious.

They physically ripped my clothes off and one of them pulled my med out. He disappeared and came back with it in a bottle of water, which they chucked around the room to each other. This was, for me, total degradation. Three of them held me down whilst one of them got on top. Two then left the room and I could hear them laughing the entire time. The third one sat on top of the partition wall, (the walls didn't go to the roof, only about three-quarters of the way) and watched. The one that was raping me kept saying things to me like, 'What's the matter? Don't you like it?'

When he was over the others came in. There was blood everywhere. I sat on the edge of the bed like a zombie. Somebody threw a med at me. Just about then, one of their girlfriends came home. It was her bed and she went berserk at the mess. She didn't care about me. I remember her yelling but I don't remember much else. I was in shock.

I waited on the front verandah for my friend to come back. She asked what had happened and I burst out crying. I was a mess. My clothes were torn and I had blood everywhere.

My major concern at this stage was what I was going to say to my parents when I got home. I was convinced that they would kill me. To this very day, as far as I'm concerned, I went home to an empty house. I can still see and hear the house that I walked into. It was dark and quiet. My mother now tells me that they were all home that day, and she tried to stop me from walking up the hallway but I kept pushing her aside. She said she kept asking me what had happened but I wouldn't answer. I have absolutely no memory of this.

I had the hottest shower that I have ever had. I tried to scrub the feeling of them touching me off. The bottom of the shower was just a pool of blood. When I tried to insert a med, it wouldn't stay in. I locked myself in my bedroom for days on end. My mother would ask me questions and I just could not answer her. I sat in front of her like a stone. My heart was breaking for her but I was hurting so badly myself that I just couldn't talk to her.

My school work suffered. I had constant tension headaches and I gave new meaning to the term 'going wild'. I tried everything to get expelled. I didn't care any more. In the end my parents brought me home to do correspondence, and it was never mentioned again until the beginning of this year when I decided to tell my parents what had happened. They were terrific, very supportive but naturally very hurt and upset that I had chosen to carry all of this alone for so long.

It has taken me years to come to grips with all the horrible things that have happened to me. I want to have a part to play in helping victims break the silence trap that society pushes them into. Thank you for taking the time to read my letter. I pray that other people will have the courage to speak out about their experiences, but also that society will care enough to hear their pleas. All people have to do is to listen, and to open their eyes. The pain is there very clearly spelled out. I can see it, why can't they?

SELF-DOUBT AND SHAME

A recurrent theme or message in many of the letters written by acquaintance rape survivors is the shame and self-doubt that they experienced; in some cases, these feelings have persisted to the time of writing. It is apparent that a number of the women question the credibility of their experience as a rape.

I just couldn't believe this had happened, I had known this man for years, helped him through his marriage break-up—talked to him for hours. I kept saying 'no, no, no'. He had some fantasy going on in his head and was not listening. I said 'I don't want this. You are doing it without my consent. You are raping me'. He laughed and said, 'Yes, and isn't it fun?'. I just lay there and cried after that. (Female, raped when she was 26)

●

I was forced to have sex by a fellow student. I kept saying I wasn't interested, that he should go home. If he wouldn't go home we could just stay on the couch till morning. He kept ignoring my no's and

118

then when we had sex he said, 'There, you liked that, didn't you'. I was young. I didn't like it at all. (Female, raped when she was 19)

For some, the shame seems to stem from their sense of partial responsibility for the rape. If they were drunk at the time, like the next writers, this appears to contribute to such self-blame.

I am not sure if I belong in your survey if you can call a survivor someone who wishes that every morning that they woke that they could die in their sleep and not a day goes by without thinking about ending my life. The night I was raped I was drunk. The two men that raped me were friends of my husband; one works for him and still does sometimes. I feel a fool for putting myself in this situation. (Female, raped when she was 38)

•

I don't think/know if my experience can be called rape or even assault. I was drunk, went willingly to his place—when pressed for sex I repeatedly said no but physically did not resist for many reasons (not physical fear really). I was a virgin previously and genuinely wanted to remain so and would have acted more strongly in defence if sober.

Although drinking willingly, I think that my drinks were spiked. Although I accompanied the man to his place, I didn't expect the events that occurred. I think that partly I didn't physically fight back because of the alcohol induced disorientation and sense of unreality (ie I didn't fully appreciate what was happening), and partly because I felt I had been stupid, unknowingly 'led him on' and I felt things had gone too far to be able to easily put a stop to the events.

Others castigated themselves for flirting.

I met my attacker, a married man, at a party—he offered to drive me home and suggested we call in to another party on the way home. At the 'party house' no-one was there and he threw me in a room and said he'd kill me. When I screamed he said it would make no difference because the neighbours were used to it.

I later found out that he was a real estate agent and had gone to the house earlier to turn on the lights, radio etc. I felt I was to blame as I knew he was married and I had flirted with him. (Female, raped when she was 18)

ALCOHOL

Two of the women above have doubted their own qualifications as rape survivors since they had been drinking at the time of the assault. The consumption of alcohol, particularly to the point of inebriation, played a role in a number of other acquaintance rapes reported in the survey. For some, it was the first time that they had been intoxicated.

I wagged school and this person bought a bottle of burgundy and a half bottle of claret which I proceeded to share with him. This was my first experience with alcohol. Unfortunately memorable. Thank you for the opportunity to 'report' this attack on myself (I still can't write the word). I hope it is helpful. (Female, raped when she was 14)

The next survivor's drinking made her feel in part responsible for the rape.

I was raped by two guys. I had a couple of drinks and someone put something in one. They dragged me to an oval and raped me. I felt it was my fault for having a drink and couldn't do anything because I was out of it. I felt till this year I was nothing and this incident really made me a fragile, insecure woman, scared of men. I am thankful to a woman counsellor who has helped me to trust this year. (Female, raped when she was 23)

SILENCE

The main reasons for non-disclosure concerned one or more of the variables discussed above: alcohol, feelings of self-responsibility and self-blame, and being a child.

I felt obligated to stay with the two guys (in a restaurant) when my girl friend slipped out. I was very naive and didn't expect two very nicely presented men, who had (so far) been perfect gentlemen to rape me. I put myself at risk—I feel stupid even now.

120

A consequence of these factors was the fear that one would not be believed. Therefore, one kept the secret.

The person who raped me was a good friend of the family. The main reason I did not tell anyone in my family was because of the fear that they would not believe me. They had known this man for 25-30 years —I was baby sitting for him. (Female, raped when she was 16)

•

I was brought up in a strictly religious family and my parents wouldn't have ever believed me as the perpetrator was also very religious and I was told these type of people would never do this type of crime. (Female, raped when she was 14)

One must read between the lines to understand the shame that stopped the next survivor from telling anyone about her victimisation until she wrote the following.

I have kept this awful secret to myself for ten years. This man knew my husband had gone out. I am a small grey haired woman and have a very good relationship with my children. This man was [a lot younger]. He had a wife and [number] children. One afternoon there was a knock at the door and he pushed his way in. He started to fondle me. I tried to fight him off but he dragged me into the bedroom, ripped my clothes off and raped me. I didn't scream as there was no-one to help me.

P.S. I have recently found out this man's marriage has broken up and also his second marriage—he has also become religious! I'm shaking as I write this but I'm glad I have told someone.

Some survivors, like the next two writers, blocked off the rape; they, and others such as them, could not disclose to anyone since they essentially shut down a curtain over the incident. Fortunately, or unfortunately—depending upon your perspective—such amnesia does not usually last forever. Also, whilst in place the effects of the assault (and its suppression) are covertly impacting on the individual and her life.

121

He suggested we 'go lie down on a bed'. I refused. He then suggested we go for a walk. I continually said 'No', but after awhile he insisted. We walked a short distance then he said 'Let's lie down'. I said 'No' and said, 'You're not getting anything from me'.

He pushed me to the ground, got on top of me and put my hands up above my head so as to hold me down. I couldn't move. I told him many times to 'get off' but as he had me in the position I was in, it was useless. I was helpless. He unzipped my jeans, pulled them down and attempted to rape me, but somehow I was able to keep my legs together so he couldn't.

Every time I think of it, all I see is him perched on top of me with his jeans down near his ankles. He forced me to masturbate him and he made a mess on me. He followed me home but didn't come inside.

Because it was a bad experience I blocked it from my mind and it wasn't until [some] months ago that I told someone.

After I'd been with my boyfriend [several] months, we were making love and he placed my arms high above my head and unfortunately it brought back awful memories. I was so upset and cried like a baby. For the first time, I decided to tell him. He couldn't have been more understanding. It's not the sort of thing you go telling people. For months I had blocked out that rape then suddenly it seemed to 're-occur' and haunt me, although it wasn't my boyfriend raping me but in my mind it flashed back because of the way my arms were placed above my head.

•

I was raped. At the time I was fourteen and a virgin. I don't really know how I felt at the time—but I definitely thought that I was to blame in some way. I felt totally ashamed, aware that this was rape, but unable to do anything about it. In retrospect, I feel I was right in hiding it, having seen the way that the courts deal with both victims and rapists.

I chose to block it out of my life. Physically I was not really injured except for bruises on my head where he had dragged me by the hair. The rape has not affected my sex life, but I am sure that my poor self image was a direct result. The rapist cried afterwards, and declared his undying love—he was [number] years old. Very ironic really, and one I am still bitter about—the violation, feeling not in control of your destiny, feeling invaded and abused. Being so young and feeling that in some way it was all my fault—that I deserved it.

Maybe it all goes back to Christian society and its concept of original sin! (Female, raped when she was 14)

Fear acted to keep the following woman silent for fifteen years.

This is the first time I've admitted that, yes, what happened to me was rape. I have not told anyone. I was and still am frightened. He knew where I lived. Fifteen years later I still have horrible dreams. (Female, raped when she was 15)

RESPONSE OF FAMILY, FRIENDS AND OTHERS

Sixty-two per cent of those raped by acquaintances had told someone about the rape. Family response was supportive in about half the cases.

Women have to be made aware they are not to blame. The person who assaulted me has been able to go on with his life while my life has been hell. I wish I was able to report this at the time it happened. Dealing with seven years of emotions almost sent me insane. I am very lucky I had the support of family and friends when I felt I was able to deal with this, which was only a few weeks ago. (Female, raped when she was 17)

Others, like the next writer, were met with disbelief or minimising. This can have lasting damage on the relationship between the survivor and the family member.

I was fifteen years old and an old mate of my father's came to stay. In young years I'd always looked at him like an Uncle. One morning as I was just about to go into the bathroom to have a shower, he came up to me in the hallway and hugged me. I didn't think twice about it. Then he asked if I had a kiss for him. Still thinking quite innocently about it I went to kiss him on the cheek and he turned my head with his hand and kissed me full on the lips. I felt his tongue in my mouth and was shocked. I jerked away a bit but wasn't sure what had happened. He then touched my breast and I quickly made the excuse about having a shower and locked myself in the bathroom.
    I cried whilst having a shower but felt so unsure of myself. I knew it didn't feel right and it was wrong for him to have done that but I was scared and felt it was my fault. I told my boyfriend's

mother at the time and she convinced me to tell my own mother. My mum shrugged it off saying that was the way he is. I told her that I didn't like it. I went and spent the next week at my boyfriend's place under the care of his mother. My own mother didn't say anything to him and let him stay at our house for the rest of his holiday.

Although it all might sound silly and it may not be what you mean, it deeply disturbed me. I hate this man. To look at him repulses me but I can never forgive her for not believing me back when I was an innocent fifteen year old and for now still thinking I made it all up.

My worst fear is to be raped. I feel I would die if it ever happens. I truly feel for anyone who is sexually abused or raped. It's the worst thing to happen to anyone. Worse then torture. At least the pain would subside in a week or so. We have to live with this all our lives. I love my parents but I can never forget.

A young victim was ignored at the time by her sister and later blamed by her mother.

My sister's boyfriend [who was eighteen]. I didn't know what was happening. My sister found out and did react but only at him. I was left thinking it was my fault. I finally told my Mum when I was twenty-four that I was raped at twelve. She said I probably deserved it (I didn't even know what happened at the time).

Friends were evaluated as supportive by 55 per cent of the acquaintance rape victims. In the next comment, the survivor's boyfriend, however, was far less than supportive.

The person that did it was the son of someone important in a small town. The police said he was a good boy. I found out he had done it [a number of] times before but people were paid to keep things quiet. He was sent [away] after my attack.

He raped me in [a place] and used my stockings to tie me to posts and stuffed my undies in my mouth. My boyfriend of two years said I had just fooled around and tried to cover up by calling it rape. (Female, raped when she was 17)

One 'friend' confidante even told the perpetrator what the survivor had said.

After reporting the rape to a friend she reported this to the rapist who was a mutual friend. He then waited a week and came back and battered me and threatened me with future violence if I didn't shut up. (Female, raped when she was 17)

Although doctors' support was not measured on the survey instrument, at least one practitioner was helpful and sympathetic.

Sixteen years after being sexually assaulted I suffered psychosomatic symptoms that were attributed by my GP to the incident. I spent some time discussing with him what had happened. His telling me I had a right to be angry helped me considerably. He was the only person I told who was supportive.

NOT REPORTING TO POLICE

A very high proportion of those assaulted by acquaintances (87 per cent) did not go to the police. Some explained that this was due to others' negative experiences.

There were experiences which stopped me from speaking up. Police handled an incident where a friend was stabbed, very badly. They interrogated me and made me feel very inferior. The perpetrator got off with a slap on the wrist. I was not going to have my case trivialised like this. The shock of being treated so viciously made me a <u>victim</u>. I went to great lengths to preserve my safety after that but wondered about my place in society. (Female, raped when she was 19)

A medical practitioner warned the next woman not to disclose to police.

The doctor I saw that night told me not to tell the police as it would not help me and only humiliate me because of their questions and tests etc. (Female, raped when she was 19)

A belief that they were in part at fault, that the rape was thus less than a 'real' rape, and that police would therefore not act was the motivation behind not reporting for several survivors.

I am a single Mum with two children. I did not report it as I felt unworthy. They wouldn't have listened and I thought I was also a decent, nice girl. I believe men will home in on someone with low self-esteem most of the time. They are weak, slimy men. Women must be more assertive. (Female, raped when she was 19)

•

The perpetrator in this case was a man who my friends (male and female) and I had accepted a lift home from, after a nightclub we were at had closed. I, in my naivety did not get out of the car when they did. I did not want to be an intrusion upon their privacy.

In my attempts to persuade him not to do it, I tried various approaches including telling him I was a lesbian although I have never had any homosexual encounters. This did not deter him; and if anything made him more determined as he told me his ex-girlfriend had left him for a woman. Knowing now, how much of a 'kick in the balls' it is for the male psycho-sexual ego to be left by a girlfriend for another woman not man, I realise it was not a smart move.

Because I had accepted the lift with him with my friends—I felt I was responsible and therefore did not report it. Also because we had been to a nightclub and I had briefly spoken to this person in the nightclub I felt this would undermine my reporting of this incident. Summing it up: it was against my will and I had given him no indication that sex was on my mind. However I did get into the car and therefore felt it was my fault.

•

Because I made a conscious decision to submit, after an initial attempt to escape was unsuccessful, that made me feel things would not go well for me police wise.

Also I never wanted to see that person again—if their story was true they were not Australian and were flying out in a couple of days time—so I just hoped they left and never came back.

Also I had offered the person a place to stay. He was a traveller I befriended on the beach. So I had asked him to stay. I had given him his own room and had gone off to my room. From my point of view there was no desire for sex and I didn't see him as untrustworthy. I offered a place to stay in a genuine spirit of friendship—the sort of safe friendship ('crash at my house!') I had enjoyed with many males.

The terrible phrase 'she was asking for it' kept knocking around in my brain. I was not asking for it but I felt as though everything about this particular rape was pointing back to me.

Also the terrible haunting of my mother's voice telling me how dreadful rape cases were—that the woman had to tell everything she did and had done in her past.

Why that should be so strong in my mind I don't know—why my mother ever told me I don't know—it was like saying, 'Don't you dare get raped', or 'If you do don't tell the police and go to court'. It's like a rape mythology which says it's the woman who is to blame. It's the woman who really gets tried, not the man, and we parents don't want the shame.

So all these reasons go together to let a rape go unreported.

Something that no-one mentions much is living after the fear.

I still find it impossible to sleep with an open window, and if I open the kids' windows I generally can't sleep and have to get up and shut them. Now my attacker didn't come through the window or break down the door and yet the fear of attack began that night with my rape.

Another woman felt that her occupation would generate disbelief.

I did not believe anyone would believe me and I felt if it had gone to court, I would have lost as at the time I was working in the X Rated video industry in an administrative role. If I had been working elsewhere I think I would have reported the incident to police. (Female, raped when she was 24)

The following survivor was warned by her assailant that she would not be believed by the police.

I realised after some time that he had planted doubts in my mind about the effectiveness of reporting the assault by saying his father was a friend of the Police Commissioner. Now, ten years later I wish I had reported it as I knew, and still do, his name. But I still think that as my past had a few men in it that I wouldn't have been successful anyway. (Female, raped when she was 18)

The lack of privacy and confidentiality due to population size was also a deterrent to another woman's reporting.

I did not report the rape as I live in a small town and have [several] teenage children. I did not want to put them through it. Also, the rapist is an ex-policeman and has lots of mates in the force! (Female, raped when she was 42)

RESPONSE OF THE POLICE

Some, like the next two women, assaulted by those they knew slightly, were met with belief and support when they went to the police.

In my case, the individual police officers were supportive, but their hands were tied by the legal system. They advised me to drop the charges. And although I still feel a sense of injustice, I am glad I didn't have to go through the humiliation and degradation of the court case. The legal system is where the problem lies. (Female, raped when she was 16)

For one child victim, the police ended up being helpful but it took a long time.

I reported my sexual assault in [date]. The perpetrator was not picked up and charged until nine months later after a number of complaints were made. My perpetrator was [over thirty] years at the time. I had reported three incidences to the police and he has been charged with five counts of sexual assault against me.

I understand the police are busy but I feel that it's a disgrace that complaints had to be made nine months later, before the perpetrator was charged. (Female, raped when she was 14)

Some had only negative comments to make about their interactions with police officers.

They brought him in for questioning, then believed his story that I was only scared 'cause I might be pregnant. They then let him go and treated me like dirt. I never heard from the police again, although he harassed me for another three months.

The gynaecologist that checked me out told me the police would only believe me if I was half dead. He believed me 'but because I had been sensible and not resisted too much the police wouldn't believe me'. He was right. However, I was not going to argue with a man with a knife at my throat. (Female, raped when she was 15)

The next two victims, like many others, were discouraged from continuing with prosecution.

I did not go ahead with charges as I was humiliated by the police questioning. They made me feel it was my fault, dirty, and it was made out that I provoked him.

I also did feel scared of the guy who had done it to me but not as bad as the police made me feel. (Female, raped when she was 18)

•

I was abducted and raped. The non help from the [name of city] police was unbelievable. They warned me 'Can you put up with having your name being dragged through the mud?' The man was later jailed on another rape charge. I am only getting counselling help now [years later]. (Female, raped when she was 27)

All of those whose perpetrator went to trial had negative experiences to recount. For some, the outcome was a not too lenient sentence for the offender.

Because of the trauma of the rape and also of the death of my mother the night after the rape I didn't want to remember.

I cooperated with the police as much as I could but it was not good enough for them. The two men got charged with Carnal knowledge; one was placed on probation; one got six months in prison.

I am over the rape—I am one of the lucky ones.

But I still cannot believe that the police could think that a twelve year old child could consent to two men, one aged over thirty and the other over twenty, having sex with her.

I wish I could take it to court now because I know, without a shadow of a doubt, they would have been convicted of rape.

The trial could prove to be another ordeal for the survivor to endure. The majority of victims whose cases went to court had to testify.

The trial was started three times due to the defence barristers withdrawing after perpetrators changed their stories. By the time the last jury got to hear the case, facts had been misplaced or lost. One of the perpetrators was also by this time arrested for another rape. I was reprimanded by the judge for stating that 'those men raped me'. (Female, raped when she was 24)

•

I found our court system did not care enough about the victim. I didn't meet the prosecutor until about one hour before the trial, etc. Police disregarded my feelings and released information to the press and always said the perpetrator probably would not be convicted, but he was. There are trials that do have a good ending. (Female, raped when she was 23)

EFFECTS

The principal symptom or masked presentation described by this group of survivors was depression. For some that depression appeared to have taken a tenacious hold.

It was in the 1970's that I was raped and people's attitudes were 'she was old enough to know about sex anyway' or 'she probably asked for it'.

The thought of going to court and having to tell what happened, sickened me and still does as I can still feel him touching me. It won't go away. I have since married and have [a number of] children. I worry about their future.

No-one knows about my experience, not my family, nor my husband. Sometimes at times, like these, when assault on women, incest and rape are in the media I find myself depressed. I cry when I hear of a child being abused or of a woman who has been raped or bashed.

Why won't the law realise that not all rape victims end up dead? Some don't even have visible scars. But rape is a very serious crime and we should have longer sentences for these offenders; most of them do repeat their crimes so let's not wait till it's our children who suffer. I hope this has helped someone understand, even if it's only the reader. Please Help Us.

•

I feel sometimes that I am only just barely a survivor. The rape was horrific for me and the continued sexual abuse by my father (as a child) has affected me enormously. But the attempted rape shocked me so much that I feel I have no emotional reserves left to fight another assault if it happened. I know that sounds dramatic, but that's how I feel. (Female, raped when she was 15 and 18)

•

After the assault I went through one year of depression. I had seven suicide attempts until I was put into a psychiatric hospital. People still do not understand, as I still suffer severe bouts of depression. It is two years later and I am lucky to get a few hours sleep, for fear of re-living the events in my nightmares. Not a day passes that I do not recall the attack in some ways. I wish he had carried out his threats and killed me.

The rape can have a long lasting effect upon the survivor's sex life.

My life, I now realise, has focused a lot on this event. I have in the past months sought marriage counselling and sexual assault counselling. But I still do not feel that my sexual thoughts and feelings will ever be healed. I just have to learn to cope better. (Female, raped when she was 17)

Some may turn to alcohol or drugs in an attempt to hide from the feelings.

It was violent gang rape both times with sodomy and severe bashing. I was very young at the time and did not think I would be able to do anything about it. They were men who did the same thing to other women. Very ashamed and humiliated. I got into drugs afterwards. I am now free of drugs since my first child. I feel the need to tell someone everything, but don't know how to go about it—it happened so long ago. (Female, raped when she was 15)

[Note to this writer and others who have kept silent for years: It is never too late to get help. Many sexual assault services run groups for survivors of past assaults.]

The rape can also act as a factor which impacted upon or influenced future sexual assaults.

This was my first sexual assault. I consider that at other subsequent (four) occasions, I pretended to be conducive to avoid the possibility of forced rape with violence. Because of fear of the situation becoming violent or abusive, I pretended it was OK for the perpetrator to demand and get sexual gratification. (Female, raped when she was 14)

HEALING

Once again, we learn that healing is preceded by sharing the secrets.

As a survivor of rape and the courts I tried to lock away all the memories. Seventeen years later I have been through a year of counselling and am finally free of the power the rape, the community and my family had over me.

I would now like to help other women with friendship, understanding, listening and being a support person. And also I would like to share my experiences, progress and new freedom somehow. (Female, raped when she was 15)

For some victims, like the next one, recovery involved mutual disclosure, one on one, with another survivor.

Capital Punishment should be brought back and it should be applicable to rape and paedophilia. Rape/incest is worse than murder. The victim has to live with it forever. You never really get 'over' it. You learn to cope but it's always there. It affects your whole personality even if you're not consciously aware of it at times. You tend to built walls around yourself because it's safer that way.

It took me a long time to let anyone get really close to me, and help me break down the barriers and talk about my true feelings. The person who helped me is the most wonderful and caring friend anyone could have. She understands me better than anybody else. She is also a victim of rape and incest. We are friends for life and we will always 'be there' for each other through the good and the bad. I just wish more people could have a special friendship like ours. I know it has helped me tremendously and always will.

I began my first adult relationship earlier this year. After the first time we made love, I told him I had been raped and was a virgin at the time. He was very supportive and concerned; he didn't want to hurt me.

I feel like my life is just beginning, the pain and memories will never leave completely, but I'm taking one day at a time. At least I know that I can love and be loved in a relationship basis. I am worthy of love and deserve to find it as much as anybody.

Question: Why is the innocent victim the one who receives the death sentence? (Female, raped when she was 12 and 13 following years of incest)

The next woman's story illustrates that counselling, in and of itself, can be a less than useful tool for healing. The quality of assistance—the requisite specialised expertise of the practitioner—is essential. For her, as in the cases of many others, healing has been a spiritual journey.

It was [a holiday] and terribly hot but the house was full of young people because the family had some male friends. Because of the heat much drink was consumed and during the later part of the evening couples began to appear.

Since I didn't want to be part of that I just quietly found my moment and slipped out the door and went to my bedroom on the pretext of going to the toilet. I went out and lay on the lawn looking up at the stars and began to think about the life I planned ahead.

Suddenly I felt him lie down beside me in the darkness and ask me why I left and I said 'To go to the toilet, I just took the long way back—anyway I'm not into this'. With that he rolled over on top of me and scratched at my dress trying to pull it up to pull my pants down. I can remember and feel again the shock of feeling his nakedness. At that stage of my life I had never seen the male body naked let alone the erection and I was a virgin.

He ripped my dress off and belted me across the face and I scratched him so much that my nails were terribly torn and for days I was picking his skin out from under my fingernails.

He forced my legs apart and entered me and the pain and tearing of me was nothing compared to the anger I felt about what he had stolen from me. I told no-one, burned the dress; he went off to the pub and came back and claimed he had been in a fight. I had more days of the holiday to go and to meet him across the table. I became such a good actress no-one knew and I retreated into myself.

Over the years I have had difficulties with relationships with men and authority figures. I was forced to go to a [specific] counsellor whose only comment to me, when after years of weekly visits and sometimes more often, I divulged this, was, 'That must have cost you a great deal to say.' I was shocked beyond belief. All I wanted was a hug! and 'You know there's a difference between physical and moral virginity!'

After [a number of] years of counselling with him I finally left him and had the opportunity to have the experience of 'Rebirthing' and a lengthy retreat which was a spiritual journey and there I dealt with the shame, guilt, agony, disbelief, rage and finally after years on the very same day, I was able to write a letter to him and forgive him and so let go.

I had so hugged my pain and ill-health as if that is what gave me meaning. There is a whole new area of reconciliation that has to be pursued and that has to be person to person, victim to oppressor and dismantling structural sin that continues to speak of human relationship in 'battle' terms. There are two victims in a rape: the male who does not know how to be a man and the woman who is so physically abused that the emotional, psychological and physiological scars remain and interfere with so much of their lives.

SUGGESTIONS FROM SURVIVORS

One woman, who after decades, is working through her hurts and issues with a counsellor, believes that the cost of good counselling is too high.

Nearly thirty years down the track from an assault on me, I am only just now able to feel the least bit comfortable talking about the assault. I still cannot remember some of the details, but, after many years of therapy, I am coming to grips with causes and effects of past deeds and actions.

Part of the cause of the assault was naivety and lack of self-esteem on my behalf. Even as I know there is no justification of rape whatsoever, a little voice says that I should have assessed the situation from the worst scenario, ie. some males will take advantage of the situation if they possibly can, therefore rape is a possibility.

The short term result of the assault was derision from members of the church fellowship I (and the rapist) was associated with at the time, due to the comment, 'She shouldn't have flirted with X; she led him on. What does she expect?'

Long term, my original lack of self-esteem (currently being worked on) had grown, culminating in a divorce, and now I'm trying to change me, so as to cope with, or leave, the alcoholic (sometimes violent) I'm now living with. ('It's all she deserves!' says the inner voice.) I believe that the incident all those years ago had a compounding effect along the way on the problems in existence then.

The point of this 'additional comment' is that, although I've had therapy of one sort or another for most of my adult life, there is a vast lack of accessible therapists, who are affordable. Currently I'm paying over one hundred dollars a week, which should really be [more], but for the discount allowed by my psychologist. Psychologists, as opposed to psychiatrists, have no rebate allocated via Medicare, or private health funds. Boy, am I paying for my mental health! Why should mental health take a vastly inferior position of importance to physical well being? It certainly doesn't give me much financial leeway to sort out current relationships.

Unfortunately, although I 'shopped around' for a counsellor, I found quite a bit of prejudice and bad information floating around the so-called 'free' therapy areas, ie. hospital care areas etc. One domestic violence counsellor recently told me she couldn't understand why women who are bashed stay with their husbands!

I would appreciate the question of funding for therapy being raised. Although I realise there may be funding for Rape Crisis, probably nowhere near adequate nevertheless, there are not enough affordable resources out there to cover all those people who don't easily fit the title 'affected by rape' and probably don't access that resource.

Others discussed the need for males to change, to be raised differently with different values about themselves, women and children.

Nothing will change in this society until our males are raised to have self-control, to feel good about themselves. At this time in our evolution, males can only feel good about themselves when they experience power over other human beings, chiefly women and children, blacks and animals.

Throughout my life I have really communicated with other people, both male and female, and it is obvious that in our generation, incest and sexual assault were rife. Most of us have suffered it some where in our lives. I confess that at times, I have viewed many of those who claim they were lucky to escape such things, as definitely in the state of denial. Many of these people seem to have a 'friend' who was subject to sexual abuse.

A number of suggestions concerned the criminal justice system. One woman spoke about the need for police attitudes to change.

Until the authorities stop accusing the victim many more women will not report their attack. If it ever happens to me again—I will hurt my attacker so he never forgets either. (Female, raped when she was 18)

Another had strong feelings about trial procedures, particularly the need to modify the role of the press.

Being so young at the time and in the middle of studying for exams I did not want to go through police interviews etc. The perpetrator was drunk—I was baby-sitting for him and his wife, who was in the next bedroom. Parents were very supportive although, like any father, my dad wanted to kill him for touching me. This experience has made me so wary and distrusting of men.

Reasons for not reporting to the police: Local girl in my town was gang raped by [a number of] men, her boyfriend was held down and made to watch. The whole town couldn't stop talking about it— everyone followed the court proceedings. The local paper thrived on the gory details.

The identity of the rape victim should be suppressed. No woman wants to be associated with rape. Getting back to this poor woman. They were found guilty and sentenced to [a low number of] years each.

You can't mention this lady to anyone without them bringing up the rape and its details. They were all released from gaol before serving their full term. They all moved back into the area. Is it any wonder she moved away?

The penalty for rape in this country is not enough. It is such a degrading, humiliating crime. More women would report rapes, I'm sure, if the media didn't have such a free hand in reporting and if the penalties were more severe. For example, to protect victims no details of the trial should be printed until the verdict has been reached. Maybe this way more women would come forward.

The need for changing societal attitudes about rape, from a young age, was stressed by the following respondent.

I feel we need greater education at school level for both male and female children to stress that rape/sexual assault is not acceptable, it is a crime and should not be accepted as 'something boys do'. We don't accept murder. This is almost as close to murder as no other crime gets as invasive—assaulting offence against the body of another human being . . . torture??

Not only rape, but also masculinity and maleness need to be redefined.

The only way to stop or reduce rape is to change the way we define masculinity. We have to get rid of the idea that power-over and domination are part of masculinity and realise they are part of a sick mind. We have to understand that a male person isn't a man if he lacks communication skills and respect for other human beings. Both have to understand that no means no and respect that. (Female, raped when she was 34)

Another woman addressed the need for the media to be controlled in order to remove violence and pornography.

I became pregnant and had to have an abortion. It was all the most humiliating experience of my life. I am currently receiving counselling and expect it will be years before I can trust, respect or have sexual relations with a man again. In the last few years I have become almost paranoid around men. Most male behaviour when I go out—the way men openly stare and leer at women makes me feel very threatened. Most men seem to have no respect for women any more and I do believe the 'sexual revolution' has made this worse. Men seem very confused about what their role is in society today. They have lost, or are losing, a lot of the 'power' they enjoyed for thousands of years, and appear not to be coping well with this. There is too much readily available violent pornographic material (videos,

137

books, magazines). Young people cannot separate the 'sex' from 'violence' in this material and learn to put them together.

There are also too many violent movies being seen by younger and younger audiences. I am amazed how many children are allowed to watch violence and sex on TV and videos—children as young as six years who've seen 'Diehard' and 'Rambo', 'Terminator' etc. and the parents say they (the children) don't understand it so it does not sink into their minds. It sinks in all right. They become numb to violence and want to be the big powerful hero! Some parents are plain stupid. They are the ones who need educating!

The last survivor in this chapter states that it is time for females to learn how to physically defend themselves

There was no Rape Crisis Centre in those days. I wish there had been. It took me over fourteen years to be able to not carry a knife on me during the day. I only carry a knife now when I go out at night and I am always ready to use it. Women should be taught to fight back. (Female, raped when she was 22)

7

BOSSES, DOCTORS, PRIESTS AND OTHERS

> He did not penetrate me, he molested me then masturbated over me. He was a church minister at a youth club. I have never told a soul, not even my husband of [number] years. From that day I lost my faith. I am frigid, but have hidden all this in the back of my mind. I will never tell anyone. I just can't. (Abused at 9 years of age)

Who was the perpetrator? Many of the respondents (14 per cent) filled in the space for 'other' which revealed that just about any type of relationship can result in a rape (for example, school bus driver, landlord, car salesman, dentist, prospective employer, welfare officer, real estate salesman, and many others.) The highest frequency of 'others' included approximately forty-eight family friends (discussed in chapter 6); twenty-nine neighbours; twenty-five employers; twelve police officers; and at least twelve clergy. (These numbers are only approximate since the respondent did not always write in an occupation such as doctor but just labelled the perpetrator as an acquaintance).

Even women consulting doctors were not safe with twenty-seven respondents naming a medical practitioner as the rapist.

What do most of these occupations and relationships have in common with each other? One shared denominator is power. The family friends and neighbours almost always involved a child victim; thus the age difference would create an element of control. Medical practitioners, clerics, police, baby-sitters, teachers and employers also potentially wield authority over those who either work for them or come to them for assistance. This manifestation of violence within a hierarchical relationship conforms to other models of such abuse within a stratified dyad: parent/child, husband/wife, guard/inmate.

One woman specifically discussed the 'authority' component in her rape by a swimming teacher.

I have never come to terms with the fact that I was sexually assaulted from the age of nine years by a person in a position of trust (swimming instructor) who was older than my father. I have never had the opportunity to talk about my feelings—discuss what happened to anyone who could enable me to 'get over it'.

I guess I once thought I was the only one something like that could have happened to but now the awful realisation has hit me that rape and sexual abuse is so common it terrifies me. That man stole my childhood, tied me up, gagged me and raped me at the age of nine—with his adult powers of persuasion guaranteed I would not tell anyone. Even to this day, although I know deep down that I wasn't to blame I still feel that possibly I was, and that if I told people now they would blame me.

The way women are portrayed on TV and in magazines and in videos has to change. We can't be portrayed as submissive objects and there should be no movies at all that contain violence and sex together. These movies do influence people. We feel happy after watching a comedy, sad after a cry, aroused after an erotic movie. What do you think people feel after seeing sex and violence? You either feel sickened by it or aroused by it.

The other common denominator among at least some of the occupations listed earlier is the component of vulnerability and trust. This is exacerbated by the fact that when one goes to a doctor, a police officer or a priest, one might already be in a vulnerable situation; to abuse an individual under those circumstances is thus doubly violent.

DOCTORS

Assault by a doctor at a very young age has resulted or influenced the following woman's life in many ways.

I now am agoraphobic, have no friends as I trust no-one, and have not been able to work for months. I am always frightened. Almost raped by strangers over ten times—exact number eludes me as I wanted to forget—as I worked shifts and used to get followed home after getting off the train and chased. I always wear running shoes now but am too frail to run and this terrifies me. I am not exaggerating or mistaken in this belief of potential attacks. (Raped by a doctor at the age of 6)

Assaults by medical practitioners can take place for a female of any age as evidenced by the next victims.

My parents blamed me. I did not understand what they were blaming me for. (Raped by family doctor when aged 8, 10-11)

•

The perpetrator was not arrested because there was not enough evidence—my word against his. (Raped by family doctor, aged 17)

•

This happened when I was ill and the doctor was called to my home. It was not reported as I knew I had no hope or the money to get a conviction and the fear of him. (Raped by a doctor, when she was 50)

•

It was not rape as defined by you but I consider it a sexual assault none the less, and by a professional person in a position of trust. (Raped by a doctor, when she was 55)

The following writers attempted to obtain some justice and help for future patients by having the medical board cancel the perpetrators' right to practice medicine. They found that such a process and its results were ambivalent at best.

I was not raped but assaulted by my doctor. I made enquires to the Medical Board—Health Department about reporting him but was told that I would have to prove it and it would be his word against mine. I decided not to put myself through such an ordeal and just decided to live with it. (Assaulted by doctor when she was 33)

•

I eventually put in a complaint to the [state] Medical Board. Eighteen months later a hearing was held. The doctor was found guilty of infamous conduct and struck off. He has appealed to the Supreme Court and is still practicing medicine subject to the outcome of the appeal. Police are now investigating, as many more victims have come forward. It took a lot of guts and support to report the doctor and I understand why few women report rape. It has been hell.

None of the survivors who were assaulted by medical practitioners went to the police. This was due, for at least one victim, to the type of molestation or sexual abuse which did not involve penetration.

I have also had experiences with a GP who made me undress unnecessarily and frequently during visits. He also fondled my breasts during examinations, but did it in such a way that I thought I would have no grounds on which to raise a complaint. I stopped seeing this GP.

•

I didn't go to the police because I was afraid I would be called insane by my attacker. (Raped by a medical practitioner when she was 50)

Aside from general practitioners, at least one psychiatrist allegedly took advantage of a patient's vulnerability

This was a result of one year's consultation during which the doctor gradually manipulated me out of much needed therapy and into a sexual relationship in which he repeatedly rejected me. I am now coming to terms with my denial and the community attitudes and only since June of this year did I realise that I should make a complaint to the unit who treat it as sexual assault. I would not have been capable emotionally of making a complaint sooner, but I am now DISTRESSED.

POLICE

Police officers have been identified as the perpetrators of rape in earlier chapters, as dates and as husbands. According to the following woman, at least one member of a police department also abused the power that he held as a law enforcement officer and perpetrated rape whilst on duty.

I went to a police station late at night for help as I had missed my last train home. I'd been to a [dance] and I was a respectable girl/woman. I called in to see if they could get me a room.

The policeman, tall, dark hair with olive skin, told me I could sleep there and he gave me a blanket and pillow. He told me to get undressed and I said, 'No, I'll sleep in clothes'. I heard him lock the door and the lights went off inside.

Next he came back and handed me a glass of beer. I said 'I don't drink'. He said, 'It won't hurt you, give you a good night's sleep'. So I drank and it made my mouth bitter. I spat it out since I had seen white powder, and I went dizzy and sleepy, and in a daze I felt myself being carried out and when I did come to I was laying naked on a bed and he was standing over me.

I reported him. He said no-one would believe me, and no-one did at the police stations.

'MEN OF THE CLOTH'

Members of the clergy were cited as sexual assault offenders in a disturbingly high number of surveys. Children, female and male, were the victims.

I was six years old, and a pupil, at [name of school and location] a priest (whose name I remember) and I am now 68—I have never forgotten his name—he put his hand up my knickers and used his fingers! I never told my mother or father—I didn't know why!

•

Every Sunday. I am now having counselling to get all that out of my system after so many years. (Female raped by priest when she was 5 through 9)

•

Celibacy in the clergy is inappropriate. I have now discovered assaulting girls was that parish priest's hobby. (Aged 7 through 10)

•

People take this wonderful opportunity to have their say in an anonymous manner. I was sexually abused in a Catholic boarding school by one of the teachers—a religious brother. I was a boy of twelve years of age. He was shifted from the school immediately but is still in the Order after [a number of] years, and once again back at boarding schools.

I found out later it was his [number] occasion of being reported. I chose to stay at the school because of my friends and the embarrassment of having to leave and trying to explain it to my home town friends if I left. I was very young.

•

You have restricted sexual assault to physical rape. I would consider that I was sexually assaulted on two separate occasions by two different Catholic priests. I was aged fourteen at the time.

The second offence was committed by an elderly (about 70) Catholic priest who, when I had to call at the [presbytery] to give a message to another priest, showed me into the front parlour. He then closed the door behind me, beckoned to me to come closer, claiming that he knew my parents. (I found out later that he didn't.) He then put his arms around me and I felt him pushing his penis up against me. I then pushed him away and got out of the room. He had been drinking (I could smell it on him) and it was only 9.30 am.

The first assault took place a week earlier. It felt more hurtful because I had trusted and knew the younger priest. When this second event occurred I knew I had a right to protect myself.

BABY-SITTER

Children are also at risk from their child care minders. For the next survivor, the violation and its subsequent secrecy and shame had a profound impact upon her as an adult. She concludes by advising parents to encourage their children to talk to them and not to keep secrets.

At eleven when you are raped you are too scared to tell anyone. I was threatened that if I told anyone ever, he would kill me. The sexual assault went on for one year and I felt so guilty because if I did not do what he said, he would hit me in the stomach.

Because he knew my family, I couldn't tell anyone. I was told to tell anyone who noticed the bruises that I had fallen over. No one ever picked up that I was being sexually assaulted.

Last year I finally was forced to tell someone because I had a Pap smear which was abnormal. I had carried an STD around for [a number of] years.

My Mum now knows about what happened. Her first reaction was to hit me. You have no idea what it feels like to be rejected by your own mother. Even now, she will ask me what happened about my supposed rape.

Why does it have to be the victim's fault?

I was only a child and I could have fallen pregnant.

I am writing this in the hope that parents and parents-to-be will think about telling their children as soon as they can understand, to always tell them about anything that happens to them, no matter what the rapist says.

Sometimes, as in the next case, a professional such as a doctor, may err in the advice given to parents by telling them not to discuss the assault with the child/victim, so that she will forget. As we have learned, over and over again, she does not forget.

Years ago the GP told Mum and Dad not to talk about it, 'The bringing up of the subject would do more damage.' My parents reported it to the police. They said he already had a record for the same thing but it was not worth them making me go to court. There is no justice for this happening. (Raped by baby sitter, aged 7)

TEACHER

We may not want to know it since ignorance may give the semblance of bliss (and we entrust our children into their care for some thirty hours a week), but according to the next survivors, children are not necessarily safe from teachers.

145

He was my teacher. For that year my family split because my father couldn't handle what happened to me. (Raped by teacher, aged 10)

Like some of the other professions already discussed, the occupation's bureaucracy seemed to protect such offenders by its failure to remove them from their positions.

As an eleven year old I had sexual harassment from one of my teachers who touched and embraced me against my will. I was too frightened and uninformed to do anything about it. Even though his reputation as a child molester is alive and known for years, he still teaches.

EMPLOYERS

A high number of women identified an employer as a sexual abuser. If rape is the tip of the iceberg which contains sexual harassment and other gender-based abuse, then the Australian work place is undoubtedly riddled with these behaviours.

For some of those who were assaulted by employers the attack took place whilst being interviewed for the position.

I was not raped but I was bailed up against a wall and fondled and kissed. I could not push him away though I tried and I escaped by telling him I would accept the job and start the next day. I tried to get some male friends to pay him a visit and they thought it was a big joke.

•

I did report this to the employment agency as I suspect he had made it a practice to rape prospective employees. He made the appointment for 5.00 p.m. in his small [type of business], bought me a small meal and flattered me. I thought the interview was genuine. Then he locked the door and overpowered me. I thought I was lucky to escape without worse injury.

•

Happened when I was being interviewed for a position: 'Be nice to the Boss' syndrome—I resisted, force was used, most degrading experience of my life.

'Boss' being a well known community identity was the reason for not reporting it to the police. Also I could not bear to go over it with a male stranger.

The social worker believed me and gave me the on-going support I needed. I was hospitalised.

In some of these scenarios, the perpetrator not only had 'boss' status to overpower and intimidate the woman, but they also were significantly older than their employees.

The perpetrator was forty years old. Initially met when I applied for a job. Started working for him then we began a relationship in which I was emotionally abused—only met on nights I worked. Obviously I realised I was not cared for, only a convenience.

One night after work he pushed me down into a kneeling position in front of him whilst he sat on the couch. He ordered me to [oral sex] until I could barely breathe. As my mouth opened gasping for air he penetrated my mouth with his penis and proceeded to ejaculate inside of me (I still become ill at the thought).

After he laughed at me, telling me I should thank him for helping improve my complexion and that all 'real women' enjoy oral sex. (Raped by her employer when she was 19)

Several of the survivors explained why they had not told anyone.

I did not tell anyone as I was only fifteen or sixteen and did not think I would be believed or that it was my fault somehow. He was underpaying me in my job and my family did not want to make waves about that as it was in a small country town so I couldn't tell them about the sexual abuse. I know he was also trying it on two other girls who worked there. His wife was pregnant. (Raped by employer when she was aged 15-16)

•

When I got home I threw up most of the night. He had a lovely family who I saw almost every day. I suffered mentally for several years and felt there was nothing I could do. He is big and fat and I could not get him off me!! It happened in the [area of work] after work hours and nobody heard my calls for help.

I have told no-one of this event, not even my husband. Many thanks to you for giving me a way of getting this off my chest. (Raped by her employer when she was 22)

One woman told no one since she could not face losing her job and having to return in disgrace to her parents.

When I was in my first job, in [certain type of business] office, I had to do certain things. I hated and despised my boss for it. He told me that I had to do it if I wanted to keep my job. He knew that to admit defeat and have to go home to my parents was highly undesirable to me—and he used this against me.

He would call me into his office whenever he chose to and made me kiss him and use my hands on his penis while he 'got off' onto the floor. When he 'got off' he would wipe the floor with a hanky and then push me out the door into my office and shut the door. I was no longer needed by him—until next time. There was no sexual feeling in it for me—just revulsion—I hated him. And he didn't consider me in any way. I was just an object for him—a thing to use. There was nothing in it for me. That didn't concern him. He was concerned to 'get off' and that was all.

I left that job and I went to the job office to see if I could get another job. They asked why I was leaving. I told them. They didn't believe me. After all, the said man was supposedly a fine, upstanding man in the community—a good citizen and a family man—he had a lovely wife and three lovely daughters! I learnt later that the girl who left the job before I took it met the same things as I.

Why do victims of employer assault remain in the situation? The following survivor described what was happening to her emotionally and how unprepared she was to cope with the situation.

I had no idea how to deal with unwelcome sexual advances. I thought I needed to learn. I was brought up to try to be attractive to men, to be nice to them, but not to defend myself against men who weren't being nice to me, i.e. were not paying attention when I said no. This guy didn't penetrate me, but he did molest me. I was assaulted by my boss continually over a period of twelve months.

The next employee did not go to the police but she did report her boss to higher management, with unsatisfactory consequences.

I did not report the rape for so long due to the perpetrator being my employer and his threats of emotional and physical kind that he would say it was with my consent. He was a person of some standing in the community, a retail proprietor—attended church and [certain community organisation]. He has also raped a male person and harassed all female staff. He has criminal convictions for [sexual offences].

Husband unsupportive; acquaintances condemning of me; community condemning of victim—slander and gossip. No rape services then either. I was sacked from my job when I told. Later on the [perpetrator] was dismissed himself after assaulting a client. The company, some years later, approached me to return because they couldn't find another employee to do as good a job as myself. (Raped by employer when she was 25)

For those who did report the rape to the police, the criminal justice system once again proved to be at best frustrating, and at the worst, unjust.

I was raped by my employer [date] at my place of work. Committal hearing [date seven months later]. I am still awaiting trial which is supposed to be [fourteen months after committal].

I am a mother of [a number of] children and now without a career because I can't go back into that sort of work again. I still cannot believe being raped turns your life upside down and the mental scars it leaves on you. The court system for a rape victim is absolutely shocking. I cannot describe the feeling, almost like being mentally raped again.

The time period for a rape trial to be heard is not fair to the victim. After being through a committal hearing in which I had to testify, I am not looking forward to the trial. I can truly understand why more people don't report rape. Also I'm concerned for my safety if my rapist is found innocent (which most of them are).

149

I believe the community should become more aware of rape in our society, and not let it still be a dirty word. It might change the jurors' minds.

•

The man that assaulted me was fifty-one years old and the owner manager of [a type of business]. He was found guilty and got a two year good behaviour bond and a $200 fine. BIG DEAL! If it ever happened again I would not seek help from the police. I would take the law into my own hands. The judicial system is a joke. My statement was conveniently lost by police. (Raped by her employer when she was 15)

Rape by an employer was not restricted to offices or urban settings as the following letter writer illustrates.

I was the only girl jillaroo on a lonely outback station. I entered the employment because my employer said he employed two other jillaroos. I was driven out to the station to find only he and I there.

His rape was not violent but intimidation was involved and it was repeated over two days until I could convince him that I would get pregnant if any more sex occurred. He was a divorcee. (Raped by her employer when she was 21)

NEIGHBOURS

Most of those assaulted by neighbours were children. As with the other (child victim) perpetrator incidents, the children usually kept their victimisation to themselves.

I never reported the rape also because I didn't want to have to go to court and tell people again and again what happened. (Raped by her neighbour when she was 11)

Rape by the man next door, for an adult woman, may be disbelieved by her husband and the police might be less than cooperative.

On the night of the rape I was treated in hospital. I was told there was no time limit to bring charges. Over the following year this man threatened me and terrorised me and when I told my then husband he didn't believe me. I have tried several times to bring charges but the police just used to say that one day he would be a victim of domestic violence.

You could hear him and his wife having violent arguments but he never hit her, to my knowledge. My husband used to say he would hate to cross him. I think that is why he raped me, because he wanted to have sex with me and I said no. He boasts that he will never get caught, I suppose that whilst society seems to prefer to believe the word of a man over and above that of a woman, nothing will change.

The police were just as bad. The detective who interviewed me had a large picture of a naked woman wearing only braces to cover her nipples and I had to sit at his desk and look at this picture whilst I was being questioned.

Because the man who raped me was our next door neighbour, who we had known for [a number of] years when the rape occurred, I knew him very well. He used to confide in me about his marital problems. They said it was my age, that I was making it all up. Eventually I took the medical report from the doctor and then they believed me, but then said I had my chance on the night.

The tragedy of any kind of sexual or physical abuse is the outstanding damage it does to you emotionally. It erodes your self esteem. You try to get help from the police and you are not taken seriously because you are female and the offender who is lying and guilty is believed because he is male.

I don't think it will ever change because men don't want it to change. Rape is taboo, men believe it isn't rape and women believe you asked for it.

OTHER: MASSEUSE

No occupation or situation is free from the risk of rape. The following letter recounts the writer's assault by a masseuse. The detail which is provided conveys more accurately than any academic's analysis or psychologist's explanation, just how an individual may shut down and not physically resist sexual abuse although resisting it 100 per cent mentally.

In [year] after having pains in my shins during an aerobics class at the recently opened [name of gym and city], one of the male gym staff suggested that I make an appointment to see the masseur, who had a small practice attached to the Gym. The only appointment available that week was on [a certain] night at either [two evening times].

I can't exactly remember. I turned up for the appointment and the male masseur told me to take off everything except for my underpants. He did not give me a gown or cover me with a towel. The masseur massaged my body for well over an hour; being my first massage I didn't want to seem foolish and didn't question the length of the time.

One of the gym staff knocked on the door to say that they were locking up and leaving. It was then that I started to realise that things weren't quite right and that I was alone with this guy in a remote area. The masseur proceeded to massage my breasts for a long time. Whilst he was very charming, very gentle and never at any time showed anger or violence, I could tell that he had lost some or all control over himself. He was in a position of power over me and utilised that to his maximum benefit.

I didn't know what to do, but my reaction was to go with things as much as I could stand. I felt he was on the brink of snapping and if I didn't comply with his desires, I would be injured. The masseur eventually pushed his hand into my underpants and entered my vagina with his fingers.

At this stage I sat up and sort of mumbled, 'no', and then ran into his small kitchenette/bathroom area and went into the toilet and locked the door. I knew then if he intended to rape me he would use force or would snap out of it and let me go. Time passed, it seemed like a long time, but I couldn't honestly tell if it was five minutes or half an hour. He called out to me that I could come out now. I walked out very slowly with my arms crossed covering my breasts. He just stood there looking at me as I got dressed. He then started talking normally as if a normal massage had just taken place. All I wanted to do was get out and away safely. I wanted to play along with whatever was going through his mind. At this stage he wanted to pretend it was all OK and nothing had happened so I got out my purse to pay him. He wouldn't accept the money. He said something about being very sorry about what had happened and that I had a very beautiful body. To me he was admitting that he had lost control, that he had abandoned his sense of right and reason. He then asked me to go to the [name of singer] concert with him. I told him I already had tickets. I got out of the building and ran to my car and drove off as fast as I could. I went to a girlfriend's house. When her mother answered the door I burst into tears and told her everything. I was surprised to see that it was [late], I had been in there for hours.

Reactions to the event were as violating and angering as the event itself. My parents said very little, but I clearly remember things like: 'Well, 8.00 p.m. was very late for an appointment', and unbelievably 'Well at least you didn't have to pay'.

I telephoned my father's business lawyer and he said that because there had been no violence and no physical struggle, and because I had not physically screamed or hit the guy, he suggested that it would be pointless to pursue the matter legally.

I went to see the gym guy who had recommended that I see the masseur the next day and told him what had happened. He was shocked and sickened and told me he would look into it. I telephoned him on the Monday. He told me the masseur said nothing had happened. I got very angry and asked him WHY I would make this event up. He said he'd look into it for me further. When I telephoned him a few days later he was very curt and said that the masseur had thought I was enjoying it. I again got very angry and he asked me in a frustrated manner what I wanted him to do and I said get rid of him out of the building. He said things about contracts and business is business and that he wanted nothing further to do with the incident, and further, not to let it stop me from going to the gym. A week later my instructor [in another sport] pulled me aside and told me that his friends from the gym had contacted him and asked him to ask me not to stop going to the gym and that 'Just because the guy fingered me I didn't need to be so upset.'

I never went back to that gym. I developed chronic bulimia concurrently with impulsive, excessive physical fitness activities shortly thereafter and I believe it was as a result of this incident.

The law needs to recognise that each person evaluates the situation such as the above at the time of its occurring. Screaming, hitting, and acting violently sometimes seems like the most wrong thing to do, the thing that will turn the situation from one where you feel you may have a chance by acting in cooperation. Just because you don't physically revolt, doesn't mean you like what is happening or want it to happen.

People need to feel they can approach the police with information such as the above. Even if charges aren't going to be laid, the police need to know about the people in society who are attempting and/or getting away with all manner of manipulative sexual behaviour.

OTHER: CLIENT

Recent cases involving prostitutes who were raped have caught the media's and public's attention (and for some, their indignation too) when judges have sentenced such rapists more leniently due to the victims' occupation. The following letter might help those who adhere to that type of sentencing and beliefs to understand that rape is about violence and not about sex; therefore the victim's sexual history is irrelevant.

I was working as a prostitute at the time of the rape. I was called out to a suburb to see a man who identified himself as [name]. He was intoxicated with alcohol and other drugs. He was charming and non-hostile, although somewhat repetitive in the initial stages. It wasn't until we had started to engage in sexual activity that I noticed he was acting strangely.

He persistently tried to insert his finger into my anus, and when I told him that his behaviour was not acceptable to me, he grew aggressive and violent. I reminded him that the time he had paid for had lapsed, and told him I was leaving. He subsequently chased me around the house, threatening me with a broken glass. He raped me orally, vaginally and anally, and slapped my face until my mouth started to bleed. This excited him even more. All the while he was talking to me in a placatory tone, as if I was a wounded animal he was easing to safety.

He blackened my eyes, punctured my chest with the beer glass and tried to kill me by strangling me. As my vision started to close in, I knew I would not survive unless I thought quickly. I picked up the glass he had discarded and thrust it between his legs. Unfortunately I didn't do much damage, but it scared him enough to unlock the door and release me.

I went straight back to the escort agency and they rang the police. All the police, from the uniforms and the detectives to the sexual assault unit, were compassionate, thoughtful and thorough. I could not fault them. They tried their best to make me comfortable, and gave me the support I so desperately needed in those early stages. The rape crisis centre was also another top class team. I was

154

on the phone to them for many a long hour in the ensuing months, and I was never made to feel like they were sick of me, or had other things to do.

The courts, however, were a different story altogether. The committal hearing was a nightmare. I have only the dimmest recollections of it due to my dependence on Valium and other prescriptions drugs given to me after the rape. At the trial, I was treated as if I were the one who had committed the crime. My previous criminal record was brought up, and the fact that I had been working as a prostitute at the time was the key to the defence case.

'How can you rape a prostitute?' they asked. Yes—I did go there to have sex with this man, but the fact that my consent was withdrawn, loudly and clearly, and that I had sustained visible injuries, was of little or no consequence.

When the police went to arrest this man, he made a statement that included 'She's just a fucking moll. I slapped her around a bit—WHO CARES???' Yes indeed, who cares? Not the twelve men and women who acquitted him. Not the Judge whose directions to the Jury included the reminder that if they thought he was so drunk that he was not aware that what he was doing was wrong, they must find him innocent!

The basis of his defence rested on that very fact. He was drunk. He told them—in an unsworn statement—that he was an alcoholic. He had absolutely no recollection of what happened, but he was sure he would never do anything like that. They obviously believed him. The fact that he had been charged with the rape (here perpetrator's record was described) was not told to the Jury. They weren't even allowed to know he had a criminal record.

The message to sex-workers was clear. Don't even think about it. If you are raped, bashed, and your life is threatened—Too bad. Who cares?

Who cares? I do.

WHY 'OTHERS'

This chapter has illustrated that one should not assume safety from sexual assault from just about any care provider or employer. Although the purpose of such an overview of potential rapists is not to frighten, it is hoped that 'forewarned' will proved to be 'forearmed'. Responsibility for rape does not

PATRICIA EASTEAL

rest upon its victims; however, if any individual can be protected from sexual assault by learning that no profession or position of 'trust' is inviolate, then one purpose of listening to the voices of some whose trust was violated, will be fulfilled.

For the survivor who was assaulted by a member of those occupations mentioned in the previous pages, and has always felt alone and ashamed—let the voices of others who have also been there wash away those feelings of aloneness and shame. As we will examine in the concluding chapter—this is in part how prevention and change can occur. One step must be the empowerment and legitimation of rape's victims.

8

STRANGERS

> In the water, hand [fingers] forced into vagina by strange
> man while he held me with hand very tight on my breast.
> Beach was deserted. Nowadays I'll only swim in public
> pools that are not very crowded and supervised and that is
> important. I never saw where the man came from. (Age 14)

As discussed earlier, a prevailing myth about rape concerns
the perpetrator. It should be clear by now that, false
mythology aside, the majority of rapists are not strangers.
Only one-fifth of the rapes in the 'Without Consent' sample
were perpetrated by strangers.

Although the shame involved in this type of rape is less
than in others, it still pervades the stories. The survivors' sense
of culpability and self-doubt about the legitimacy of the act as
rape, particularly if the threat of force or the lack of consent
was the defining feature of the assault instead of force and/or
a weapon, are recurrent threads or themes in many of their
stories.

LOCATION

Rape by a stranger can take place anywhere, from a car to the
beach to the victim's home.

> I had lost my bus fare and walked, thought I was lost and a man
> offered to take me home around 6pm (I had been to ballet classes). I
> didn't arrive home until late—about 9-10pm. (Female, raped at age of
> nine)

•

> I was raped in my own home. He threatened my life and told me if
> he was ever caught he had a friend he would pay $100 to come and
> shoot me. (Female, raped when she was 25)

•

It was in the middle of the night and he said he would hurt my children if I told anyone or didn't do what he wanted. I was so frightened that I almost didn't call the police but the thought of 'him' coming back made me wake up to myself. (Female, raped when she was 25)

•

I was sexually assaulted and thrown in a gutter. I screamed and went berserk, he ran off and the police couldn't find him. (Female, raped when she was 16)

•

The perpetrator attacked me at knife point in the middle of the day on making my way back from [name] Beach. Public Holiday Australia Day (lots of people around) I was dragged into the bushes. He apparently has attacked five other women since. (Female, raped when she was 24)

•

What I am going to tell you might be hard to believe but it is the truth. This is what happened to me. It was about 6.30 pm. on the beginning of [month] 1989. I was sitting in front of a sand dune down at [place] just as the sun was setting. Suddenly someone came up behind me, threw his jumper over my head and locked my head in the corner of his arm. He then led me up the beach to a more secluded place. It felt so unreal. Nothing like this had ever happened to me before.

We stumbled along for about five minutes with his jumper still over my head and then he said 'Now get down on you tummy'. He sounded almost sorry for what he was doing. He also sounded a bit desperate and I tried to calm him down and get him talking. All this happened in less than a minute. When this didn't work in desperation I called out 'Jesus help me'. There wasn't another person on the beach to stop him, but as soon as I said that he leapt up and ran as fast as he could. He was close to doing it but he never raped me. I got up walked back to my car, drove to my boyfriend's place not far away and told him what happened. I was pretty shaken up but unhurt in any way.

•

Looking at cards in DJ's at Christmas in a crush of people felt a hand up my skirt try to pull my pants aside. I will never, never go to big sales or big events like football, concerts etc. (Age 17)

•

After evening class while waiting for a bus, man tried to force me to hold his penis (erect). When I tried to get away some boys in a car stopped. But that was even worse, it seemed like hours but it was only minutes before the bus came. Nowadays I get taxis home from evening classes. (Age 18)

MALE VICTIMS

In the 'Without Consent' sample 30 per cent of the male survivors were victims of a stranger rapist. As the following show, most were perpetrated by men against boys.

Both times was oral sex but as I had no sex talks at home did not know what it was for many years. I did not even know about oral sex with my wife until I was about twenty-seven. There was no physical harm so I did not know it was wrong. (Male, aged 10 and 14)

•

Feelings of anger and revulsion towards all male homosexuals and criminals still remain to this day. (Male, raped when he was 11)

•

Only last week starting to acknowledge the abuse and its effect on me since—but where and how does a male get help? There is nothing but pain, shame and guilt—a life of feeling like you are two people: a respected Dad and on the other a worthless, twisted shit for letting yourself be abused. Sixteen years on I've told someone and I'm crying silently every time I think of it. But where can I get help? (Male, raped when he was 16)

One man described his rape by a group of females.

Being a male raped by women. I feel shamed as I was the victim, being abused by the women. I was drunk at a pub and was touched-up, so I left. Was followed bashed and raped in the front yard of house. All three women had vaginal intercourse with me whilst others sat on neck and legs to restrain me.

Two other male survivors were adults when sexually assaulted.

I was raped by a bisexual male after getting him away from a transsexual friend who was much more vulnerable than me. I believed I would not have the support of the law as I am physically male. I would also have been ashamed/embarrassed to report the assault.

I went along with it in the hope I could talk him into using a condom (I am terrified of AIDS). My submissiveness seemed to make him lose interest and he did use a condom and his aggressive behaviour subsided. He did not injure me otherwise. He simply relieved his sexual urge and I was able to get rid of him. Men like him are a risk we take. He was drunk.

I don't see myself as gay—I relate to men as a woman, and I have several caring friends.

•

I couldn't go through all the dealings of the examinations of the rape knowing that the group of men wouldn't be caught. I didn't have decent descriptions of the men (approximately ten—raped by two). The police told me that the description given was not detailed enough. The police did ask me if I was raped but I denied it. I didn't tell anyone about the rape until one year after. Just coming to grips with it now, over three years later. (Male, raped when he was 21)

CHILDREN AS THE VICTIMS

Although the primary risk of sexual assault for children comes from within the family, 19 per cent of those, when 16 years of age or younger were raped or molested by strangers.

The assault did not involve penetration of the vagina—only fingers between the labia. I woke up to discover this happening. It was on an overnight country train. My mother was in the compartment but I never told her. Why? So threatening to her as well as me and we never saw the man again. (Female, aged 11)

160

For some, the consequences have lasted well into their adult lives, for others to the present.

I was abducted and raped and left by the side of the road otherwise unharmed. The incident was never discussed and my parents chose to believe that nothing had happened to me. I felt guilty and thought God had punished me as I was a Catholic. I have been able as a mature adult to come to terms with the incident and feel neither guilt nor hate. (Female, raped when she was six; 36 years earlier)

•

At age nine sex was considered shameful. At first the rape was about sex not power, so I found it difficult to tell anyone. I also blocked out the rape from memory and can only recall certain parts of the experience.

One writer told of her retribution years after the crime took place.

The first time I was sexually assaulted was when I was eight years old. My little sister and I had gone to watch a local soccer game, one street away from our home. While we were there, we met some of the kids from the neighbourhood and with them was this older teenage male. He started chatting to me, saying how pretty I was, bought me and my sister an icecream and drink. Then he asked my sister to go and play as he wanted to show me the soccer trophies. So stupid me went, and bang, dragged off into the surrounding scrub, clothes ripped off, kept telling me to shut up, he was very big and heavy, breathing on me, kissing very hard, hurting me, I kept saying stop, no good, eventually he let me go. I got my sister and ran home, hid my clothes and had a bath.

I told my parents two days later. My father was a policeman. He was very angry at me. Gave me a hiding, because he said I had been stupid and should have known better and that I was irresponsible because my little sister could have got hurt. My father never reported it. They didn't take me to the doctor, they just said it was my fault, because I took the drink and icecream and next time I would know better. The next time!!

I saw the perpetrator five years ago when I went home to visit some of my friends in my old hometown. He's an old man of 50+

[*sic*], I guess. I was out walking my particularly large dog when he came by on his bike, so I followed him, I saw where he lived and with whom, guess his elderly mother. I know this because she called him son.

The next day I took my dog out again and waited. There he came riding by, smiling, giving me and the dog the eye. I gave the order and the dog went for him, knocked him off his bike, grabbed his trouser leg and chewed. He started yelling, 'Lady get your dog off me'.

I stood there and looked over him and thought you pathetic old creep, terrified by a dog hey? I don't know what came over me but I said to him, 'How does it feel arsehole, scared are you? You don't remember me, but I know who and what you are'.

I called the dog off, he jumped up screaming I'm some sort of crazy woman (which I probably was at that moment). But all I could do was laugh, gee it felt good. Don't get the wrong idea I'm not mad, but whatever came over me that day, certainly was the catalyst for making me feel better for what had happened at that time and the events that followed for years to come. Justice was served in some way.

•

Abducted—child abuse. As soon as he let me go I walked home and told my parents who were advised by the police not to proceed as it was a small town. Ran into the man later [when she was 15] but mother felt it was too late to do anything and shocked I still remembered. (It was a subject not talked about so I hadn't.)

Many years later when I told a step grandfather as an adult, he reacted as if it was quite exciting and started using me after that. I later remembered he had sex with my girlfriend when she was 12-14. As a child I hadn't taken it on board. (Aged 3 when abducted)

PACK RAPE

Although there was no specific question dealing with pack rape on the survey, a number of survivors described rape perpetrated by a group of males.

I was scared they would kill me. This threat was used throughout the assault. These 'men' decided to gang rape me; one in the mouth, one in the anus, and one in the vagina. After each had finished, they shuffled themselves around and started again—it was in essence a 'multiple rape'. I was just glad it was over and I was alive—dirty, but alive.

•

Seven men, one admitted he was guilty, got gaoled for a couple of months, then released. He never left me alone. I left my home town and have spent most of the time in hospital. Suffering still never got any help until a few months ago. Thanks, hopefully something will be achieved! (Aged 15 when raped by seven males)

•

I want to tell you about a dear friend of mine who committed suicide six years ago because of the men who terrorised her and I when we were young. The rapes and 'gang bangs' were too numerous to count. She tried suicide twice and was successful the second try. They would pick her up off the street and throw her in the car. They all got away with it. It is all true and so horrific it sounds unbelievable. Her story is ghastly and I witnessed it many times, because of her they would leave me alone.

We were both fifteen years old. There were many times she thought they would murder her—knifes and guns were held against her. She is dead and can't speak for herself now, so I will. It was fifteen years ago now so I will put her age down at that! She died when she was twenty-four.

Tied up and raped by Bikies in [name of place]. Escaped and lay down on the road and run over by a car and caravan. Fractured pelvis in places and loss of muscle in the back of her leg. Recovered, returned home and picked up that night and raped by five men on a concrete floor in their house. Abducted off the street going to meet me! We did not walk the street, we were only 15 and it was the only way to get around. We were both called sluts and no-one really cared including my mother.

•

This incident happened at [name of town] as I was on my way to visit my flatmate's sister. These teenagers took turns with only one in the room at a time. They told the last boy it was his turn. By this time I could not stop howling, so he took me out the window and drove me back to [name of place]. He kept crying all the way back to my flat and could not apologise enough for his friends' behaviour. I even insisted I make him coffee to calm down before driving home. I think he would have more lasting nightmares than me. I never found out any names but he rang me at my work the next day to make sure I was OK. Never heard from him again. (This boy did not rape me.) (Female, raped when she was 19)

THE EFFECTS OF THE RAPE

The aftermath of rape can go on for years. As the following survivors tell us, fear is one of the lingering memories.

I contemplate suicide a lot. My whole life is really stuffed. I feel so alone. I'd often read about rape attacks and thought 'that would be terrible'. Mate, it's worse than terrible . . . It's a friggen nightmare that seems to go on for eternity. It's been almost [number of] years for me, they say time heals all wounds, my soul has been shredded and I sometimes wonder whether it will heal at all, but somehow I can 'grin through the shit' but, there are times when I wonder . . .

And what have I learned from being raped?? I'm fearful of walking in the daylight, even though the attack was at night; I don't enjoy going to nightclubs even though I love dancing; I've put on a lot of weight, not enough to worry about though; I'm unemotional; I get depressed; I can't cry; I never used to worry about the clothes I wore or the things I did or said, now I feel I'm being watched all the time by some pervert, as my attacker said he had been watching me for quite a while. I'd really like male intimacy but saying it and doing it are two different matters.

•

I was made to feel guilty as it if was my fault—the police were very sceptical and I felt that my friend doubted me. I am still very bitter and the guy swore he would get me again. I live in fear in another state and am married and have a new home but I'm still afraid. (Female, raped when she was 22)

There also may be physical consequences.

For twenty years I had recurrent nightmares that I was fighting with my fists for my life—that I screamed out but was unable to make a sound. In fact at the time of the rape I screamed out and was heard by a neighbour but he didn't investigate because he knew that his own daughter was in bed asleep. I suffered a pregnancy and miscarriage as a result of this rape. (Female, raped when she was 21)

•

Rape is a crime of violence—very underestimated. It changed my life. I was very lucky to survive as I was almost strangled, very dizzy passed out with pressure on throat. I had incontinence—urine, still need medication, to have pain voided. It is a constant reminder and I can only now talk about it. I have had to undertake further psychological counselling for post-trauma stress.

My family are unaware. It is a strain on my husband. My attacker was on some sort of drugs—he broke into my hotel room. (Female, raped when she was 25)

And, it can affect the woman's feelings about men and/or her willingness and capability of having long-term relationships.

It is now 21 years after my rape and at last I am having counselling in an attempt to resolve the feelings associated with it. I was a virgin when I was raped and it was a shocking introduction to men and sexuality. It has affected my life considerably and I only hope I can sort it out now. (Female, raped when she was 16)

•

I only very recently sought help from rape crisis, I feel very alone and withdrawn inside. If it were not for the help and one to one counselling on a regular basic I wouldn't be able to cope.

I'm extremely angry at what men do to women. I've not only been raped but I've lost everything I had previously with [the particular church]. I feel robbed and scattered in so many pieces. I lost all my friends so the consequences from this rape have been a domino effect. I am very angry.

•

The fear I experienced at the time of rape was so intense that I complied with all wishes and shut my mouth. This has left me with huge feelings of anger and resentment and powerlessness.

•

165

I can still see his face. I could draw it but wouldn't want to. I often wonder if he has/had a family and whether he ever felt guilty or sorry. It's frustrating not knowing and I rarely tell anyone about my opinions of rape etc. I am happy now though. (Female, raped when she was 27; nine years earlier)

If penetration does not occur, the consequences for the victim can be just as traumatic as one woman writes.

I was [a number of] months pregnant. The perpetrator jumped bail and was later apprehended in [another State] after he started cashing his dole cheques. He didn't get away. He was caught at the scene of the crime just before penetration occurred and due to this I felt, in some people's eyes, it wasn't as bad an assault. I disagree because I endured the fear, the humiliation and degradation and some of the physical injuries. The police said if it had gone any further the charges would have been harsher, but they also said that I probably wouldn't have been around to tell of them.

The last two letters in this section come from survivors who are both eloquent, angry and determined not to be victimised again.

This took place in [year]. I was part of the Kings Cross 'hippie culture' at the time and operating as a prostitute escort. Being raped by the pimps was from their point of view showing me how the system worked. Even in 1969 you could not pick up men on the streets of Sydney without paying someone for 'protection'. I was lucky I found other work and we'd have to live on what I could earn as a waitress.

My life—well I accepted the rape in Kings Cross a long time ago. I've been thumped around by my husband for three years until I left him and a couple of other blokes—although all of these thumpings were to 'shut me up' not connected to sexual assault in any way. Point is there came a day when I was crawling around the floor begging 'please don't hurt me' and since then (I left that bloke too) whenever it's even looked like a man was likely to threaten me I'm the one who has frightened him away. As I said, I've been lucky—I never had children to worry about, only myself, and I've never met a man who didn't back off, mind you that is because I think they have always thought I was a complete loony. Since I decided I would [not be passive] (and I really would—I have been in a situation where I was prepared to—and it worked) rather than be humiliated ever again.

But I'm not a man hater, I just think men are <u>allowed</u> by our society to use the excuse of 'being tried beyond the point of reason'. What a lot of Codswallop!! I do think that until the society demands of men a great deal more in the way of self-control they will always blame someone else for rape.

Sorry about the rave—and thank you for reading this.

•

There is no justification for rape. To me it is somehow worse than murder. I have to live with the nightmare every day until I die. The physical act does not disappear ever. But it is the mental aspect that will drive me to my grave. Last year I had my [number] child, a girl. Not long after I had a nervous breakdown. God help anyone who hurts my darling girl.

Years may go by—but you will never forget the horror. The most absolute feeling of all the most helplessness, scared and numb of feelings—you cannot describe it to anyone. He has your life—he has your body—he has your mind all in the palm of his hand. And till you die—if you survive, you will feel those feelings forever. This is what rape is all about. It is a fear that to me has not died as the years roll bybut becomes more intense and fearful. A face in a crowd—a program on T.V.—something someone says—a smell—for me it's rotten oranges—the way a stranger or a friend looks at you—holding my baby daughter—seeing my husband naked—going to the beach—talking to my best friend—a song—for me all these things and one more—the knife—cutting up vegies for my children's dinner or just making a sandwich—makes me being raped [number] years ago an everyday nightmare.

They say that only murder is a life taken—well after you have been violently raped at knife point anally that is also a life taken—the life you so freely enjoyed previously as you knew it is gone forever. But you still have to live—put on a happy face—sometimes I think it would be much easier to have died. I wouldn't be the person I'm now. I hate myself sometimes—to get dressed up and look pretty seems almost a crime—because in your head you go back and think does this warrant someone else raping me again—should I look and be ugly and then they won't even try?

I didn't report my rape. I had heard of one girl who took her attacker to court and the bastards held up her underpants in the court while she was there. I could not go through that. The help of family and friends is very vital in helping us, but when all is said and done it is only us that has to live with it.

He who did this has no regrets—they have no conscience—they have no remorse. That makes it harder to deal with. I am the victim—no one else. You must deal with every case as a whole new one. There is no such thing as an 'everyday' rape. Every situation concerning the victim is so varied.

I certainly hope that someone has taken the time to read this properly. It is from the heart and soul from a living violent crime survivor. It wasn't easy. It will never be. Please help us.

THEY DID NOT TELL

Although research has shown that women raped by strangers are more likely to disclose to someone (due to society's view of this as a 'real' rape), some of the survivors of stranger rape (22.5 per cent) had kept their assault a secret until they filled in the survey. Others waited years before disclosing. Why? Shame and a feeling of responsibility for their own victimisation.

The rape was at gunpoint and I was too ashamed to tell anyone. (Female, raped when she was 15)

•

Trauma was dramatic and I did not think I could repeat the story and till this day have not. (Female, raped when she was 23)

•

I did not tell anyone because I felt awful and they would probably say I was 'asking for it'. It happened in a caravan park where we were staying. He was 10 or so years older than me. My Dad would have killed him if he had known who it was and we believed that the law wouldn't do much—only hurt and shame me. (Female, raped when she was 14)

•

As I was under the influence of alcohol I felt somehow that affected whether people would believe me. (Female, raped when she was 17)

Fear of the perpetrators' threats also kept the victims silent.

It was a stranger. I was terrified afterwards and was too scared to tell my parents as we were brought up strict Lutherans. My parents still do not know today. (Female, raped at the age of 12)

•

I was a thirteen year old girl returning home from a swim early evening in summer. I was grabbed and held in a panel van for approximately 30-40 minutes and raped by five or six young men. I was threatened with my life and reprisals if I told anyone. I was battered, confused, angry, shameful and shocked and to this day have only spoken to a girlfriend and my brother-in-law recently about my ordeal.

•

I was walking along [name] promenade at 6.30 in the morning and a jogger followed me and pulled me into an underground carpark and made me masturbate him. I felt shame and dirty because I didn't fight him and relief that the incident wasn't worse. I have never told anyone about this before. Why aren't women safe to walk our streets? Why does half our population have to be fearful of what the other half takes for granted? (Female, raped when she was 25)

DID NOT REPORT TO THE POLICE

Slightly more than one half of the survivors of rape perpetrated by strangers did not report to the police. Again the decision was most often based upon their own feeling of responsibility or, in the children's cases, the parents' view that a trial would be disturbing for the survivor.

I was hitchhiking and had put myself in the position so I thought it was my own fault. I had to tell someone straight away, though I was very scared. It was a male friend who I was going to visit. He was very supportive and wanted to go to the police but I didn't. (Female, raped when she was 22)

●

In my case the rapist broke into my flat, cornered me in the bathroom when I was having a shower and threatened me with a knife. He wore a stocking over his head and was a total stranger. After I escaped I didn't report it to the police because I didn't think I could give them enough information to catch him as I couldn't describe him. I was also afraid that he'd try again and maybe next time I wouldn't live.

So it wasn't that the police were at fault—I just didn't think I could tell them anything useful. (Female, raped when she was 28)

●

Two years later this same perpetrator was found guilty of the rape of a 16 year old girl in a public toilet. He had strangled her and left her to die. She was found and was hospitalised for several months. I didn't report because I didn't believe in the effectiveness of the law. My self-esteem was extremely low and self-guilt extremely high.

●

Did not report to the police as this stranger had my car number and address and name. I was at a caravan park [name] that was very isolated. He was the caretaker. He tried to drive us (i.e. me and my two children twelve and four years old) over a cliff in the rain. He threatened the children and I played along to get him to drive us home to the caravan from his house saying I'd be late for dinner at the nearby club.

My comments: Overwhelming feeling of revulsion, dirty. He was over 50 years old. Most important factors in retrospect; playing along, pretending it was 'pleasant' doing as he wished to survive. Thank God it worked.

I was afraid for my children both at the time he grabbed them, put them in the car. I had that fear when he said, 'You come and see my house. You'll get wet in the van, make some tea, etc.' I had to pretend everything was normal for the kids' sakes.

I was physically sick during the 'act'. I wanted to vomit. Prior to this he insisted that I have a shower (kids and I were at the beach so I was only in a swim costume). 'It's cold, you'll feel better' . . . but of course I had no change of clothes. The door did not shut and he came in and pushed me into the shower . . . the fear became a fear of being killed not just being raped. I had to use my wits as I was determined to survive and to save my kids. He had forced them to stay in the other room. The youngest fell asleep. He locked the doors. There was no escape as it was up a mountain track and I couldn't have got away with the kids.

Prior to this he raced the car up to the edge of the cliff and slithered all over the rocky road and said 'It would be easy to go over the edge you know'. You can see it was a matter of my not showing fear and pretending. He drove like a mad man coming down the mountain, running the car towards trees etc.

Afterwards I told the next family (another single mother and her sons) who arrived to use the van about him and then on the way home the people who had loaned us single mums their van were horrified and contacted the park owners (I think). They didn't suggest the police etc, as I was so afraid he'd come to my house (he had said he would). I later told my mother's friend and I had a test at the doctor's to check I hadn't caught anything. I was afraid to report it.

RESPONSE OF THOSE THEY TOLD

Fifty-nine per cent of relatives were supportive if the offender was a stranger.

The support I got from my family and my friends saved my sanity. (Female, aged 21, raped by three men)

•

My family were (and are) of great support to me. Unfortunately I often get the impression from men (i.e. boyfriends, dates, etc.) to whom I told the story that they didn't believe me. Personally I have managed to some extent to forget, mainly because my assailant was mentally disturbed. He was committed to an asylum. (Female, raped when she was 8)

However, many others encountered hostility and blame.

One of the worst aspects of the rape was the lack of support from people, especially my mother, who clearly blamed me absolutely for the rape and has never acknowledged my feelings. (Female, raped when she was 17)

For the child/victim the most frequently mentioned parental response was denial; not to talk about it so that it would go away . . . but it did not go away.

After the police interviewed me at home, the crime was never mentioned ever again. I spoke to my mother about it when I was in my twenties. She was shocked that I still remembered. WHAT A JOKE! (Female, raped when she was 9)

•

Twenty years after the attack in the park my memories are coming to the surface of what happened. My family never dealt with it. It was not addressed—pushed aside. It must be addressed for survivors to be able to get help and try and live. (Female, raped when she was 5)

•

Not much help when I was twelve. I was told to forget it. I had to act as if it had never happened. I was so scared of men, even my brothers.

•

The police said, 'She won't remember it and nothing really happened so I suggest you let it all drop,' which my parents did and it has never been discussed. It is taboo but had oral sex with the perpetrator and he would have penetrated me if I hadn't been wearing a tough swimsuit under my clothes. It was very, very traumatic. (Female, raped when she was 10)

•

This assault was blocked from my memory until I was 28 then it slowly surfaced as I got to know more of the inner me. I remember telling my mother that I was bleeding and sore. My mother was very naive about sexual matters and thought I started my periods and the whole incident was never discussed again. (Female, raped when she was 17)

RESPONSE OF THE POLICE

Although the police response did not differ significantly by offender, there was some variation. Almost one half were supportive if the perpetrator was a stranger. Police supportiveness has increased over the past twenty-five years.

The two young men were not found although the police had line ups. I found the detectives very kind and understanding. They made me feel comfortable—I have nothing but praise for them—I am still affected by the attack and feel if they'd been caught I would feel better now. (Raped by stranger at age 21)

•

I was not actually raped but had been beaten and was unconscious and was about to be raped when my husband came home. In the struggle which followed between my husband and the attacker, my husband was stabbed twice and as a consequence he nearly died several times in the following few days. As a result our case may have been treated differently if only I had been attacked, but I found the police very helpful at the time of attack and also leading up to the court dates and sentencing time.

•

The man who raped me still has not been found.

Our house belonged to a [certain person and occupation] and when my parents bought the house we had harassment from the time we moved in.

One night I was home by myself for only two hours. There was a knock on the front door. I answered and a man with a knife and a balaclava on pushed me inside and raped me. He cut my body as he cut my clothes off! He raped me brutally and then just left telling me that if I told anyone he would kill my parents.

I was so badly hurt and scared, so I rang my parents' friend who was a lawyer as soon as the rapist left. He rang the police. The police, detectives and a policewoman all came to the house. All the police and detectives were so good to me. I was taken to police headquarters to the rape crisis centre. The rape crisis police took statements from me, my parents then arrived and the police were very good to them as well. I was taken to the hospital by the police with my mother, and three lady doctors examined me. They were also very good to me. I spent three days in hospital and all the time the police, detectives and rape crisis people were excellent.

The rapist was never found but I received $16,000 from the Victims of Crime. I never had to go to court, a lawyer handled everything. Nobody was ever nasty to me except a lot of my parents' friends, who just did not believe it happened. That was the worst part of it all, a lot of school friends and my parents' friends did not give us any support at all. The detectives on my case gave me enormous support and used to come to my house every three weeks for a year after the rape just to see if I was all right. The rape crisis centre did the same.

I became very sick emotionally and had to see a psychologist for almost three years after the rape. I am now happily married with a baby but the last ten years have been a nightmare! I never went back to school after the rape—I was too emotionally sick and in hospital a lot. The support I received from police, detectives doctors and the rape crisis centre was excellent. I would always tell a rape victim to please report the rape.

•

I found that having a support person from 'Victims of Crime' at the police station before I arrived of great benefit. The police called her after receiving my call. I could then give my statement freely as well as receive the support and comfort I needed so badly. I knew I could not have said anything in front of family or friends. (Female, aged 31)

However, even when the rapist was a stranger, the police may have been reluctant to act and/or were not necessarily sympathetic.

The police were males, inept, uncommunicative, uncaring, terse, could not relate to a very traumatised teenager (me), did little to offer referrals—NIL help. Had NO comprehension of the event at all! Wrote down a different message. I was left hopelessly stunned. No medical examination took place. No counselling or discussion offered. No attempts to really get me to talk. No signs of communicating competence exhibited, two males who appeared hardened, tired and antipathetic [sic]. No follow up communication of any kind took place. I wanted to see this criminal caught. No invitation to contact them if I saw him again—NO nothing!

I look back now and am absolutely dumb struck. Why do we have such inept people on the job? I bear scars to this day—internal physical and if it wasn't for good, kind counsel from caring people I would have been quite a mess. (Female, raped when she was 16)

•

I was kept three hours in the police station, overhearing disbelieving comments about me. I only wanted to be taken home safely. I complained after and CIB [Criminal Investigation Bureau] called a couple of times explaining they get a lot of 'made up' stories. (Female, raped when she was 37)

•

I would just like to add the following: I reported my attack to the police but they treated me like the perpetrator instead of the victim. The police photographer said that I was one of the 'worst assault cases' he had ever seen, with regard to the physical assault side of it. I was taken to a Rape Crisis Centre in a Women's Hospital where it was declared after all the tests had been done, that I had had 'forced sexual intercourse', so it was proven forensically that I had been raped.

Even with all the forensic evidence the police still did not believe me, and treated me like a piece of garbage. They even told me that 'they couldn't be bothered looking for the guy' because it was a dark night and my description of the guy was 'sketchy'. I felt ashamed, dirty and terribly guilty, and the police treated me as such. To make matters worse, they [the police] FORCED me into signing a FALSE REPORT about it, so I got charged for that. They told me horror stories of going to court etc. and how I would be made to look and feel. And so, in my then frame of mind I went along with the false report.

They played on my feelings at the time; degradation, humiliation, shame and disgust. Even ten years later, I would never ever report a rape to the police if it happened again. I just couldn't cope with going through that again. I just hope that one day the judicial system will change, and treat victims the way they should be, with compassion and understanding. Thank you for letting me get this off my chest.

PS Because of the police attitude toward me, my family and friends began to have doubts about what happened. And that made me feel really good!!!! (Female, raped when she was 21)

•

I reported the attack to the police. I was examined at the hospital the following day and I have never had any follow up from the police. The toy dagger which was used in the attack was taken as evidence but was never returned even though numerous enquires were made about its whereabouts. I was living in a predominantly Aboriginal town at the time and the police would not believe that I felt the perpetrator was not an Aboriginal. And yet eighteen months later an Aboriginal activist in a neighbouring town accused me of stating that the perpetrator was an Aboriginal. (Female, raped when she was 25)

•

The perpetrator broke into my motel room and asked to have sex with him. When I refused he bashed me unconscious. When I woke up he had ripped my clothes off and was having anal intercourse with me. I started struggling again and eventually got away and jumped off the balcony and went naked up to the Reception desk. The motel owner called the police who asked me if I could identify an Aboriginal man. I told them he was not an Aboriginal and the motel owner told them the man's name and that in fact he too was staying at the motel.

The police then asked me why I was alone in [the town] and said that any woman unescorted in [their town] was only asking for trouble as it was full of blacks and transients.

They interviewed the perpetrator and came back to me saying that it was not possible that he had committed the assault as he was an executive for a [product] firm and stayed in [town] about once a month. They also said that they had told him to stay away from me and I wouldn't have any trouble from him.

They told me to get cleaned up and get dressed and they would take me to the hospital to have my injuries taken care of and stitches in my head.

During the interview the police kept yelling at me and telling me that it was a black man that had done this to me and that in fact an Aboriginal was known to be loitering near the motel.

The police said it would be better for me to forget the whole matter as I would be in a lot of trouble if I laid charges against this man. The way the police treated me and accused me at the aforementioned interview instilled deeper feelings of desperation that (a) I was powerless to stop or receive any justice. There is no justice. (b) No-one wants to believe you, they blame you instead.

●

It was nine years ago. The police appeared to doubt my story despite obvious signs, but the sexual assault unit was very caring. (Female, raped when she was 49)

●

The police that arrive at the scene when [the rape is] first reported should be made to do some studies on how to question and treat the victim. As in my case my son who was five at the time was sitting right next to me as they questioned me, which I didn't realise until days later as I was in shock at the time. That stinks to put it mildly. (Female, raped when she was 25)

●

I find it difficult to evaluate because the police dealing with my case did not understand enough about rape situations and so in trying to be nice to me and making comments like 'well he had good choice' and meaning it as a compliment, in fact confused the issue and made me feel that the line separating the police from the rapist was in fact negligible. (Female, raped when she was 21)

Some felt discouraged by the police in taking their cases to court.

The police found the guy who was around forty years old, married, two children. The guy lied about a few incidents. They [the police] came to my house and went over the statement with me again and pointed out the differences. They then told me to ring them and let them know if I still wanted to take the rapist to court. At this stage my parents knew what the detective said to me, so because of the fact I didn't stay at my parents the following week, they rung the police without my consent and told them that I didn't want to go through with it.

Following this, I don't think police should take an answer about this case from my parents, as I was very destroyed. I don't care how long I was to wait but I just wanted to see this guy sentenced if not anything else. (Female, raped when she was 16)

For others such as the next writer, the police were willing to take the case to court but recognised her inability to cope.

The attacker climbed through an unlocked window of my unit at 2.00 a.m. I had never seen him but he had seen me [at local shopping centre] and followed me earlier in the week.

After the attack I was threatened with a knife and he left about three hours later threatening to deny everything if I reported him. He had told me about his family enough for police to identify him—he was a known house breaker and rapist.

I learned from the police in the ensuing weeks that he has been to court on rape charges before but has always got off. His previous major rape was a [child]—he got a suspended sentence for that one!! Other rapes reported were not taken seriously by the police as he said the women 'had led him on'.

I was in deep shock and obviously deeply disturbed by the attack. I was taken care of by doctors and I received regular visits by police and I identified a photo but apparently it could not be taken as conclusive evidence because I 'hesitated' at the first shot! Eventually they found him and he was questioned. He produced an alibi from a person which was after proved to be untrue. The attacker finally admitted the crime but said he would get a good lawyer (the one who got him off last time) and shoot me down in court.

I think the police realised I was not strong enough to take a court case appearance and dropped all proceedings. I was under psychiatric care for over a year constantly, then over the next ten years suffered nightmares, anger etc. I had to move interstate to get away from bad memories. When I came back to [the town] the nightmares resumed.

The police had the unit fingerprinted etc. but although they found evidence of hair etc they said the attacker would have to volunteer specimens—they could not force him to give specimens. After a year they said they were getting rid of all evidence (standard procedure apparently) so I requested they burn the bed sheets they had taken as evidence.

THE HOSPITAL EXPERIENCE

Reporting to the police usually involved a doctor's examination which could be an added trauma if not performed with some sensitivity.

After being sexually assaulted I told my [relative] who contacted the police. I was still very scared, because during the assault I was sure the man would kill me. I was not offered any counselling or anyone at all to talk to. I'm not sure if the Rape Crisis Centre existed in 19XX.

The very worst part, which made me wonder if we should have told the police at all, happened at the hospital. The police took me to a hospital to get some specimens of semen from my anus.

The doctor put me in a room and told me to remove all of my clothing. At that point I just wanted to cry. I thought it was unnecessary to remove all my clothing. I felt humiliated and very alone.

Sometimes now when I am under a lot of stress, I wake up in the night with an intense, excruciating pain in my anus, which becomes very tight. Also I have frequent sexual thoughts. (Female, raped in her youth)

•

The Sexual Assault Clinic at [name] Hospital were very good, but although I consented to a medical examination, I was not guaranteed a female doctor. Can you imagine how distressing it would be to be examined by a man several hours after the rape?! I also had to walk a distance from the counselling room to the examination room , past a public entrance, in the clothes I was raped in! Very unpleasant. (Female, raped when she was 20)

•

The police said as I was nine years old at the time it was my fault for going with him. He was my big brother's age, and we had only been on the beach five minutes, waiting for Dad.

The boy said, 'Come on. We will go and get some worms, just up in the mangroves'. So me and my sister who was five at that time went with him.

He grabbed me, threatened my sister if she watched, and he raped me. My parents took me straight down the police station. I was examined at a private doctor's, and then the hospital at [name]: both internal exams, and as bad as the rape, they really hurt me.

The police found the boy and then told me it was pointless charging him as he was a bit retarded, and had just got a job, but they told my father to give him a belting.

We had to move house after that, as he kept walking past smirking at us all the time, and my parents were frightened for us girls. I must add if my Dad had taken police advice, he was that angry he would have killed the boy.

Note from mother:
And as this girl's mother, I would never put a child through that again. Better to say nothing, than be accused of being a willing party. My daughter still sleepwalks and can't go outside in the dark on her own at [number] years old.

RESPONSE OF THE COURTS

A family member living in a different household from the victim, a stranger rapist, and a date were the most likely to be imprisoned. However, even in the case of the 579 strangers, only ninety-two went to court with an even smaller number, sixty, found guilty and imprisoned.

I was the first in a line of twelve others. The offender was not caught for four years. In most instances a condom was used so that identification was difficult. He was not linked to my assault, but when he was caught he admitted to mine and many others including some who had not reported the rape. He received nineteen years.

Few of the victims whose perpetrators went to court felt that the outcome was harsh enough.

This man was placed on a good behaviour bond—I was not the first child he had approached to enter his car to show him where a certain street was—I was the fifth! I got his rego number and told my Dad who informed the police straight away. (Female, raped when she was 11)

•

My rapist was given a more lenient sentence because he pleaded guilty and was drunk. I was not informed of the trial date and read about it in the newspaper!!!' (Female, raped when she was 34)

•

I was raped by number one in the vagina, anus and mouth plus beaten up. Guy number one got four years, three and a half years non-parole and was out in one year. The other three totally got off so what's the point of all the pain on my part. (Female, raped when she was 18)

•

A close friend of mine was also raped. She took it through the courts and the perpetrator was let off on a good behaviour bond. We supported each other.

Her case is the reason I didn't follow through with mine. I have gone through enough hell without the courts putting me through more!

•

There is something wrong with the justice system. If it doesn't change, criminals are always going to get off free. My rapist was found guilty on assault and threats, but not rape. So all he got was 300 hours community work.

I was angry, and I felt like I had just wasted my time reporting it. The police knew he was guilty, and they wanted him to go to jail as much as I. But the decision is not up to them, it's up to the court.

On a lot of rape cases, they always put more men than women on the jury which is unfair. They should have half and half, because some men would think the women deserved what she got.

I think the system stinks. If judges don't turn their thinking around, criminals are always going to think they will get off or won't get much time to do in jail.

Police sometimes must think that they do all their work for nothing when a criminal walks out of court a free person.

PS: I still have sexual problems since the rape.

•

I believe the courts give no priority to rape cases—it seems I am fairly lucky as some cases take two years to get to trial. I believe Victoria sets a priority and trials must be held within four months. The victim is the least considered person. Has no legal support, ie. lawyer to object on her/his behalf. Very 'alone'.

Police initially were very attentive but of course they go on and have new cases to attend to every day. So the victim is in a state of limbo 'dreading' the trial but also wanting to get it over with. Inquisitive about the rapist 'Where is he?' 'Is he meeting bail conditions?' but feels like a 'nuisance' asking.

Never been in a court before. Have heard stories about how terrible rape trials are, how the victim is the one who goes 'on trial'. Guilt has to be the worst thing. Could I have prevented it happening? Why didn't I fight harder? Why didn't I scream louder? Guilt because I survived, others have been killed or seriously injured. Guilt—he has a wife and family—I may put him in gaol. I hope so.

The long delay for the trial numbs me. The initial elation of surviving, of his being arrested, my being able to pick him out of an identification photo line up. The anger I felt at a total stranger forcing his way into my own home and taking what he wanted. These feelings have all numbed and I tend to wonder if I have the energy to go through with a trial. Friends (acquaintances) have tired of the initial shock, horror—'seven day wonder' so I have a private hell. Maybe a trial will help purge the system. But what if . . . the jury doesn't believe me . . . takes pity on him and his young family . . . his ethnicity scares the jury . . . racism! I now know he has prior rape convictions . . . the jury don't and won't know. He can get the best lawyer—I am just a witness for the prosecution.

•

Three out of the four were found guilty. Was told the fourth man had powerful father. Police advised me to drop anal charge and should only charge for assault—I did not. He got three months at a camp (not jail). I received seventy-eight stitches and also had a glass bottle kicked inside my vagina. I can no longer have children. (Female, raped when she was 17)

•

The only reason the perpetrators were arrested and the police were supportive, I believe, is because they were known offenders.

After three months of imprisonment the offenders were released on appeal. The judge (elderly age) made a 'technical error'. He neglected to inform the jury that as the verdict was undecided they could return for further deliberation. I asked for a lawyer, besides the Crown, and was refused. I also asked for a closed court and was refused. But when the Crown prosecutor asked me to return to court he almost begged me and assured me of the 'closed court' which I now know I was entitled to in the beginning.

I would also like to add that whilst in court I objected to some lines of questioning, much to the disgust of the judge, hence defending myself to some degree.

I felt like I was on trial. My character was degraded, exaggerated. There were two of them, how could I fight?? Even the rape crisis people turned against me because of the twisted evidence. It's not fair how you only get a Public Prosecutor and the men have top barristers who tear you to shreds for a hefty pay packet. The system's all wrong. I wasn't even granted any compensation and I was pregnant when the assault took place. I wouldn't go to court again—gross misjustice!! (Female, raped when she was 18)

•

Police Rape Squad and CIB were very supportive, partly because the rapist was a prison escapee, partly because I was (a) a virgin and (b) a [occupation] and I was lucky to get good people. I did not contact a Rape Crisis Centre because I had good support. The rapist got a sentence of nineteen years.

I consider that I was lucky—the police who dealt with my case were most supportive and continue to keep in contact with me. However I do not have much faith in the court system at this stage. (Female, raped when she was 37)

•

In reference to adult sexual violence you may not consider an eleven year old girl an adult, but he was an adult. I was certainly treated like one by the police and in the court case making out I was some young cheap tart. Going to court is not for every rape victim—I would only recommend it for those who could cope mentally and emotionally. I think it has made me too strong of a person; natural emotion or love does not come naturally any more. Now that I have had [a number of] children, [a number] of them sons, I hate my husband showing flirtation or degrading me in front of them. You wonder what they will think is okay to do to a woman when they are older.

Suggestions from the Survivors

Considering the volume of reported negative experiences with the criminal justice system, it is not surprising that a number of writers included a recommendation concerning that area.

The interview by two male police was one of the most embarrassing and demeaning experiences I have ever experienced.

So after the actual horror of the rapes, one from past memory was not inspired to undergo yet another aggressive, insensitive, demeaning attack of non-understanding from policemen.

One would hope that psychological training for police has developed far more sensitive approaches to victims of rape.

•

Why so long for a 'priority' case—aggravated sexual assault?

Why bail for a rapist, a potential murderer who lived three blocks away?

I had to move. (Female raped when she was 19)

•

Unfortunately when I was raped (which took me a while to accept) I was too young and unaware of where to seek help. I know though that there would have been no way I could have gone through the emotional hurt of a court case. I hope what you are doing will allow the system to change so that justice can be done. No-one deserves to be raped once and then have to go through it again to prove it. It's just not right! (Female, raped when she was 16)

•

Please keep this in the public arena—to be debated and discussed. 'Without Consent' was a good beginning. Maybe more emphasis on the criminal aspect of the sexual assault and the innocence of the women assaulted. Total ideological shift from 'victim blaming' needed. (Female, raped when she was 12)

•

Testifying at court was devastating. Perpetrator didn't have to testify —why?

How come the accused can appeal if found guilty but not the victim if the perpetrator is found innocent?

There should be more counselling for the victim's spouse/boyfriend and family—they are victims too. (Female, raped when she was 21)

•

I believe a central computer profiling system of sex offenders should be introduced and be available to the police of all states. As is the case with the FBI in the USA. (Male, raped when he was 14)

•

Rapists get off scot free and it's time the justice system was overhauled. Women should appear as judges before the rapists. Rapists then wouldn't get off so lightly.

X rated videos should be banned altogether. Men watching these often go out and rape after watching pornography. (Female, raped when she was 25)

•

It is irrelevant as to the number of years a rapist serves imprisonment unless he gets professional counselling to understand himself, his anger and his need for power. I believe that the man who raped me will continue to rape other women when he is released from prison. (Female, raped when she was 32)

Others addressed the need for more macro-level change concerning societal attitudes about men and women and the myths about rape.

Rape is not only about dominance. It is also about (anti-social) behaviour. Sex penalties are not severe enough or appropriate. Men would fear penalty of castration. Would be better if most of the judges and prosecutors in these cases were females as most of the victims are females (if not children). Judges and lawyers who had some personal experience with rape would be even better. Victims must have a say in punishing the offender.

The problem is based within society—the legal system is just one side issue. It will always be difficult to convict a person of rape where there is no evidence of violence, the two people were alone together and it is just one person's word against another. Therefore the focus

185

needs to be on social values and ways to reduce the acceptance of rape.

The legal system must be sensitive to the accusing person's feelings at all stages, from reporting to court trial and if <u>insufficient evidence was available to convict</u> the accused it can be just that, rather than a vindication. (Female, raped when she was 26)

•

Unless attitudes within our law institutions and society in general change towards this most vicious of crimes and towards women, Australia will continue to produce such alarming levels of rape, sexual assault and domestic violence. I would hope that this survey is a beginning in the quest to change such a situation. (Female raped by five men at age 15)

•

At twelve years of age I was pack raped at the show. It took me over ten years to seek therapy for this owing to the fact I was very young and naive at the time. What distresses me now is that at [my current age] and after much therapy I still can't forgive or forget and still have a very low regard for men, and I think I always will. My husband is very timid and patient, I'm sure that's why I married him, yet I still can't trust him 100 per cent which is pretty distressing for both of us—out of ten of my closest girlfriends, eight of them have been raped; most of them repeatedly by fathers or relatives.

Men's attitudes have obviously got to alter dramatically in Australia if it is ever going to be equal for women. I think that penalties for rapists, especially child molesters, are far too lenient and need immediate review. Also I think we need to take more drastic measures in educating men <u>before</u> they rape. Until we do this it will continue to happen. The saddest thing is it doesn't just affect you while you're being abused. It stays with you and haunts you forever and changes your whole outlook on life. It also changes the lives of your loved ones. The rapist never thinks of that.

•

I was raped in Queensland last year. Since the rape, my life has basically been ruined. I am unable to work, my personality is totally different. I feel angry at a society that continually puts women down in a sexual way.

I decided to apply for compensation. Because it is through Queensland I have had so many problems. So many people have been unsupportive of my claim and have tried to put me off. Even a solicitor that I contacted warned me that I might receive nothing. How is this possible? Apparently in Queensland it is not enough to have suffered a rape. You then have to go on and prove that you have been adversely affected and that you have suffered a 'loss'. Because there is no official tribunal, it goes to the Attorney-General's department. There are no guidelines as to what I may receive, if anything. I can not depend on any legal help—they offer assistance, at my expense, but no guarantees.

I have had to go around asking people to write reports for me, and paying $350.00 for a psychiatrist's report as well as spending many hours trying to write a personal report. For all this, and for all I have gone through, I may receive nothing. It just doesn't seem at all fair.

Apart from the financial side, I want the society to recognise what I've been through. Our society still can't talk about it. The ABC program showed that the real reasons behind why men (and some women) rape still is a taboo subject.

I find I have lost so many friends, and even family and close friends just seem to want me to forget all about it and get back to the way I used to be. Well, it just isn't possible. Why doesn't somebody make a program about that, so that the general public can start to understand it all better. Why do we always seem to hear all the horrible details of rapes, and not the reasons for them, which run deep in our society.

Being raped is every woman's nightmare, yet it is one we all face every day without feeling that we have any power to stop it.

It took me about two months to realise it had really happened to me. Even now, it just all seems like a terrible dream. I just wish that society could start to nurture and look after its victims, not make it a continued nightmare for compensation. (Female raped when she was 30)

•

Three years after the assault I found the courage to tell a family member. Their most unsupportive reaction devastated me and has made my healing more painful than it needs to be. I basically was not believed and was told to leave my past where it belongs—in the past. I have since received most needed and valued support and

187

counselling from the Rape Crisis Centre. Until the stigma associated with being a rape victim is removed (a stigma that exists with no other crime) women will NOT report.

In our society, one does not hesitate to identify themselves as a victim of an armed robbery or hold-up, or most other types of violent crime. And they receive the support and sympathy that is needed. But when it comes to identifying yourself as a victim of rape or sexual assault, there is such a stigma associated with this that women cannot even tell their families and the people close to them, never mind telling complete strangers. The stigma results in women being blamed for rape/sexual assault, and thus society fails to put the full responsibility where it belongs—with the rapist.

The only way that rape is ever going to begin to decrease in our society is if we put the full responsibility for the prevention of rape on men's shoulders and stop treating women like they are the criminals. Women have absolutely nothing to gain by 'making up' a false rape complaint. It's just one of the many rape myths. (Female, raped when she was 17)

•

I didn't want to be known as a victim of rape—even my boyfriend told me it was my fault.

Also men rape because they want to—they are socialised to rape. There is an acceptance in the community (male and female) of rape. There is an acceptance of anti-social behaviour in men—look at who commits crime! The socialisation process starts at home, often a poor male role model or an absent one is a contributing factor. Mums can't do it all! I propose parenting lessons for everybody and radical changes in our misogynist society. Women are in pain! (Female, raped when she was 19)

•

Increased self-defence classes for women FREE with child care provided.

•

A psychologist should be available to victims and be present while the victim is interviewed by police.

There should be better education in schools to both males and females about rape. Police need to be more compassionate and stop treating victims as the villain.

•

At the time of the assault I was ignorant as to what was actually happening and the power exerted by the male was considerable. I eventually talked my way out of it. MORE programs about rape are needed to make EVERYONE aware of the problem and so as to make women not feel so alone. (Female, raped when she was 18)

STRANGER DANGER PROTECTION

One letter writer discussed the precautions that she took subsequent to her rape.

I was living with my teenage daughter and I didn't want to worry or frighten her, but I became suddenly VERY safety conscious and this with my injuries endorsed her suspicions. Since then I've taken a women's self defence course and my daughter and I, without being really paranoid, are both alert to possible dangerous situations—e.g. street lighting when looking for a new flat, outside lights etc.

Indeed, it must be acknowledged that we do not live in a utopian world nor in a society that is amenable to radical change. Therefore, it is important that precautionary measures are adopted by women. Until women can indeed 'take back the night' and be safe from violence both on the streets, in their homes and within their relationships, there are ways to minimise the potential danger. The steps outlined below are an aggregation of some suggestions outlined by the Sydney Rape Crisis Centre (1990) and other readings. The list in no way is intended to put, or even imply that, the responsibility for rape rests with the victims.

- Learn self defence not only to fight back but to become more assertive and able to detect danger.

- Use deadlocks; install a peep-hole; and be wary of strangers.

- Leave your car in a well lit area; have your key in your hand; shift parking places occasionally; and check seats before entering the vehicle.

- Stand straight and walk with a firm step on the street; do not carry too many objects; and wear clothing which does not impede running.

- Wait for trains in well lit areas; sit near the aisle; and let someone know how you are travelling and when you expect to arrive.

- Book a taxi by phone; sit in the back seat; and be dropped a short distance from destination.

- If hitchhiking, ask the driver for his destination; sit close to the door; and carry something for self-protection.

INTO THE LIGHT

If we bring the fungus into the sunlight, it will not grow. Over time it will wither and die. So too with the aftermath and pain of sexual assault at the level of the survivor and so too with the incidence of rape within a society. How? First, let us look at the victim and the process of her healing. Then, we will see how this can contribute in the long run to changes at a societal level. However, just to complicate matters, we will see how the reverse can also work: cultural shifts at the belief level and within the structures of society such as the criminal justice system can impact on the individual and her willingness to report and talk about the crime. Concurrently, the laws and police and other structures are of course markedly affected by changes in the attitudes held by members of a society. A picture is worth a thousand words: the interrelationship between all of these components is illustrated in Figure 1.

THE INDIVIDUALS' RECOVERY

'Don't talk', 'Don't trust', and 'Don't feel', are the three rules which dominate households where addiction, abuse or other types of dysfunction are present[1]. It would appear that a high proportion of adult victims of rape are survivors of childhood sexual assault and therefore grew up with these rules. It is theorised that, as a consequence of growing up in this type of environment with these rigid norms, there is an increased likelihood of the children developing certain personality traits

---

1. Aside from the literature cited on these rules and other aspects of the dysfunctional family (Beattie 1989; Bradshaw 1988; Wegscheider-Cruse 1985), the model described in this paper has also been confirmed by the author who has spent considerable time as a volunteer interacting with women who were sexually, physically, or emotionally abused as children.

and behavioural patterns of survival. Low self-esteem and deeply embedded feelings of shame may lead to alcoholism, drug abuse, other forms of dependency, and/or adult relationships marked by victimisation (Finkelhor 1979; Gelinas 1983; Whitfield 1979).

Figure 1: Dynamics of rape within Australian culture

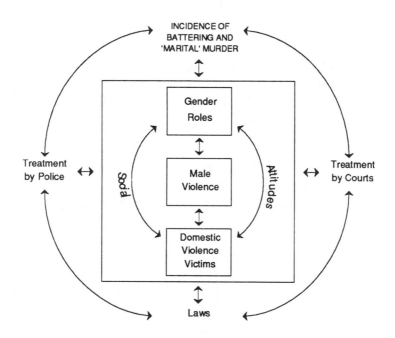

Presentation of this theory is not intended in any way to impute the blame for adult rapes upon the adult child survivor of sexual assault. It does, however, help us to understand why so many of the women who responded to the 'Without Consent' survey were victims of rape many, many times in their lives—most often first as children.

Further, an adult woman who is raped, but is not a survivor of assault as a child, also learns these rules very quickly unless she is met with support and openness.

Don't Talk

The incest victim or the child who is abused (or the adult victim who senses that she would be judged) learns secrecy. Not only does she not talk to anyone outside of the home, but within the family, the violence is also not discussed. The equilibrium of the dysfunctional system requires that its members do not rock the boat. Violating the code of secrecy would jeopardise the status quo. The 'Don't talk' rule is therefore mandatory and will usually be both explicit, 'We do not talk about this to anyone'; or implicit through the on-going denial of the child's perception of reality. She can't tell anyone about something that she has been told, in a variety of ways, has not occurred.

We have seen in many of the comments and letters that the 'Don't talk' rule is also frequently set into place even when the rapist is a stranger or from outside of the family. 'Don't talk to her about it and then she will forget'. She does not forget.

The 'Don't talk' rule is also a by-product of two other factors: her own sense of shame (discussed below) and because of it, she assumes the responsibility for the abuse; and the idea that such violence becomes so normative that it is no longer exceptional but just a part of her reality: the bizarre becomes normal.

Don't Trust

The girl who grows up in a troubled family is taught by experience that her parents—their promises, their behaviour and even their rules—cannot be trusted. (The adult woman also may have learned that society and its practitioners are not to be trusted). Too often the child has been told that, 'It will never happen again', or that, 'This time, the family really will go on that trip'. Additionally the rules are always being changed without her being told. Broken promises and inconsistency are earmarks of such family systems.

A child learns to trust when she is nurtured and treated with love, consistency and caring. The abused child is not. She does not learn to trust in her parents or in their love. Within a continuum of degree, this lack of trust in others would take place for any child who is abused within or outside of the family. And, it takes place for the adult woman who encounters non-support from those to whom she discloses about the assault.

The incest victim, the battered child, the childhood sexual assault survivor grows up with a deep void within; a lack of self or self-worth. In its place is a core of shame which continuously says to that child, 'You are the one responsible for this. You are bad.' She has probably been told either overtly or indirectly that this is the case. Besides, if adults are a child's gods then the cause of such evil must emanate from her, the child. In direct and tacit ways, Australian culture also blames the rape victim and, as we have heard over and over again in these pages, as an individual socialised with those messages, she also takes on the responsibility and self-blame for her own victimisation.

Don't Feel

When he starts to touch her, she leaves her body and watches from a distance. She does not feel the pain or the anger because she isn't really there. But, the hurt and the rage are in there buried beneath layer upon layer of denial, shame, and later perhaps food, alcohol, drugs or relationships.

When he touches her, she learns not to feel the rage because if she does, it will mean more pain for her. She learns not to feel the pain because there is no one or no way to make it feel better. So, the feelings stay inside, medicated later on perhaps.

And that is the process of surviving. Not talking, not trusting and not feeling do not help the child to heal but they do enable her to live through it. If you have heard all of the voices in these pages, then you have heard the answer to how to heal from sexual assault. Let's listen to another woman.

I feel that I concentrated too heavily on the four rapes and that I didn't quite tell you about how I have benefited from therapy.

Three years after the rapes I realised that I was a victim of child abuse and psychological incest, and I believe that this may have predisposed me to the four rapes. I have been doing intensive therapy for four years now and I have improved dramatically.

I want you to know that rape survivors can recover.

Today I am at my normal weight after having battled with anorexia for [a number of] years, I feel safe in my role as a woman and I am again sexually attracted to men. I am meeting healthy, kind, mature men and women who respect me for who I am.

I am planning to specialise in [a type of helping occupation]. So life is looking better for me. I think that receiving help has allowed me to become a whole woman again.

The rules must be broken, one by one. First, the survivor must unearth the secrets and talk. We are only as sick as the secrets we keep. Given the low trust levels of those who have been violated, beginning to share what happened is not easy; it is simple but definitely not easy. As we have seen from many of those who wrote in, the safest listener may be a professional who has been trained in the area of sexual assault or another survivor who is already into the on-going process of recovery.

Appendix II will be a guide to both types of listener since support groups may provide a chance to meet other survivors.

Increased funding: More monies are critically required in order to meet both the following issues and to make a statement to the community about the importance of assistance for victims of rape. The idea that a survivor in some areas is basically asked to save her crisis for up to three months until counselling becomes available is a statement of the low priority Australian society and governments have of this women's issue. Seventy per cent of the survivors in this survey who tried to obtain assistance from a sexual assault service were unable to receive assistance immediately. Yet Rape Crisis Services were perceived by most survivors as far more supportive than police, family or friends.

Increased 24-hour services: Currently not all crisis agencies have the resources to maintain service around the clock.

Increased services to bush areas: Those in remote areas need to have crisis and on-going counselling made available to them.

Increased services for adult children survivors: As sexual assault becomes a less shameful act for a victim to reveal, and through the inevitable 'acting out', more and more adults who have experienced assault whilst children, are needing assistance.

Multicultural services: Crisis services and advocacy are sorely required by both the Aboriginal and the non-English speaking communities. In both areas a major part of that service must be to make it user or culturally friendly and to encourage access.

Trust is developmental. It will not happen over night. How could it? For so long the survivor has not been able to trust and had what should be a basic right for all people violated, over and over again. Many who have worked through the issues of their sexual assaults have found that the growth of trust is not only slow but also a part of what many refer to as a spiritual journey. Somewhere in the process of disclosure, affirmation and validation, hopefully the woman can begin also to trust in herself—in her integrity as a human being and in her reality of the past. We have heard women doing just that, at various points along the continuum, throughout the previous pages.

Part of the healing process is extraordinarily painful; again we have witnessed that from some of the survivors. Those symptoms of sexual assault mask feelings of pain and anger that must be released and felt—not a pleasant process but certainly a rewarding one as the survivor moves from fragmentation and lack of centeredness to some sort of wholeness.

The next survivor is fittingly one of the last of the voices to be heard; fittingly because her voice is more powerful than many. She has apparently been in the process of healing which has given her some empowerment with a bit of humour.

I have been threatened with rape so many times I have lost count. I believed that these threats were genuine and would have resulted in an attack if I had handled them in a different way. Most of these threats were made whilst I was a member of [an occupation that is largely male]. I found the following statements defused the situation and had quite a profound effect, that is, they all backed down.

1.   A genuine statement that I would report them, that is, 'If you lay one hand on me I will report you to the police/your superior so fast that your feet won't touch the ground and you will spend your life in prison, so who's the most powerful now?'

2.   A statement that I will not allow anyone to make me their victim. i.e. 'I believe that reading a comic or eating an apple is effective in turning them off'.

3.   Make a statement about male performance anxiety. That is, 'You get three tries and if the earth doesn't move, you're out!' or 'If you attempt to rape me I will tell everyone what size your penis is and whether you are any good or not and I might just lie a little and say you are smaller than you actually are.'

(Note: The preceding is not necessarily a safe response in every potential rape situation. Unfortunately there does not seem to be any set advise on the best response other than to use one's intuition.)

The recovery of the individual can have an impact on the rest of the system. If more and more women flood the criminal justice system and speak up about their victimisation then society and its structures such as the courts and the police may be pressured to respond. And, of course, the individual's healing can also be affected by the other components. It is not a one-way flow, but a dynamic interchange.

CHANGING THE CRIMINAL JUSTICE RESPONSE

The criminal justice system can play a major role in changing attitudes and preventing both rape and the re-victimisation of the victim. However, as illustrated in Figure 1, the criminal justice system is influenced by the prevailing beliefs of the culture. Just as norms about rape cannot be understood without perceiving how they fit within an existing cultural framework, the workers in the criminal justice system cannot be seen in isolation from societal beliefs. It is therefore not sufficient to change legislation; new laws are hollow promises of what could be if they are not accompanied by shifts in the attitudes and behaviour of the police and the judiciary.

The Laws and the Courts[2]

There has been significant law reform in reference to sexual assault in every state and territory of Australia. Rape legislation has always been set apart from other criminal laws with implicit or tacit rules such as a mandated prompt reporting to validate that a crime had taken place. In the past (and in some cases to the present) rape laws centred around the protection of the defendant's rights. Thus historically, the victim's dress/appearance at the time of the assault, her previous sex life, her physical resistance, and quick reporting were significant components of the trial. In a variety of ways, the victim became the prosecuted. This has changed to an unknown, but probably limited, degree if the experiences of the 'Without Consent' sample are representative.

One reform model (for example, New South Wales) has been to create several graded offences of sexual assault to replace the old charge of rape. By offering different levels of seriousness, it was hoped that convictions and reporting would increase; this would appear to have taken place in New South Wales (Carter 1991) although there were no such increases following a similar innovation in California (Polk 1985).

The legal definition of rape or sexual assault has also been broadened to include penetration of the mouth or anus by any body part or object. This is substantial progress from old laws which narrowly defined rape as vaginal penetration by the penis. In addition, in at least some jurisdictions such as the ACT the victim's evidence can be given in camera with a support person present and a victim's name cannot be published without her consent (Follett 1986).

---

2. The literature on law reform in the area of sexual assault is voluminous. Material presented on this subject was integrated from numerous of these sources (Carter 1991; Franzway et al. 1989; L'Orange & Egger 1987; Scutt 1990).

The requirement for the judge to warn the jury against convicting on the word of the victim alone (corroboration) has been removed; however the judge still has the discretion to deliver such a warning. Further, in many jurisdictions, at the statutory level, the assumption that a woman has to physically resist to constitute a bona fide rape has been removed. Again, the gap between laws and practice has been apparent.

A woman is no longer supposed to abdicate her sexual rights in marriage; a wife's consent is no longer to be implied. However, the reality is that few rapes by cohabiting spouse/rapists are either reported or tried. Even estrangement has proven problematic. Extreme violence appears to be a necessary component in the marital rape for it to be deemed as a criminal act. Certainly the change in legislation has not resulted in a flow of marital rape cases through the courts. In September 1991 a man in Tasmania was sentenced for the rape of his wife (Browne 1991). This was the first marital rape trial in that state although immunity was abolished in 1987. The couple were estranged. *More reform is needed in this area.*

Other problems which require legislative change include the continuation of judges' discretion in allowing evidence about the victim's sexual history; the admissibility of unsworn testimony by the defendant whereas the victim is cross-examined; and the issue of consent. The last is perhaps the most problematic. Consent needs to be defined clearly such as in the Western Australian legislation which states that consent must be freely given without force, threat or intimidation (Rape Reform 1986). The consent/non-consent dichotomy may be too narrow to allow for women's experience since the laws are made and interpreted by males (Smart 1990). Thus it needs to be spelled out or it ends up with a definition used in practice that is based upon sexist attitudes. Consent needs to be more specifically defined in all jurisdictions removing the attention from the victim to the defendant. The absence of 'no' does not mean consent; the expression of 'yes' does mean consent. All jurisdictions need to eliminate any reference to physical resistance as necessary either directly or indirectly.

In addition, many researchers have expressed dismay at the light sentences in general which are dispensed to rapists by the judges. Do the current sentences reflect the horrific nature of this violent crime? Heavier penalties and a more offender-oriented trial should contribute to improved deterrence. Those in the 'Without Consent' sample who had taken their perpetrator to court had experienced lower rates of imprisonment in recent years.

Many of the voices we have heard through these pages have decried the lenient treatment that their perpetrator received in the courts, as the following survivor comments:

It is clear that these rapists only worry about if they are going to get caught and how many years they will get. The victim never gets over rape and the punishment to the offender should be more severe. The offender should be publicly whipped, with signs on him saying he's an [expletive] who has committed rape. The rapist should be publicly humiliated, should be made to feel the shame, humiliation and helplessness of being tied up and whipped. This is the correct way to punish the rapist. Instead of protecting them by shielding them from publicity and the public when rape is a crime against the community as much as theft or robbery are.

The rapist is getting away with too much. The easy treatment they get in court has got to change and they should be put on trial, not the victim.

Please keep on doing shows to stress the injustice victims receive through the court system so our attitudes towards this crime can be seen as just that, a crime which is not excusable. Please put on TV commercials that aggressive behaviour towards women is not acceptable. Aggressive behaviour is not macho, it is a crime!

As indicated above, many of the new laws still retain old elements which are to be used at the discretion of the judges, for example, allowing testimony about the victim's past or the corroboration rule. Further, although new legislation may remove a concept, it does not stop judges from raising it in their remarks to the jury or in their sentencing. For instance, although Victorian law now says that force is not an issue, judges' remarks have implied their persistent view that a struggle is necessary (Scutt 1993a).

Traditionally, and to the present, the victim is frequently re-victimised in the court-room. In no other violent crime is the victim subjected to the type of scrutiny and interrogation that befalls the rape victim in the court. She has traditionally been shown as either pure and chaste—hence a bona fide victim or impure, a 'bad' woman. Thus, a judge in Victoria recently gave a rapist a less severe sentence since the victim was a prostitute who, the judge felt, would not be as psychologically affected by rape (Scutt 1993b; Stuart 1993). This type of attitude and trial experience have to change in order to encourage both more survivors to report and prosecute and to increase the sanctioning of rapists.

The laws may change but unless the attitudes of the judges and juries change, the impact of new legislation is limited. Prevention requires increased education of the judiciary. They must be taught what rape is and its impact on the victim. Judges must be required to receive training in issues concerning rape. Unless this training is mandatory, it is doubtful that those who need it the most would attend. The main purpose would be to confront stereotypes and myths which differentiate between 'real' or legitimate rape and others (husband, boyfriend, date). New appointees should receive such training prior to working at the bench; however, a workshop should be offered periodically. No judge should be permitted to hear a rape case unless she or he has been certified as having received the course.

Lawyers should also be required to receive a similar type of training. All law schools should include such a component which should be at least one half of a course length if not an entire class (in other words, not a one hour lecture). No lawyer should be permitted to be a participant in a rape case unless she or he has received such training.

Police

Prevention of rape requires increased training and education about both sexual assault and its impact on the victim. The perceptions of many of the survivors in the 'Without Consent' sample have been found in other studies. A high proportion of callers in several phone-ins have reported negative experiences with law enforcement officers. These include not being believed, feeling judged, blamed or ridiculed, treated in an insensitive manner, and talked out of proceeding with charges (Report to the Women's Coordination Unit 1984; Corbett 1993). In Victorian research, police were found to hold a more stereotypical view of rape victims than were other occupations and their responses to victims were still orientated around what they considered to be indicators of a valid rape: prompt reporting, resistance, and emotional distress (Cabassi 1990). Interviews with police have confirmed their adherence to the myths: that women contribute to their own victimisation and that violence is a natural part of masculinity (Carter 1991).

There have been some changes in police practices in charging offenders: the number of police designated 'unfounded reports' has apparently dropped during the past decade (Broadhurst 1990). However, this must be placed in the context of what had been traditionally an extremely high level of 'unfounded' designations (Scutt 1988). Thus, a recent Victorian study found that only one out of three victim reports ended in police charges (Brereton 1991). Within the 'Without Consent' sample, more women were reporting to the police in recent years than ten, fifteen and twenty years ago and a higher proportion of these reports were culminating in arrest. However, the anecdotal evidence certainly verifies all of these other researchers' findings. The women whose experiences have been recounted in the current study confirm that, for many, the police response was inadequate at best and re-victimising at worst.

I lost trust for Australian legal system—there is no justice. Also the police were very insensitive and did not believe me until they found out that the same man had been charged twice before—also charges were dropped.
In court I was made to feel that I was the one on trial.
Therefore if my daughter or myself will be raped, in the future, I would not report it to the police knowing how you get treated it is not worth going to court.

There is some indication, as shown in Appendix I, that there has been improvement in police treatment of rape victims over the last twenty-five years. However, it has not been enough. Changing police attitudes must be a part of prevention. The sexist nature of the police sub-culture and its preponderance of males make this a highly problematic hope for the future. They can, however, be retrained about the reality of rape and what it does to its victims. Supportive and sympathetic interviewing techniques could be taught. All jurisdictions need to establish very unambiguous protocols for police to follow when they are interacting with a sexual assault survivor. These pro-cedures should be developed in conjunction with sexual assault services and reflect the sensitivity and understanding about rape that they have hopefully been taught.

In each jurisdiction police should set up an operational plan for dealing with sexual assault victims that involves liaison with local sexual assault services. If the police have Orders which dictate how they should respond then discretion which permits abuse could be minimised. Police performance vis-à-vis rape victims needs to be continuously monitored to ensure adherence with whatever strict procedures are mandated.

CHANGING SOCIAL ATTITUDES

There can be no real substantial change in either the incidence of rape, its reporting and the degree of shame carried by its victims without the shifting of public attitudes. A major effort must be made at repudiating the false myths and stereotypes concerning rape that were discussed in Chapter 1. It is hoped that this book goes some way in doing just that. It is just a tiny step that must be replicated in other forms in order to continue to bring the secrets out into the light where they can be seen; their truth can be used to repudiate the false myths that flourish in the shadows of secrecy maintained by the patriarchy.

Aside from changing views about rape, it is also necessary to change attitudes about sex, romance and consent. In part this could be the outcome of fundamental shifts in attitudes about females. Without these essential changes in the values and behaviour relating to males, females, power, and the ethos of violence, there will be little transformation in the incidence or reporting of rape. For, if rape is more common in patriarchal and misogynist cultures, then one goal must be the equality of females in all areas of the society and a value system which does not generate antipathy towards women and gender stratification. As one survivor writes:

Rape and incest reflect an attitude to women and children that is part of patriarchal attitudes and the world generally, one of power—over, control, exploitation and brutality.

For the violence to stop and for this planet to survive we all need to change our attitudes. We need to review the 'feminine', the gentle, the young, we need to respect the 'other'.

Men—I do not hate you, I understand the conditioning and forces that bring out violence in you. But I beg you PLEASE CHANGE before every life form on this planet pays the price of your violence and exploitation.

Rape is, therefore, an act of domination which cannot be seen as isolated from the masculine structures of the society in which it takes place. Prevention and reporting require attitudes about the nature of rape, the nature of male/female relations to be modified. The attitudes that promulgate male violence need to be changed and women's relatively powerless position within Australian society should be radically transformed.

As stated at the beginning of this book, one major shift must be to recognise how erroneous many of the beliefs about rape are. Through these pages we have heard about the reality of rape: the who, how, why, and consequences. It is vitally important that the potential victims learn that the greatest risk of rape is from someone they know.

- Learn assertiveness.

- Learn self defence.

- Know your sexual rights as a person and as a partner.

- Be cautious about going to a date's home or having him to yours, particularly if alcohol has been consumed. Most rapes do not occur outside; they take place in the victim's home. Most rapes do not involve strangers; the offender is more likely to be a date or an acquaintance than someone you do not know.

- Understand that rape does not have to involve physical force. If an acquaintance, date, or spouse insists on having sex with you without your free and willing consent, he is committing a criminal act.

It is not the author's intention to terrify young girls and women about the dangers of sex and/or men. It is this author's intent, however, to inform these young girls and women about the potential risk and to encourage some caution—not fear— but prudence and awareness.

One key to change lies in reaching the next generation, the children in Australia. The school, through its curriculum, material, definitions of appropriate/inappropriate behaviour and role modelling are critically important. A non-partisan body needs to be created in order to assure all Australians that their children are receiving non-gender harassing education. Gender equity programs should be set up in all school districts. Clear statements of what constitutes harassment and violence must be made, communicated and affirmed through serious sanctions.

Thus, at least one by-product of gender equity programs and other basic shifts in power politics can be the empowerment of females.

One other thing I would like to say is that I feel girls especially need to be taught how to say 'No' and to be taught self-defence in school which is something needed in today's environment, instead of teaching all this stuff we never really have any use for.

The media is a vital link in changing societal attitudes about rape and about other forms of violence and gender inequities. While the focus is often placed on pornography and physical violence, it is important to recognise that more covert examples of sexism are rampant throughout the media. As one survivor commented:

The media, television shows have a lot to answer for in the way they portray women as being a meat market; who ask for what they get in the way they look. In fact contribute to the crimes and are criminals by sending out the wrong message that to rape women is okay.

If we need to teach males that 'no' means 'no', then the television soap operas viewed by so many of an impressionable age should stop presenting visual and verbal messages which state or imply the opposite. Research is sorely needed in this area and should be funded by the government as a prerequisite to policy formulation.

LAST WORDS

The path ahead is not an easy one, neither for the individual survivor nor Australian society as a whole. Not easy but definitely necessary. It will require a concerted effort by governmental bodies, other structures within our culture and the survivors themselves. It is not easy to break the silence. It hurts to tell your story once again and re-live the pain and terror and to feel the ambivalence of those who listen. Not easy but definitely necessary for healing.

I believe that your book will encourage women to not keep their secrets, but to expose the rapists and to seek help.

As I say, 'we are rewarded in being sick, and punished for being well' by society. I have been shunned for telling people the truth about myself but I still believe that women need to tell the truth. I am glad that you want to expose Australia's vilest secret, for Australia really needs to know.

REFERENCES, FURTHER READINGS & INFORMATION

Alder, Christine 1985, 'An exploration of self-reported sexually aggressive behavior', *Crime and Delinquency*, vol. 31, no. 2, April, pp. 306-31.

Beattie, Melody 1989, *Beyond Codependency*, Collins Dove, Melbourne.

Belknap, Joanne 1989, 'The sexual victimization of unmarried women by nonrelative acquaintances', in *Violence in Dating Relationships*, eds Maureen A. Pirog-Good & Jan E. Stets, Praeger Publishers, New York, pp. 205-18.

Black, Claudia 1980, *It Will Never Happen to Me*, Medical Administration, Boulder, Colorado.

Bonney, Roseanne 1985, *Crimes (Sexual Assault) Amendment Act 1981 Monitoring and Evaluation, Interim Report No. 1: Characteristics of the Complainant, the Defendant and the Offence*, New South Wales Bureau of Crime Statistics and Research, Sydney.

Bowker, Lee H. 1983, 'Marital rape: a distinct syndrome?', *Social Casework*, vol. 64, no. 6, June, pp. 347-52.

Bownes, Ian T., O'Gorman, Ethna C. & Sayers, Angela 1991, 'Rape—a comparison of stranger and acquaintance results', *Medical Science Law*, vol. 31, no. 2, pp. 102-9.

Bradshaw, John 1988, *Bradshaw on: The Family*, Health Communications, Deerfield, FL.

Brereton, David 1993, 'Rape prosecutions in Victoria', in *Women and the Law*, Conference Proceedings No. 16, eds P. Easteal & S. McKillop, Australian Institute of Criminology, Canberra.

Broadhurst, R.G. 1990, 'Counting rapes: reporting and recording practices in Western Australia', *Criminology Australia*, vol. 2, no. 1, July/August, pp. 8-10.

Broadhurst, R.G. & Maller, R.A. 1992, 'The recidivism of sex offenders in the Western Australian prison population', *British Journal of Criminology*, vol. 32, no. 1, Winter, pp. 54-80.

Browne, Roland 1991, 'Developments in Tasmania's rape laws', *Legal Service Bulletin*, vol. 16, no. 6, p. 286.

Bullock, Jackie (Narrator) 1992, Surviving Rape: A journey through grief. Audio visual, United States.

Burgess, Ann Wolbert & Holmstrom, Lynda Lytle 1977, 'Rape trauma syndrome', in *Forcible Rape: The crime, the victim, and the offender*, eds D. Chappell, R. Geis & G. Geis, Columbia University Press, New York, pp. 315-28.

Cabassi, Julia, 1990, 'Police response to rape', *Hearsay*, vol. 24, no. 3.

Carmody, Moira 1990, Sexual Assault of People with an Intellectual Disability, final report prepared for the Women's Coordination Unit, Parramatta, NSW.

Carmody, Moira 1984, 'The fear of rape', *Social Alternatives*, vol. 4, no. 3, pp. 21-22.

Carter, Meredith 1991, 'Judicial sexism and law reform', *Legal Service Bulletin*, vol. 16, no. 1, February, pp. 29-32.

CASA House 1992, *A Pastoral report to the churches on sexual violence against women and children of the church community*, Centre Against Sexual Assault, Royal Women's Hospital, Melbourne, in collaboration with the Women, Church and Sexual Violence Project Advisory Group with representatives from the Uniting Church in Australia, the Catholic Church, the Anglican Church, Churches of Christ and the Salvation Army, CASA House, Melbourne.

Chappell, Duncan 1989, 'Sexual criminal violence', in *Pathways to Criminal Violence,* eds N.A. Weiner & M.E. Wolfgang, SAGE Publications Inc., Newbury Park, CA., pp. 68-108.

Cobb, Kenneth, A. & Schauer, Nancy R. 1977, 'Michigan's criminal sexual assault law', in *Forcible Rape: The crime, the victim, and the offender*, eds D. Chappell, R. Geis & G. Geis, Columbia University Press, New York, pp. 170-86.

Corbett, Lea 1993, 'Lunar landscapes: the dark side of sexual assault and the law', in *Women and the Law*, Conference Proceedings No. 16, eds P. Easteal & S. McKillop, Australian Institute of Criminology, Canberra.

Crime Victims Research and Treatment Center 1992, *Rape in America*, National Victim Center, Arlington, VA.

Criminal Justice Newsletter 1992, 'Rape found 5 times more common than earlier studies indicated', *Criminal Justice Newsletter*, vol. 23, no. 7, April, pp. 6-7.

David, Jennifer, Stubbs, Julie & Pegrum, Francis 1988, 'Services for victims of crime in Australia: Directory and bibliography', Report to the Criminology Research Council, held in the J.V. Barry Library, Australian Institute of Criminology, Canberra.

Easteal, Patricia 1993, *Killing the Beloved*, Australian Studies in Law, Crime and Justice, Australian Institute of Criminology, Canberra.

---------- 1992a, *'Rape'*, Violence Prevention Today, No. 1, Australian Institute of Criminology, Canberra.

---------- 1992b, 'Battered woman syndrome: what is reasonable?' *Alternative Law Journal*, vol. 17, no. 5, pp. 220-23.

Evans, Patricia 1992, *The Verbally Abusive Relationship: How to recognise it and how to respond*, Bob Adams, Holbrook, MA.

Feldman-Summers, Shirley & Norris, Jeanette 1984, 'Differences between rape victims who report and those who do not report to a public agency', *Journal of Applied Social Psychology*, vol. 14, no. 6, November-December, pp. 562-73.

Finkelhor, David 1985, 'Marital rape: The misunderstood crime', *National Conference on Domestic Violence*, Seminar Proceedings No. 12. ed. Suzanne E. Hatty, Australian Institute of Criminology, Canberra, pp. 203-14.

---------- 1979, *Sexually Victimized Children*, The Free Press, New York.

Flowers, Ronald B. 1987, *Women and Criminality: The woman as victim, offender, and practitioner*, Greenwood Press, Westport, Connecticut.

Follett, Rosemary 1986, 'Reform of sexual offences legislation', *Lobby*, Summer/Autumn, pp. 5-6.

Franzway, Suzanne, Court, Dianne & Connell, R.W. 1989, 'Sexual Violence', *Staking a Claim: Feminism, bureaucracy and the State*, Allen & Unwin, Sydney, pp. 104-29.

Gelinas, D.J. 1983, 'Persisting negative effects of incest', *Psychiatry*, vol. 46, no. 4, pp. 312-32.

Gilmour, Kate 1990, 'Violence and sexual assault', in *The Scandal of Family Violence*, ed. Anne Amos, Uniting Church Press, Melbourne, pp. 26-31.

Girelli, S.A., Resick, P.A., Marhoefer-Dvorak, S. & Hutter, C.K. 1986, 'Subjective distress and violence during rape: Their effects on long-term fear', *Victims and Violence*, vol. 1, no. 1, pp. 35-46.

Girelli, S.A., Schwartz, J., Williams, H. & Pepitone-Rockwell, F. 1981, 'Construction of a rape awareness scale', *Victimology*, vol. 6, no. 1, pp. 110-19.

Going to Court: Information for women who are victims of sexual assault 1986, Women's Coordination Unit, New South Wales Premier's Department in conjunction with the New South Wales Sexual Assault Committee, Sydney.

Green, Lorraine 1987, 'South Australian research on common perceptions about rape', *Legal Service Bulletin*, vol. 12, no. 2, April, pp. 77-78.

Horley, Sandra 1991, *The Charm Syndrome: Why charming men can make dangerous lovers*, Macmillan, London.

---------- 1988, *Love and Pain: A survival handbook for women*, Bedford Square Press, London.

Jones, Ann & Schechter, Susan 1988, *When Love Goes Wrong: What to do when you can't do anything right*, Century Hutchison, New York.

Kissane, Karen 1993, 'Rape's Rough Justice', *Time*, vol. 8, no. 4, pp. 38-39.

Koss, Mary P., Dinero, Thomas E., Seibel, Cynthia A. & Cox, Susan L. 1988, 'Stranger and acquaintance rape', *Psychology of Women Quarterly*, no. 12, pp. 1-24.

Koss, Mary P. 1989, 'Hidden rape: Sexual aggression and victimization in a national sample of students in higher education', in *Violence in Dating Relationships*, eds Maureen A. Pirog-Good & Jan E. Stets, Praeger Publishers, New York, pp. 145-68.

Law Reform Commissioner 1976, *Rape prosecutions: court procedures and rules of evidence*, Law Reform Commission, Melbourne.

L'Orange, Helen & Egger, Sandra 1987, 'Adult victims of sexual assault: An evaluation of the reforms', *Proceedings of a Seminar on Sexual Assault Law Reform in the 1980s: To where from now?*, Institute of Criminology, Sydney University Law School, Sydney, pp. 12-38.

Main, Nikki 1991, 'HIV and rape', *National Aids Bulletin*, vol. 5, no. 2, March, pp. 36-38.

Matchett, Ruth 1988, 'Beyond these walls: Domestic violence in Queensland', *Channel '88*, vol. 4, no. 88, November, pp. 1-3.

McSherry, B. 1993, 'Legislating to change social attitudes: the significance of Section 37(a) of the Victorian Crimes Act 1958', in *Without Consent: Confronting adult sexual violence*, Conference Proceedings No. 20, ed. P. Easteal, Australian Institute of Criminology, Canberra.

Mishkin, Barry D. 1989, 'Date rape—terror from a friend', *Australian Police Journal*, vol. 43, no. 4, pp. 155-57.

Muehlenhard, C.L. 1989, 'Misinterpreted dating behaviors and the risk of date rape', in *Violence in Dating Relationships*, eds M.A. Pirog-Good & J.E. Stets, Praeger Publishers, New York, pp. 241-56.

National Committee on Violence Against Women 1991, *National Strategy on Violence Against Women*, Office of the Status of Women, Canberra.

Naffin, Ngaire 1984, 'South Australia's rape law: A specific focus for investigation', *Legal Service Bulletin*, vol. 9, August, pp. 158-162.

Nancy, W. 1991, *On the Path: Affirmations for adults recovering from child sexual abuse*, HarperSanFrancisco, San Francisco.

New South Wales Child Protection Council 1992, Out of court videotaping of the statements of children who are the alleged victims of child sexual assault in New South Wales, Sydney. Researched and written by Fran Waugh, revised and edited by Eithne O'Donovan, cover title 'Discussion Paper'.

New South Wales Child Sexual Assault Task Force 1984, *Community consultation paper*, Government Printer, Sydney.

New South Wales Government. Violence Against Women and Children Law Reform Task Force 1987, *Consultation paper*, Government Printer, Sydney.

NiCarthy, Ginny 1987, *The One Who Got Away: Women who left abusive partners*, Seal Press, Seattle.

---------- 1986, *Getting Free: You can end abuse and take back your life*, Seal Press, Seattle.

NiCarthy, Ginny & Davidson, Sue 1989, *You Can Be Free: An easy-to-read handbook for abused women*, Seal Press, Seattle.

Peretti, Peter O. & Cozzens, Nancy 1983, 'Characteristics of female rapees not reporting and reporting the first incidence of rape', *Indian Journal of Criminology*, no. 11, July, pp. 119-24.

Polk, Kenneth 1985, 'Rape reform and criminal justice processing', *Crime and Delinquency*, vol. 31, no. 2, April, pp. 191-205.

Pittman, Lise 1990, 'Surviving sexual assault', *Parity*, vol. 3, no. 4, pp. 7-8.

Real Rape Law Coalition 1992, 'No Real Justice', *Family Violence and Sexual Assault Bulletin*, May.

Reekie, Gail & Wilson, Paul 1993, 'Rape, resistance and women's rights of self-defence', in *Without Consent: Confronting adult sexual violence*, Conference Proceedings No. 20, ed. P. Easteal, Australian Institute of Criminology, Canberra.

Reform 1986, 'Rape reform', *Reform*, no. 44, October, pp. 192-93.

Report on Sexual Assault Phone-In 1984, Appendix VI on the report to the Women's Coordination Unit of the NSW Premier's Department.

Roxburgh, Tor 1989, *Taking Control: Help for women and children escaping domestic violence*, Greenhouse Publications, Melbourne.

Safety in numbers (no date), videorecording Swinburne Film and Television School, Hawthorn, Vic.

Sandra's Garden n.d, [video], Melbourne, AFI.

Sandford, Linda 1991, *Strong at the Broken Places: Overcoming the trauma of childhood abuse*, Virago, London.

Schwartz, Judy, Williams, Heather & Pepitone-Rockwell, Fran 1981, 'Construction of a rape awareness scale', *Victimology*, vol. 6, no. 1, pp. 110-19.

Scott, Dorothy & Hewitt, Lesley 1983, 'Short term adjustment to rape and the utilization of a sexual assault counselling service', *Australian & New Zealand Journal of Criminology*, vol. 16, June, pp. 93-105.

Scutt, Jocelynne A. 1993a, 'The incredible woman: a recurring character in criminal law', in *Women and the Law*, Conference Proceedings No. 16, eds P. Easteal & S. McKillop, Australian Institute of Criminology, Canberra.

---------- 1993b, 'Rape, prostitution and the chaste woman', in *Without Consent*, Conference Proceedings No. 20, ed. P. Easteal, Australian Institute of Criminology, Canberra.

---------- 1990, *Women and the Law*, The Law Book Company Limited, Sydney.

---------- 1988, 'Women and the police', in *Police in our Society*, eds Ian Freckelton & Hugh Selby, Butterworths, Sydney, pp. 26-43.

---------- 1980, *Rape Law Reform: A collection of conference papers*, Australian Institute of Criminology, Canberra.

Sexual Abuse Self-Help Association 1992, *Not In My Family*, Sexual Abuse Self-Help Association (Western Australia) Inc., Midland, WA.

Shotland, R. Lance & Goodstein, Lynne 1983, 'Just because she doesn't want to doesn't mean it's rape: An experimentally based causal model of the perception of rape in a dating situation', *Social Psychology Quarterly*, vol. 46, no. 3, pp. 220-32.

Smart, Carol 1990, 'Law's truth/women's experience', in *Dissenting Opinions: Feminist explorations in law and society*, ed. R. Graycar, Allen & Unwin, Sydney.

Special Report: Rape and other sexual offences 1976, Criminal Law and Penal Methods Reform Committee of South Australia, Government Printer, Adelaide.

Stewart, Libby 1990, 'Beyond survival of sexual assault', *Community Quarterly*, no. 18, pp. 14-23.

Stuart, Donna 1993, 'Who is on trial? The criminal justice system and the treatment of sexual assault survivors', in *Without Consent*, Conference Proceedings No. 16, ed. P. Easteal, Australian Institute of Criminology, Canberra.

Surviving Sexual Assault (no date), video recording produced for Sexual Assault Referral Centre by the Video Production Unit Health Department of WA, Perth.

Sydney Rape Crisis Centre 1990, *Surviving Rape: A handbook to help women become aware of the reality of rape*, 2nd edn, Redfern Legal Centre Publishers Ltd, Sydney.

The London Rape Crisis Centre 1984, *Sexual Violence: The reality from women*, the Women's Press Handbook Series, Women's Press, London.

Trachtenburg, Milton S. 1989, *Stop the Merry-Go-Round: Stories of women who broke the cycle of abusive relationships*, Tab Books, Blue Ridge Summit:

Warshaw, Robin 1988, *I Never Called It Rape: The Ms report on recognizing, fighting and surviving date and acquaintance rape*, Harper & Row, New York.

Whangarei Rape Crisis Centre 1989, *My Body Belongs To Me: What to do about sexual violation*, Whangarei Rape Crisis Centre, Whangarei.

Women's Legal Resources Centre 1990, *Compensation for Victims of Sexual Assault*, Women's Legal Resources Centre, Sydney.

Walker, John, 1993, *Crime in Australia 1992*, Australian Institute of Criminology, Canberra.

Weatherburn, Don & Devery, Christopher 1991, 'How violent is Australia?', in *Australian Violence: Contemporary perspectives*, eds D. Chappell, P. Grabosky & H. Strang, Australian Institute of Criminology, Canberra, pp. 23-39.

Weekley, K.J.C. 1986, *Rape: A 4 year policy study of victims*, South Australian Police Department, South Australia.

Wegscheider-Cruse, Sharon 1985, *Choice Making*, Health Communication, Florida.

Westbury, Virginia 1991, 'Women hating—an Australian talent?', *Bulletin*, 8 October, pp. 82-84.

Whitfield, Charles 1979, 'Children of alcoholics: treatment issues', *Services for Children of Alcoholics*, NIAAA Research Monograph 4, Washington.

Wilson, Paul 1989, 'Sexual and violent crime in Australia: rhetoric and reality', *Current Affairs Bulletin*, vol. 65, no. 10, March, pp. 11-17.

Young, Marlene A. 1991, 'Sexual assault: the crime and its consequences', *NOVA Newsletter*, vol. 15, no. 7.

•

The following resources were extracted from book lists supplied by:

The Feminist Bookshop
Shop 9, Orange Grove Plaza
Balmain Road, LILYFIELD 2040
Tel:(02) 810 2666. Fax: (02) 818 5745

Adams, Caren, *Free of the Shadows: Recovering from sexual violence*

Adams, Caren, *Nobody Told Me It Was Rape: Acquaintance rape and exploitation*

Anonymous, *Growing Through the Pain: The incest survivor's companion*

Ayers & James, *It's OK to Say No: Activity book*

Ayers & James, *It's OK to Say No: Colouring book*

Bart, Pauline & O'Brien, Patricia, *Stopping Rape: Successful survival strategies*

Bass, Ellen & Davis, Laura, *Courage To Heal: For survivors of sexual abuse* (2 cassettes)

Bass, Ellen & Davis, Laura, *Courage To Heal Workbook: For men and women survivors CSA*

Bass, Ellen & Davis, Laura, *Allies in Healing: For partners/friends of incest survivors* (2 cassettes)

Bass Ellen, *I Never Told Anyone: Writing by women survivors*

Bass Ellen, *Outgrowing The Pain: Writings by women survivors of CSA*

Bass Ellen, *Beginning To Heal: For survivors of abuse*

Bloch, Douglas, *Words That Heal: Affirmations and meditations*

Blume, Sue, *Secret Survivors: The after effects of incest*

Boumil, Marcia, *Date Rape: The secret epidemic*

Butler, Sandra, *Conspiracy Of Silence: The trauma of incest*

Courtois, Christine, *Healing The Incest Wound: Adult survivors in therapy*

Driver, Emily, *Child Sexual Abuse: Feminist perspectives*

Dworkin, Andrea, *Woman Hating: Sexism and male violence*

Dworkin, Andrea, *Mercy: A novel about sexual violence*

Estrich, Susan, *Real Rape: How the law victimises women*

Finney, Lynne, *Reach For The Rainbow: For survivors of sexual abuse*

Fraser, Sylvia, *My Father's House: A memoir of incest and of healing*

Fredrickson, Renee, *Repressed Memories: Recovery from sexual abuse*

Gallagher, Vera, *Becoming Whole Again: For women survivors of CSA*

Gordon, Margaret, *Female Fear: The social cost of rape*

Gulliver, Penny, *Self Defence For Women: Australian video and guide*

Hart-Rossi, Janie, *Protect Your Child From Sexual Abuse: A parent's guide*

Hennekens, Candace, *Healing Your Life: Recovery from spousal abuse* (2 cassettes)

Herman, Judith, *Trauma and Recovery: The aftermath of violence*

Herman, Judith, *Father Daughter Incest: Abuse or power in the family*

Hooper, Carol Ann, *Mothers Surviving: Child sexual abuse*

Jarvis-Kirkendall, Carol, *If She Is Raped: Healing child sexual abuse*

Johnson, Janis, *Mothers Of Incest Survivors: Another side of the story*

Johnson, Kathryn, *If You Are Raped: What every woman needs to know*

Kehoe, Patricia, *Helping Abused Children: For incest workers*

Kehoe, Patricia, *Something Happened And I'm Scared To Tell: A book for young victims of abuse*

Kelly, Liz, *Surviving Sexual Violence: Survivors not victims*

King, County, *He Told Me Not To Tell: A parent's guide*

King, County, *So What's It To Me? Activity guide: for boys*

King, County, *Helping Your Child To Be Safe: Particularly for Asian children*

King, County, *Healing Celebration: A manual for facilitators: adult survivors of CSA*

King, County, *Top Secret: Teen sexual assault information and discussion guide*

LaFontaine, Jean, *Child Sexual Abuse: The evidence*

Lena, Dan, *Sexual Assault: How to defend yourself*

Levy, Barrie, *Dating Violence: Young women in danger*

Maltz, Wendy, *Sexual Healing Journey: Surviving sexual abuse*

McEvoy, Alan, *If She Is Raped: For husbands, fathers, male friends*

McNaron, Toni, *Voices in the Night: Women speaking about incest*

McShane, Claudette, *Warning! Dating May Be Hazardous: Sexual, physical and verbal abuse*

Rowland, Judith, *Rape: The ultimate violation*

Sakheim, David, *Out of Darkness: Satanic and ritual abuse*

Saphira, Miriam, *Sexual Abuse of Children: Information and help*

Search, Gay, *Last Taboo: Sexual abuse of children*

See, Helena, *Reclaiming Our Days: Meditations for incest survivors*

Spies, Karen, *Everything You Need To Know About Incest: Classroom discussion*

Spring, Jacqueline, *Cry Hard And Swim: The story of an incest survivor*

Stanko, Elizabeth, *Intimate Intrusions: Women's experience of male violence*

Thomas, T., *Surviving With Serenity: Daily meditations for survivors*

Thomas, T., *Men Surviving Incest: Sharing the process of recovery*

Turner, Janine, *Home Is Where It Hurts: Guidance for victims of sexual abuse*

Utain, Marsha, *Scream Louder: Healing with an incest survivor*

Walsh, Deirdre, *Surviving Sexual Abuse: Help for survivors*

Ward, Elizabeth, *Father Daughter Rape: A feminist analysis*

Wegscheider-Cruse, Sharon, *Learning To Love Yourself: Finding your self-worth*

APPENDIX I

As stated in Chapter 1, almost 3,000 surveys from survivors of sexual assault were received at the Australian Institute of Criminology. The responses were coded, entered into the computer and analysed. Some of the results of that analysis appear in this appendix.

To correspond with the structure of the book, most of the tables are organised by the relationship of the perpetrator to the victim. In a sense this provides a summary of what we have learned through the voices of the survivors about their ages, injuries, disclosure, reporting to police, and the responses of the latter, friends and families, and the courts. The numbers illustrate that there are some differences in these variables based on whether the rapist was a husband, father, date, stranger or acquaintance. They also show in stark percentages the painful reality of rape and often, at best, ambivalent reactions from those to whom the survivors may turn.

Several caveats concerning the methods and the findings must be provided. Once the returns began to come in, it became obvious that for some questions the choice of responses had been too limited and this resulted in a high number of 'other' answers. (This was in part the consequence of distribution through newspapers, a data collection source with restricted space requirements.) Another difficulty arose from one newspaper's failure to correctly define the meaning of numbers in the Likert scale. Therefore, the five point scale had to be reduced to three in the analysis (agree, neutral, disagree).

Table 1
Age at the time of sexual assault, by gender of survivor

	Gender		
	Male (n=97)	Female (n=2665)	Total (n=2762)
Age when raped	%	%	%
0-10	32.0	15.7	16.2
11-16	38.1	27.2	27.6
17-19	12.4	18.2	18.0
20-29	8.2	26.5	25.8
30-49	8.3	11.4	11.3
50+	1.0	1.0	1.0
Total	100.0	100.0	100.0

Notes: 1. In 90 cases age was unknown.
2. Apparent inconsistency in sum total is attributable to rounding error.
3. If a respondent gave a range of ages and stated that (s)he had been raped many times but only filled out one survey, the youngest age was recorded.

Table 2
Number of times sexually assaulted, by gender of survivor

	Gender		
	Male (n=91)	Female (n=2551)	Total (n=2642)
Number of times assaulted	%	%	%
Once	48.4	39.2	39.5
Twice	17.6	19.5	19.5
3-5	11.0	22.0	21.7
6-10	5.5	4.2	4.3
More than 10	17.6	14.7	14.8
Total	100.0	100.0	100.0

Notes: 1. In 210 cases this variable was unknown.
2. Apparent inconsistency in sum total is attributable to rounding error.

Table 3
Relationship of the rapist, by survivors' age at time of assault

Relationship of rapist	Age at the time of rape						
	0-10 (n= 448) %	11-16 (n= 755) %	17-19 (n= 492) %	20-29 (n= 707) %	30-49 (n= 313) %	50+ (n= 27) %	Total (n= 2746) %
Stranger	14.5	22.0	22.8	21.2	22.4	29.6	20.8
Acquaintance	14.3	31.8	31.3	24.6	18.8	22.2	25.4
Date	0.0	7.7	15.0	10.3	5.4	0.0	8.2
Husband/De facto	0.0	0.5	6.1	23.1	27.8	3.7	10.4
Estranged husband/De facto	0.0	0.1	1.0	4.0	8.6	3.7	2.3
Family member living with	35.5	11.4	1.6	0.3	1.3	3.7	9.5
Family member living apart	12.3	5.3	1.0	1.0	1.0	0.0	4.0
Boyfriend	0.0	5.4	10.2	6.1	4.8	3.7	5.5
Other	23.4	15.8	11.0	9.5	9.9	33.3	14.0
Total	100.0	100.0	100.0	100.0	100.0	100.0	100.0

Table 4
Survivors' physical injuries by relationship of the rapist

| | Physical Injuries | | |
Nature of relationship to perpetrator	Yes (n=1193) %	No (n=1367) %	Total (n=2560) %
Stranger	55.6	44.4	100.0
Acquaintance	41.4	58.6	100.0
Date	45.0	55.0	100.0
Husband/De facto	66.5	33.5	100.0
Estranged Husband/De facto	52.4	47.6	100.0
Family member living with	36.9	63.1	100.0
Family member living apart	21.9	78.1	100.0
Boyfriend	49.0	51.0	100.0
Other	38.4	61.6	100.0

Figure 2
Tell anyone? By rapist's relationship to survivor

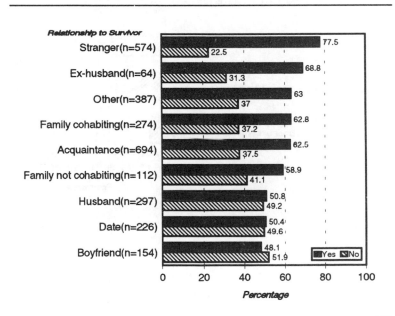

225

Figure 3
Why survivors did not report assault to police

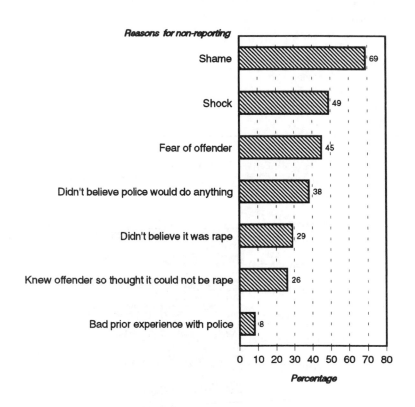

Table 5
Why rape was not reported to the police, by rapist's
relationship to the survivor

Relationship to rapist	Did not believe it was rape	Did not believe police would act	Shock	Shame	Prior bad experience with police	Fear of perpetrator	Knew perpetrator
	%	%	%	%	%	%	%
Stranger (n=237)	19.0	33.9	42.8	53.2	7.5	23.9	0.0
Acquaintance (n=613)	20.2	29.0	41.4	62.5	6.9	30.3	17.8
Date (n=214)	24.3	33.6	36.0	62.6	3.3	23.8	21.0
Husband (n=262)	23.7	40.1	34.0	34.0	8.0	61.1	29.0
Ex-husband (n=262)	13.0	50.0	19.6	45.7	10.9	50.0	21.7
Family together (n=233)	24.5	17.2	35.2	45.5	4.3	42.5	23.6
Family apart (n=108)	21.3	13.9	33.3	44.4	3.7	38.0	20.4
Boyfriend (n=140)	30.0	31.4	31.4	57.1	5.0	28.6	43.8
Total (n=2270)	18.9	25.9	32.2	45.6	5.3	29.9	16.7

Note: The columns exceed 100 per cent since many respondents identified
more than one reason.

227

Figure 4
Who did the survivors tell?

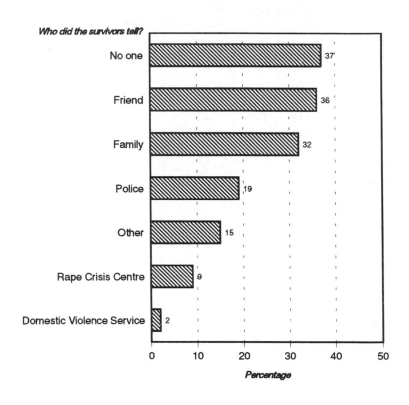

Table 6
Reporting to the police, by relationship of the rapist to survivor

| | Reported to police | | |
| | Yes, Reported to Police (n=540) | No, did not report to Police (n=2281) | Total (n=2821) |
Relationship of Rapist	%	%	%
Stranger	43.5	56.5	20.5
Acquaintance	13.4	86.6	25.1
Date	6.6	93.4	8.1
Husband/De facto	13.0	87.0	10.7
Estranged Husband/De facto	29.2	70.8	2.3
Family member living with	15.6	84.4	9.8
Family member living apart	6.9	93.1	4.1
Boyfriend	9.1	90.9	5.5
Other	14.0	86.0	13.9
Total	100.0	100.0	100.0

Notes: 1. 31 cases were excluded from the analysis.
2. Apparent inconsistency in sum total is attributable to rounding error.

Table 7
Survivors' reporting to the police, by injuries

| | Reported to police | |
| | Yes, reported (n=531) | No did not report (n=2049) |
Survivors' injuries	%	%
Yes, injuries	62.0	42.6
No injuries	38.0	57.4
Total	100.0	100.0

Note: 272 cases are excluded because of unknowns.

Table 8
Reporting to the police, by time since the rape occurred

Reported to police?	Years since rape took place					
	0-5 (n=501)	6-10 (n=444)	11-15 (n=492)	16-24 (n=726)	25+ (n=590)	Total (n=2753)
	%	%	%	%	%	%
Yes, reported to police	30.1	22.5	18.3	16.1	13.7	19.6
No, did not report to police	69.9	77.5	81.7	83.9	86.3	80.4
Total	100.0	100.0	100.0	100.0	100.0	100.0

Note: 99 cases are excluded since time since rape was unknown.

Table 9
Survivors' assessment of those to whom they reported

	Agency or person told				
	Police (n=544)	Rape Crisis Centre (n=262)	Domestic Violence Service (n=64)	Family Member (n=910)	Friend (n=1014)
	%	%	%	%	%
Supportive	42.3	74.4	50.0	49.1	61.5
Neutral	20.8	10.7	16.5	17.0	19.5
Non-Supportive	36.9	14.9	34.4	33.8	21.0
Total	100.0	100.0	100.0	100.0	100.0

Notes: 1. 441 cases where survivor told 'other' are not included.
2. Apparent inconsistency in sum total is attributable to rounding error.

Table 10
Survivors' assessment of police response, by relationship
of rapist to survivor

| | Response | | | |
| | Supportive (n=623) | Neutral (n=176) | Non-Supportive (n=211) | Total (n=1011) |
Relationship of rapist	%	%	%	%
Stranger	49.2	18.7	32.1	100.0
Acquaintance	40.0	23.2	36.8	100.0
Date	26.7	26.7	46.7	100.0
Husband/De facto	28.2	30.8	41.0	100.0
Estranged Husband/De facto	47.4	10.5	42.1	100.0
Family member living with	27.9	25.6	46.5	100.0
Family member living apart	37.5	25.0	37.5	100.0
Boyfriend	35.7	7.1	57.1	100.0
Other	43.6	18.2	38.2	100.0

Table 11
Survivors' assessment of police response, over time

| | Years since rape took place | | | | |
| | 0-5 (n=151) | 6-10 (n-100) | 11-5 (n=90) | 16-24 (n=117) | 25+ (n=81) |
Response	%	%	%	%	%
Supportive	57.6	41.0	43.3	32.5	30.9
Neutral	16.6	20.0	28.9	21.4	19.8
Non-Supportive	25.8	39.0	27.8	46.2	49.4
Total	100.0	100.0	100.0	100.0	100.0

Note: Inconsistency in sum totals can be attributable to rounding error.

Table 12
Assessment of family response, by relationship of the rapist

| Relationship of rapist | Response | | | |
	Supportive (n = 444) %	Neutral (n = 157) %	Non-Supportive (n = 304) %	Total (n = 905) %
Stranger	58.8	14.7	26.5	100.0
Acquaintance	51.1	17.7	31.2	100.0
Date	25.0	27.5	47.5	100.0
Husband/De facto	42.6	23.0	34.4	100.0
Estranged Husband/De facto	63.2	10.5	26.3	100.0
Family member living with	31.6	19.1	49.3	100.0
Family member living apart	43.5	8.7	47.8	100.0
Boyfriend	62.9	17.1	20.0	100.0
Other	52.6	18.2	29.2	100.0

Table 13
Assessment of friends' response, by relationship of the
rapist

| | Response | | | |
| | Supportive (n = 623) % | Neutral (n = 176) % | Non- Supportive (n = 211) % | Total (n = 1011) % |
Relationship of rapist				
Stranger	67.4	11.6	20.7	100.0
Acquaintance	55.9	19.7	24.5	100.0
Date	47.7	26.7	25.6	100.0
Husband/De facto	68.2	15.9	15.9	100.0
Estranged Husband/De facto	91.3	4.3	4.3	100.0
Family member living with	54.1	23.0	23.0	100.0
Family member living apart	50.0	18.8	31.3	100.0
Boyfriend	71.4	18.4	10.2	100.0
Other	65.7	17.1	17.1	100.0

Note: Apparent inconsistency in sum total is attributable to rounding error.

Table 14
Outcome of reporting to police, by relationship of rapist to survivor

	Perpetrator Arrested?	
Relationship to perpetrator	Arrested %	Not arrested %
Stranger (n=245)	38.4	61.6
Acquaintance (n=93)	46.2	53.8
Date (n=16)	25.0	75.0
Husband (n=43)	25.6	74.4
Ex-husband (n=17)	35.3	64.7
Family together (n=38)	42.1	57.9
Family apart (n=9)	77.8	22.2
Boyfriend (n=16)	25.0	75.0
Other (n=50)	28.0	72.0

Note: In 17 cases the nature of relationship was unknown although arrest did take place.

Table 15
Outcome of reporting to police, by injuries

	Injuries	
Offender Arrested?	Injuries (n = 324) %	No Injuries (n = 195) %
Arrested	43.5	28.7
Not Arrested	56.5	71.3
Total	100.0	100.0

Note: In 25 cases injuries were unknown although arrest did occur.

Table 16
Outcome of reporting to police, by time since assault

			Years since rape took place			
Offender Arrested?	0-5 (n=148) %	6-10 (n=103) %	11-15 (n=87) %	16-24 (n=111) %	25+ (n=77) %	Total (n=526) %
Arrested	50.0	30.1	42.5	29.7	33.8	38.2
Not Arrested	50.0	69.9	57.5	70.3	66.2	61.8
Total	100.0	100.0	100.0	100.0	100.0	100.0

Note: In 22 cases time since assault was unknown although an arrest took place.

Table 17
Outcome of judicial system, by relationship of rapist to victim

	Judicial outcome				
Relationship to perpetrator	Guilty, imprisoned (n=92) %	Guilty, released (n=38) %	Innocent (n=4) %	Dismissed /dropped (n=13) %	Total (n=5) %
Stranger (n=92)	65.2	17.4	7.6	9.8	100.0
Acquaintance (n=38)	39.5	28.9	18.4	13.2	100.0
Date (n=4)	0.0	0.0	25.0	75.0	100.0
Husband (n=13)	23.1	61.5	0.0	15.4	100.0
Ex-husband (n=5)	40.0	20.0	20.0	20.0	100.0
Family together (n=17)	41.2	17.6	0.0	41.2	100.0
Family apart (n=6)	66.7	0.0	16.7	16.7	100.0
Boyfriend (n=3)	66.7	33.3	0.0	0.0	100.0
Other (n=19)	42.1	21.2	26.3	10.5	100.0

Note: Inconsistency in sum totals can be attributable to rounding error.

Table 18
Outcome of judicial system, by injuries

	Injuries	
	Yes, injuries	No injuries
	(n= 141)	(n = 55)
Judicial outcome	%	%
Guilty, Imprisoned	51.1	52.7
Guilty, Released	23.4	20.0
Innocent	11.3	10.9
Dismissed, Dropped	14.2	16.4
Total	100.0	100.0

Table 19
Outcome of judicial system, over time

	Years since rape took place					
	0-5	6-10	11-15	16-24	25+	Total
Judicial	(n=67)	(n=37)	(n=37)	(n=33)	(n=24)	(n=198)
outcome	%	%	%	%	%	%
Guilty, Imprisoned	46.3	43.2	54.1	69.7	54.2	52.0
Guilty, Released	25.4	21.6	24.3	12.1	20.8	21.7
Innocent	11.9	24.3	2.7	9.1	4.2	11.1
Dismissed, Dropped	16.4	10.8	18.9	9.1	20.8	15.2
Total	100.0	100.0	100.0	100.0	100.0	100.0

Note: Inconsistency in sum totals can be attributable to rounding error.

APPENDIX II

The following directory of sexual assault services has been drawn from *Surviving Rape* (Sydney Rape Crisis Centre 1990) and *Services for Victims of Crime in Australia* (David, Stubbs & Pegrum 1988). All entries were checked during the compilation of this publication but since changes to telephone numbers are inevitable, it would be wise to check the relevant local directory.

NATIONAL

Kids Help Line Telephone: 008 073 008
Service Description: Kids Help Line is a national service delivering free 24-hour telephone counselling and information about local available support services and resources to young Australians from 5 to 18 years old.

AUSTRALIAN CAPITAL TERRITORY

Rape Crisis Centre TELEPHONE: (06) 247 2525 (24-hour service)
PO Box 31 LYNEHAM 2620.
Hours: 9.00 a.m.-5.00 p.m. Mon-Fri

The Incest Centre TELEPHONE: (06) 249 6070
PO Box 92, CANBERRA CITY, 2601
Hours: 9.00 a.m.-5.00 p.m. Mon-Thurs
SERVICE DESCRIPTION: Full range of services including counselling, referral and training other workers in the area of child sexual abuse.

Children at Risk Unit TELEPHONE: (06) 244 2152
Woden Valley Hospital

Child and Adolescent Unit TELEPHONE: (06) 205 1469
Woden Valley Hospital

Woden Youth Centre TELEPHONE: (06) 282 3037; (06) 282 3631
John Bynon (for men who have been sexually abused)

Canberra Incest Survivors Association TELEPHONE:
(06) 247 4981
PO Box 171, DICKSON, 2602

**Catholic Social Services: Marriage and Family Counselling
and School Social Work** TELEPHONE: (06) 295 3832
42 Canberra Avenue, FORREST, 2603
Hours: 9.00 a.m.-6.00 p.m. Mon-Fri
SERVICE DESCRIPTION: Crisis intervention, counselling and
referral for victims of domestic violence, child sexual assault,
incest and child abuse and their families and teachers.

Domestic Violence and Crisis Service TELEPHONE:
(06) 248 7800
Hours: 24-hour service

Janice Horne TELEPHONE: (06) 251 3535
PO Box 261, Belconnen, 2617
SERVICE DESCRIPTION: 'Out front' member of a support group
getting training for the survivors who become facilitators for
more groups

Police Sexual Assault Unit TELEPHONE: (06) 245 7236

Tamar
Mary Cutts & Shona Chisholm TELEPHONE: (06) 248 8290
(Please ring for an appointment)
7 Amaroo Street, REID, 2601
SERVICE DESCRIPTION: Counselling for adult survivors of childhood sexual assault

NEW SOUTH WALES

Department of Health, NSW Sexual Assault Services
SERVICE DESCRIPTION: The Department of Health coordinates a 24-hour statewide network of counselling and medical services for all adults and child victims of sexual assault (recent or in the past) in the area of sexual assault, child sexual assault, and incest. Services provided include: Crisis intervention, on-going counselling and support; referral; telephone information and counselling; information about criminal justice system; lobbying; court support; medical; community education.

NSW Child Protection Council TELEPHONE: (02) 262 1655
Level 11, 95-99 York Street, SYDNEY, 2000
SERVICE DESCRIPTION: The role of the Child Protection Council is to coordinate and monitor the government's four-year child Sexual Assault Program. The Council conducts mass media community education campaigns and produces and distributes a wide range of publications including a comprehensive *Directory of Services for Child Victims of Sexual Assault and their Families*. This Directory is available free of charge at the above address. Other useful publications are: *Child Sexual Assault: How to talk to children. No Excuses, It's often closer to home than you think, Reporting Child Sexual Assault*, in 10 community languages.

Sydney Rape Crisis Centre TELEPHONE: (02) 819 6565
PO Box 188, DRUMMOYNE, 2047
SERVICE DESCRIPTION: 24-hour telephone service; phone counselling; crisis counselling; individual and group work; information and support on medical and legal matters.

NORTHERN METROPOLITAN REGION

Sexual Assault Centre TELEPHONE: (02) 438 7580;
(02) 438 7111 (AH)
Royal North Shore Hospital, Pacific Highway,
ST LEONARDS, 2065

SOUTHERN METROPOLITAL REGION

Royal Prince Alfred Sexual Assault Centre TELEPHONE:
(02) 438 7580; (02) 438 7111 (AH)
King George V Hospital, Missenden Road,
CAMPERDOWN, 2050

Women's Health and Sexual Assault Education Unit
TELEPHONE: (02) 555 1665
PO Box 648, ROZELLE, 2039

Child Abuse Team TELEPHONE: (02) 692 6624;
(02) 519 0466 (AH)
The Children's Hospital, CAMPERDOWN, 2050

Sexual Assault Centre St George Hospital TELEPHONE:
(02) 250 2494; (02) 350 1111 (AH)
Belgrave Street, KOGARAH, 2217

Bankstown Sexual Assault Service TELEPHONE: (02) 790 0055
Bankstown Community Health Centre, 47 Stanley Street,
BANKSTOWN, 2280

WESTERN METROPOLITAN REGION

Westmead Sexual Assault Centre TELEPHONE: (02) 633 7940;
(02) 633 6333 (AH)
Grevillea Cottage, Westmead Hospital, WESTMEAD, 2145

Wentworth Sexual Assault Service TELEPHONE: (047) 32 0512;
(047) 32 2577 (AH)
Nepean Hospital, Parker Street, PENRITH, 2750

Community Health Centre TELEPHONE: (047) 31 1777
113 Henry Street, PENRITH, 2750.

Macarthur Sexual Assault Service TELEPHONE:
(046) 29 2111 (BH)
Campbelltown Health Centre, Cnr Moore & Cordeaux Streets,
CAMPBELLTOWN, 2560

Prospect Sexual Assault Service TELEPHONE: (02) 622 8111;
Hospital (02) 622 611
Blacktown Community Health Centre, Main Street,
BLACKTOWN, 2148

Whitlam Sexual Assault Service TELEPHONE: (02) 601 2333;
(02) 600 0555 (AH)
Community Health Centre, 205 Northumberland Street,
LIVERPOOL, 2170

Central Administration TELEPHONE (02) 217 5986;
(02) 217 5981
Policy Analyst, Women's Health Unit, Department of Health,
Level 19, McKell Building, Rawson Place, SYDNEY, 2000

Education Coordinator TELEPHONE: (02) 217 5981;
(02) 217 5987; (02) 217 5981
Women's Health Unit, Department of Health, Level 19 McKell
Building, Rawson Place, SYDNEY, 2000

Dympna House TELEPHONE: (02) 97 6733
PO Box 22, HABERFIELD, 2045
SERVICE DESCRIPTION: Incest Counselling Centre.
Hours: 9.30 a.m.-5.30 p.m. Mon-Fri with appointments and
groups in evening if needed by working women.

WISN TELEPHONE: (02) 516 1138
Women Incest and Child Sexual Assault Survivors Network

Child Abuse and Prevention Centre TELEPHONE:
(02) 344 5111; (02) 344 7646
33 Bundock Street, RANDWICK, 2025

Camperdown Children's Hospital Child Protection Unit
TELEPHONE: (02) 519 0466
Pyrmont Bridge Road, CAMPERDOWN, 2050
Hours: 24-hour service; crisis referrals through social worker
on call
SERVICE DESCRIPTION: Multi-disciplinary child protection unit;
child assessment and counselling of victims of physical and
sexual child abuse, and their families.

Prince of Wales Hospital Child Abuse Team TELEPHONE:
(02) 399 4430/4431; (02) 399 0111 (AH)
High Street, RANDWICK, 2031
SERVICE DESCRIPTION: Crisis intervention for child victims of
physical and sexual abuse.

Initial Self Help and Lobbying League (I Shall) TELEPHONE: NFP at this stage
PO Box 276, ENGADINE, 2233
SERVICE DESCRIPTION: Moral, emotional and physical support for non-offending parents of victims of child sexual abuse and incest. Lobbying for change in access laws.

Dept. Family and Community Services—Child at Risk Services TELEPHONE: (02) 689 8111; Crisis Line: (02) 818 5555
31-30 Macquarie Street, PARRAMATTA, 2150
Hours: 24-hour service
SERVICE DESCRIPTION: Crisis intervention for youth/children—victims of physical and sexual abuse. There are about 700 field officers and specialists working in the area throughout NSW. For further information ring FACS at the above number or check local telephone book.

The Cottage Family Care Centre TELEPHONE: (046) 26 6308
Cnr Allman St & Oxley-Moore Bypass,
CAMPBELLTOWN, 2560
Hours: 8.30 a.m.-4.30 p.m. Mon-Fri
SERVICE DESCRIPTION: Specialised child care centre for 0-5 year old victims of child abuse—physical, emotional and sexual and neglect. Also includes counselling and support for the parents of the children.

CENTRAL COAST

Sexual Assault Centre TELEPHONE: (043) 25 9111
Gosford Hospital, GOSFORD, 2250

Central Coast Sexual Assault Service TELEPHONE: (043) 92 4444
Wyong Hospital, Pacific Highway, KANWAL, 2259

**Child Sexual Assault Unit, Central Coast Community
Women's Health Centre** TELEPHONE: (043) 24 2533
10 Fielders Street, WEST GOSFORD, 2250

HUNTER REGION

Sexual Assault Centre TELEPHONE: (049) 69 4022;
(049) 26 6234 (AH)
Cnr Stewart Avenue & Parry Street, NEWCASTLE WEST,
2303

Upper Hunter Sexual Assault Service TELEPHONE:
(065) 43 1777; (049) 26 6234 (AH)

Musswellbrook Community Health Centre TELEPHONE:
(065) 33 4422
Musswellbrook District Hospital, Brentwood Street,
MUSSWELLBROOK, 2333

Sexual Assault Service TELEPHONE: (065) 52 2799
Community Health Centre, 22 York Street, TAREE, 2430

ILLAWARRA REGION

Wollongong Women Against Incest (WWAI) TELEPHONE:
(042) 29 6240
170 Corrimal Street, WOLLONGONG, 2500

Sexual Assault Centre TELEPHONE: (042) 20 1408;
(042) 29 8233 (AH)
Wollongong Hospital, Crown Street, WOLLONGONG, 2500

Sexual Assault Service TELEPHONE: (044) 21 3322;
(044) 21 3111 (AH)
Department of Health, 4 Collins Way, NOWRA, 2541

NEW ENGLAND

Sexual Assault Service TELEPHONE: (067) 68 3240;
(067) 66 1772
Social Work Department, Tamworth Base Hospital,
Dean Street, TAMWORTH, 2340

Community Health Centre TELEPHONE: (067) 66 2555;
(067) 661722 (AH)
180 Peel Street, TAMWORTH, NSW, 2340

SOUTH WEST REGION

Sexual Assault Service TELEPHONE: (060) 23 0340;
(060) 23 0370; 23 0310 (AH)
Albury Base Hospital, Wodonga Place, ALBURY, 2640

Sexual Assault Service TELEPHONE: (069) 23 4816;
(069) 23 4815; (069) 23 4818
Wagga Health Centre, Docker Street, WAGGA WAGGA, 2650

Griffith Community Health Centre TELEPHONE: (069) 62 3900
39 Yambil Street, GRIFFITH, 2680

CENTRAL WEST

Sexual Assault Service TELEPHONE: (068) 52 1000
Forbes District Hospital, Elgin Street, FORBES, 2871

Sexual Assault Service TELEPHONE: (063) 62 1411
Orange Base Hospital, Dalton Street, ORANGE, 2800

Central West Sexual Assault Service TELEPHONE: (063) 33 1311
Bathurst Base Hospital, Howick Street, BATHURST, 2795

Sexual Assault Service TELEPHONE: (068) 95 2600
Condobolin District Hospital, Madeline Street,
CONDOBOLIN, 2877

SOUTH EAST REGION

Sexual Assault Service TELEPHONE: (048) 21 5755; 008 024 934
Community Health Centre, Goldsmith Street, GOULBURN,
2580

Sexual Assault Service TELEPHONE: (063) 82 1522 Young
Community Centre, Lynch Street, YOUNG, 2594

Sexual Assault Service TELEPHONE: (064) 92 9196;
(064) 92 9177 (AH)
Canning House, 10 Canning Street, BEGA, 2550

Sexual Assault Service TELEPHONE: (064) 52 2777
Community Health Centre, PO Box 10, COOMA, 2630

Sexual Assault Service TELEPHONE: (06) 99 1432; (06) 97 2266
Community Health Centre, PO Box 729, QUEANBEYAN, 2620

ORANA AND FAR WEST REGION

Sexual Assault Service TELEPHONE: (068) 85 8999;
(068) 85 8927
Community Health Centre, PO Box 790, DUBBO, 2830

Coonabarabran Sexual Assault Service TELEPHONE:
(068) 42 2111 (24-hour service)
Coonabarabran District Hospital, Edwards Street,
COONABARABRAN, 2357

Dunedoo Sexual Assault Service TELEPHONE: (063) 75 1408
Dunedoo War Memorial Hospital, Sullivan Street,
DUNEDOO, 2844

Child Sexual Support Worker, Dept FACS, Parkes Area
206 Clarinda Street, PARKES, 2870
Hours: At any time at discretion of FACS
SERVICE DESCRIPTION: Provision of support to child victims of sexual assault, throughout reporting and disclosure, police interviews, doctors appointments, court appointments and interviewing, 'waiting' periods. Service provides support from the *same* worker throughout what is often a protracted period of legal proceedings.

Community Health Centre TELEPHONE: (08) 088 5800;
(08) 088 0333 (AH)
Broken Hill Base Hospital, PO Box 457, BROKEN HILL, 2880

NORTH COAST

Sexual Assault Service TELEPHONE: (066) 52 2866;
(066) 52 2000 (24-hour service)
Community Health Centre, 38 Gordon Street,
COFFS HARBOUR, 2450

Grafton Sexual Assault Service TELEPHONE: (066) 42 3933
Grafton Community Health Centre, Arthur Street,
GRAFTON, 2460

Sexual Assault Service TELEPHONE: (066) 21 8000
Lismore Base Hospital, PO Box 419, LISMORE, 2480

Sexual Assault Service TELEPHONE: (075) 36 0440;
(075) 36 2431
Community Health Centre, Keith Compton Drive,
TWEED HEADS, 2485

Sexual Assault Service TELEPHONE: (065) 83 1066;
(065) 83 3944
Community Health Centre, Hastings District Hospital,
Morton Street, PORT MACQUARIE, 2444

Child Sexual Assault Unit, Manning Support Services
TELEPHONE: (065) 52 5747; (065) 52 1817
67 Pulteney Street, TAREE, 2430
Hours: 9.00 a.m.-4.30 p.m. Mon-Fri
SERVICE DESCRIPTION: Short and long-term counselling for
victims of child sexual assault and non-offending family
member. Court preparation and support. Groups for
caregivers and victims; community education.

NORTHERN TERRITORY

Ruby-Gaea, Darwin Centre Against Rape TELEPHONE:
(089) 45 0155
PO Box 42082, CASUARINA, 0811
Hours: 9.00 a.m.-6.00 p.m. Mon-Fri
SERVICE DESCRIPTION: Counselling, support, emergency
accommodation and support during legal and court
procedures for women and children who have been raped at
any time.

Sexual Assault Referral Centre TELEPHONE: (089) 227 156
PO Box 40596, CASUARINA, 0811
Hours: 8.30 a.m.-5.00 p.m.. Appointments can be arranged
outside these hours
Crisis Line in Darwin can also provide assistance

ALICE SPRINGS

Sexual Assault Referral Centre TELEPHONE: (089) 515 880
Department of Health and Community Services, Helm House,
Cnr Bath Street & Gregory Terrace, ALICE SPRINGS, 0870
Hours: 8.00 a.m.-4.30 p.m. Mon-Fri. Emergency help is also
available 24-hours.

Alice Springs Women's Shelter TELEPHONE: (089) 526 075

Dawn House Women's Refuge TELEPHONE: (089) 27 4581;
(089) 27 8341
134 Vanderlin Drive, WULAGI, 0812
Hours: 24-hour service
SERVICE DESCRIPTION: Refuge for women and children
providing counselling, accommodation and a wide range of
services targeting women and children who are victims of
sexual assault, domestic violence, incest or child abuse.

Salvation Army Women's Refuge/Community Centre
TELEPHONE: (089) 72 1332; Crisis Line: (089) 71 0338
PO Box 736, KATHERINE, 0851
Hours: 24-hour service
SERVICE DESCRIPTION: Crisis invervention, counselling,
information, referral, accommodation, food and support at
police station and in court.

QUEENSLAND

Brisbane Rape and Incest Crisis Service TELEPHONE:
(07) 844 4008; Crisis Line: (07) 844 4008
14 Brook Street, HIGHGATE HILL, 4101
Hours: 24-hour service
SERVICE DESCRIPTION: Crisis service for rape victims

Zig Zag Women's Resource Centre Inc. TELEPHONE:
(07) 57 1900
1/124 Brunswick Street, FORTITUDE VALLEY, 4006
Hours: 9.00 a.m.-5.00 p.m. Mon-Fri
SERVICE DESCRIPTION: Resource centre for young women
between the ages of 12 and 25 years. Zig Zag is involved in
supporting incest survivors through self help group.

The Cairns Rape Crisis and Incest Unit TELEPHONE:
(070) 31 3590
7 Miller Street, Parramatta Park, NORTH CAIRNS, 4870

Southport Sexual Assault Service TELEPHONE: (075) 91 1164
PO Box 1924, SOUTHPORT, 4215

Sunshine Coast Rape Crisis Services TELEPHONE: 008 012 023;
Crisis Line: (074) 43 4334
Parker Street, MAROOCHYDORE, 4558
Hours: 9.00 a.m.-5.00 p.m. Mon-Fri
SERVICE DESCRIPTION: Offers a 24-hour 7-day a week telephone
counselling service. Also offered is face-to-face counselling,
public education by way of talks to any organisations, support
service for clients in need through medical, legal and police
investigation, on-going support to client and families suffering
from rape and incest.

The Tableland Women's Rape and Incest Crisis Centre
TELEPHONE: (070) 91 2334
15 Beatrice Street, ATHERTON, 4883

North Queensland Combine Women's Services Incorporated
TELEPHONE: (077) 75 7555
Rape Crisis Service, 50 Patrick Street ,AITKENVALE, 4814

Department of Family Services TELEPHONE: (077) 22 1110;
Crisis Line: (Brisbane) (07) 227 5903, 24-hour service
Cnr. Walker & Stanley Streets, TOWNSVILLE, 4810
Hours: 9.00 a.m.-5.00 p.m. Mon-Fri
SERVICE DESCRIPTION: Involvement and responsibility for child
protection offering services to victims and their families
including perpetrator.

Queensland Health Department TELEPHONE: (077) 79 0333
Division of Youth Welfare and Child Guidance, Institute of
Child Guidance, Palmerston Street, VINCENT, TOWNSVILLE,
4814
Hours: 9.00 a.m.-5.00 p.m. Mon-Fri
SERVICE DESCRIPTION: Clinical multi-disciplinary community-
based child and family psychiatric service, dealing with
victims of child sexual assault/abuse and incest.

**Aboriginal and Torres Strait Islander Corporation for
Women, Rape Crisis Service** TELEPHONE: (077) 844 1146
PO Box 443, Woolloongabba, 4102

The Women's Sexual Assault Service TELEPHONE:
(079) 53 4522
PO Box 3509, NORTH MACKAY, 4740

Logan Women's Health Centre Rape Crisis Service
TELEPHONE: (075) 808 9233
PO Box 788, WOODRIDGE, 4114

Rockhampton Women's Health and Referral Centre, Rape Crisis Service TELEPHONE: (079) 226 585; 008 017 382
PO Box 6395, ROCKHAMPTON MAIL CENTRE, 4702

Whitsunday Sexual Assault Unit TELEPHONE: (079) 465 211
PO Box 183, AIRLIE Beach, 4802

Mookai Rosie-Bi-Bayan Rape Crisis Service TELEPHONE: (079) 465 211
PO Box 78, SMITHFIELD, 4878

Townsville Aboriginal and Torres Strait Islander Corporation for Mental Health, Rape Crisis Service TELEPHONE: (077) 21 4611/4605
PO Box 2292, TOWNSVILLE, 4810

SOUTH AUSTRALIA

Adelaide Rape Crisis Centre Inc. TELEPHONE: (08) 293 8667 (office); Crisis Line: (08) 293 8666
PO Box 164, PLYMPTON, 5038

Judith House Inc. TELEPHONE: (08) 266 0550
PO Box 208, GREENACRES, 5086
Hours: 24-hour service
SERVICE DESCRIPTION: Therapeutic residence for young women between the ages of 14 and 20 who are survivors of sexual abuse. Also an Outreach service: for young women between ages of 16 and 25 years who are homeless and survivors of child sexual abuse.

Rape and Sexual Assault Services TELEPHONE: (08) 345 0222
ext 7659, (08) 243 6836 (AH)
Queen Elizabeth Hospital, 28 Woodville Road, WOODVILLE
SOUTH, 5011
SERVICE DESCRIPTION: A medical and counselling service for
victims of sexual abuse and assault; male and female,
adolescent and adult, which may be utilised in the acute
period or may be sought by adult and adolescent survivors of
child sexual abuse.

Victims of Crime Service TELEPHONE: (08) 231 5626
337 King William Street, ADELAIDE, 5000

Adelaide Children's Hospital Child Protection Service
TELEPHONE: (08) 204 7245; (08) 204 7000 (AH)
King William Road, NORTH ADELAIDE, 5006
SERVICE DESCRIPTION: Child maltreatment, assessment and
treatment service

Flinders Medical Centre—Child Protection Service
TELEPHONE: (08) 204 5511; (08) 204 5484
Flinders Drive, BEDFORD PARK, 5042

Crisis Care Unit TELEPHONE: (08) 232 3300; 008 188 118
Hours: 4.00 p.m.-9.00 a.m. Mon-Fri; weekends and public
holidays 24-hour service

Sexual Assault Unit, SA Police Department TELEPHONE:
(08) 207 5716
Adelaide Police Station Building, 1 Angas Street,
ADELAIDE, 5000
Hours, 24-hour service

TASMANIA

Sexual Assault Support Service (SASS) TELEPHONE:
(002) 31 1811
PO Box 217, NORTH HOBART, 7002
Hours: 24-hour servuce
SERVICE DESCRIPTION: Community-based crisis call service
which provides immediate and on-going support and
counselling by phone or face-to-face for women and children
who have been sexually assaulted at any time in their life. The
service also provides community education programs and
liaison between agencies.

Clare House Child and Adolescent Psychiatric Unit (South)
TELEPHONE: (002) 71 8612
26 Clare Street, NEW TOWN, 7008
Hours: 8.45 a.m.-5.00 p.m. Mon-Fri
SERVICE DESCRIPTION: Clare House is a mental health facility
offering assessment and therapy for young people (0-18 years)
and their families, where the young person is deemed to have
an emotional or behavioural problem.

Child Protection Unit TELEPHONE: (002) 30 2921;
008 001 219 (AH)
5th Floor, Kirksway House, Kirksway Place,
BATTERY POINT, 7000
Hours: 24-hour service
SERVICE DESCRIPTION: The Child Protection Unit provides a
service for children who are reported as suffering physical,
sexual or emotional abuse or being at risk of suffering such
abuse. Child protection officers protect and support child
victims by providing counselling, practical assistance, referral
to support organisations and where appropriate alternate care.

NORTH-WESTERN REGION

North West Sexual Assault Support Service TELEPHONE:
(004) 31 8675
PO Box 1090, BURNIE, 7320
Hours: 9.00 a.m.-5.00 p.m. Mon-Fri (A telephone answering
machine operates after hours)
SERVICE DESCRIPTION: Primarily face-to-face counselling
support for women, men and children who have been sexually
assaulted at any time in their life plus support for other family
members. Education programs for the communityand for
professionals are also provided. (Note: It is anticipated that
telephone counselling will increase once a 24-hour service is
established in October 1994.)

Burnie Child and Adolescent Service (North West)
TELEPHONE: (004) 34 6277
7 Bourke Street, BURNIE, 7320
Hours: 8.45 a.m.-5.00 p.m. Mon-Fri
SERVICE DESCRIPTION: The Burnie Child and Adolescent Service
is a mental health facility offering assessment and therapy for
young people (0-18) years and their families, where the young
person is deemed to have an emotional or behavioural
problem.

Child Protection Units TELEPHONE: (004) 34 6277;
008 001 219 (AH)
Reece House, 46 Mount Street, BURNIE, 7320
Hours: 24-hour service
SERVICE DESCRIPTION: The Child Protection Unit provides a
service for children who are reported as suffering physical,
sexual or emotional abuse or being at risk of suffering such
abuse. Child Protection Officers protect and support child
victims by providing counselling, practical assistance, referral
to support organisations and where appropriate alternate care.

Child Protection Units Telelphone: (004) 21 7818;
008 001 219 (AH)
84 Best Street, DEVONPORT, 7310
Hours: 24-hour service
Service Description: The Child Protection Unit provides a service for children who are reported as suffering physical, sexual or emotional abuse or being at risk of suffering such abuse. Child Protection Officers protect and support child victims by providing counselling, practical assistance, referral to support organisations and where appropriate alternate care.

NORTHERN REGION

Laurel House: Northern Sexual Assault Support Service
Telephone: (003) 34 2740
PO Box 1062, LAUNCESTON, 7250
Hours: 24-hour service
Service Description: Telephone and face-to-face counselling support for adults and children who have been sexually assaulted at any time in their life, plus community support for the mothers of children who have been sexually assaulted.

Oakrise Child and Adolescent Service (North) Telephone: (003) 36 2867
Kelham Street, LAUNCESTON, 7250
Hours: 8.45 a.m.-5.00 p.m. Mon-Fri
Service Description: Oakrise is a mental health facility offering assessment and therapy for young people (0-18 years) and their families, where the young person is deemed to have an emotional or behavioural problem.

Child Protection Unit TELEPHONE: (003) 36 2338;
008 001 219 (AH)
Suite 1/23 Brisbane Street, LAUNCESTON, 7250
Hours: 24-hour service
SERVICE DESCRIPTION: The Child Protection Unit provides a service for children who are reported as suffering physical, sexual or emotional abuse or being at risk of suffering such abuse. Child Protection Offices protect and support child victims by providing counselling, practical assistance, referral to support organisations and, where appropriate, alternate care.

VICTORIA

Telephone Service Against Sexual Assault (TelSASA)
Telephone: (03) 349 2466 (BH); (03) 349 1766 (AH);
008 806 292 (metro barred)
PO Box 4313, Melbourne University, PARKVILLE, 3052

Broadmeadows Community Health Service TELEPHONE: (03) 301 9777; Crisis Line: (03) 301 9777
Cnr Pearcedale Parade & Coleraine Street,
BROADMEADOWS, 3047
Hours: 9.00 a.m.-11.00 p.m. daily; 9.00 a.m.-5.00 p.m. (office) Mon-Fri
SERVICE DESCRIPTION: Crisis intervention, counselling and support, telephone information, repairs, legal advocacy (mainly for children) and some court support.

Centre Against Sexual Assault (CASA House) TELEPHONE:
(03) 344 2233; (03) 347 3698; Crisis Line: (03) 344 2210
CASA House, 270 Cardigan Street, CARLTON, 3053
Hours: 24-hour service
SERVICE DESCRIPTION: Counselling, advocacy, support and care
of victims of sexual assault. Medical services, follow up
medical care, interpreter service, consultation, telephone
support, advice and information.

Collingwood Community Health Centre TELEPHONE: (03)
419 6155; Crisis Number: (03) 419 6155
154 Sackville Street, COLLINGWOOD, 3066
Hours: 8.30 a.m.-7.30 p.m. Mon-Fri; 9.00 a.m.-12.00 noon Sat
SERVICE DESCRIPTION: Multidisciplinary health centre, medical,
nursing, physiotherapy, podiatry, pharmacy (free) and bi-
lingual social workers for all residents including victims.

Loddon Campaspe Sexual Assault Service TELEPHONE:
(054) 41 0222
PO Box 126, BENDIGO, 3550
Hours: 24-hour service
SERVICE DESCRIPTION: Crisis intervention, on-going counselling
and support, referral, telephone counselling and information,
financial assistance, court support and information about
criminal justice system.

Monash Medical Sexual Assault Centre TELEPHONE:
(03) 550 2289; Crisis Number: 550 2289
Clayton Road, CLAYTON, 3168
Hours: 24-hour service
SERVICE DESCRIPTION: A 24-hour specialist counselling service
for all victims of sexual assault and all non-offending family
members/partners.

North East Centre Against Sexual Assault TELEPHONE:
(03) 450 5770; (03) 459 3190; Crisis Number: (03) 450 5770
9 Martin Street, HEIDELBERG, 3084
Hours: 24-hour service
SERVICE DESCRIPTION: Provide requested services of crisis intervention, emergency medical assistance, on-going counselling and support, referral to other agencies, telephone information and counselling, court support and information about criminal justice system.

Warrnambool Sexual Assault Unit TELEPHONE: (055) 61 2821
Warrnambool Base Hospital, Ryot Street,
WARRNAMBOOL, 3280
Hours: 24-hour service, 8.30 a.m.-5.30 p.m. Mon-Fri (office)
SERVICE DESCRIPTION: Counselling and support service for adult and child victims of sexual assault including crisis intervention, on-going counselling and support, referral, self-support groups, court support and information on criminal justice system.

Western Region Centre Against Sexual Assault (West CASA)
Telephone: (03) 687 5811
53 Ballarat Road, FOOTSCRAY, 3011
Hours: 24-hour service, Mon, Wed, Fri 9.00 a.m.-5.00 p.m.,
Tues, Thurs, 11.00 a.m.-7.00 p.m. (office).
SERVICE DESCRIPTION: Counselling and support to survivors of sexual assault, their friends and relatives, information provision, community education, crisis intervention, referral and self-support groups.

Royal Children's Hospital Child Protection Unit TELEPHONE: (03) 345 6391; (03) 345 5522 (AH)
Flemington Road, PARKVILLE, 3052
Hours: 24-hour service
SERVICE DESCRIPTION: Assessment and treatment of children and their families who have been sexually or physically abused.

Domestic Violence and Incest Resource Centre TELEPHONE: (03) 347 1866
60 Elgin Street, CARLTON, 3053
Hours: 9.00 a.m.-5.00 p.m. Mon-Fri
SERVICE DESCRIPTION: Telephone crisis counselling and referral, library, worker consultation, facilitation of incest support groups, general information on all aspects of incest and domestic violence, legal advice and information about criminal justice system

Broken Rites Collective TELEPHONE: Kerry (03) 830 5280; Chris (03) 387 8407; Mavis (03) 328 3318
PO Box 345, CANTERBURY, 3121

Women's Information and Referral Exchange TELEPHONE: (03) 654 6844
3rd Floor, 238 Flinders Lane, MELBOURNE, 3000
Hours: 9.00 a.m.-9.00 p.m. Mon-Fri
SERVICE DESCRIPTION: Information and referral service for women—largely victims/survivors of domestic violence/ assault and sexual assault.

Ballarat Base Hospital Crisis Centre TELEPHONE:
(053) 32 1771; Crisis Line 32 1771
Ballarat Base Hospital, BALLARAT 3350
Hours: 24-hour service
SERVICE DESCRIPTION: A sexual assault unit dealing with current and past cases providing crisis intervention, on-going counselling and support, information about criminal justice system and court support.

Wimmera Sexual Assault Service TELEPHONE: (053) 81 9111
Horsham Base Hospital, HORSHAM, 3400

Geelong Rape Crisis Centre TELEPHONE: (052) 22 4318;
Crisis Line (052) 22 4802
291 LaTrobe Terrace, GEELONG, 3220

Goulburn Valley Centre Against Sexual Assault TELEPHONE:
(058) 31 2343
63 Edward Street, SHEPPARTON, 3630
Hours: 24-hour service

Kalparrin Centre Against Sexual Assault TELEPHONE:
(051) 34 3922
PO Box 1124, MORWELL, 3840

Mallee Sexual Assault Unit TELEPHONE: (050) 22 3444
1 Jenner Court, MILDURA, 3500

Upper Murray Centre Against Sexual Assault TELEPHONE:
(057) 22 2203
PO Box 438, WANGARATTA, 3677

WESTERN AUSTRALIA

Sexual Assault Referral Centre TELEPHONE: (09) 340 1820; (09) 340 1830
PO Box 842, SUBIACO, 6008
SERVICE DESCRIPTION: 24-hour counselling and medical service providing crisis intervention, referral, information about criminal justice system and court support etc.

Selby Clinic, (Health Dept, WA) TELEPHONE: (09) 382 0666
2 Selby Street, SHENTON PARK, 6008
Hours: 9.00 a.m.-5.00 p.m.
SERVICE DESCRIPTION: Child, adolescent psychiatric health service for survivors of sexual assault, incest, child abuse.

Sexual Assault Referral Centre TELEPHONE: (099) 64 1853
PO Box 2153, GERALDTON, 6530
Waratah Women's Support Centre TELEPHONE: (097) 912 844
PO Box 644, BUNBURY, 6230

Eastern Goldfields Sexual Assault Referral Centre
TELEPHONE (090) 911 922
15 Dugan Street, KALGOORLIE, 6430

Port Hedland Sexual Assault Refersault Referral Centre TELEPHONE
(091) 732 329
PO Box 93, PORT HEDLAND, 6721

Child Sexual Assault Centre TELEPHONE: (09) 340 8222
Princess Margaret Hospital, Thomas Street, SUBIACO, 6008